ELIZA BERRY

A SECOND CHANCE

Daniella Colombo

Pluto Press

Cover Photography (adapted): Enrique Meseguer
https://pixabay.com/users/darksouls1-2189876/

ISBN: 978-1-7399989-0-5

This book is dedicated to:

Tony

…and to all those non-humans amongst us.

CONTENTS

— CHAPTER ONE —

Drop Dead!

Look! Don't be fooled. This world isn't as it seems, and if you focus hard enough, I reckon you'll see it too...

Now, to be clear, I don't know what's going on, but things got really weird about a month ago, when Cecelia Latimer joined our school; she's incredible, sophisticated and smart. You know the sort... if I'm honest, she's everything I'm not and my lame attempts to make friends with her fail dismally.

Of course, she soon became Miss Popular. Everyone loves her, including the teachers, so reporting her for terrorising me is an utter waste of time. All Ms Sherbetton, our head teacher, says is, "Your oddness attracts negativity, Eliza Berry. Try to be more normal!" Normal! She can talk. Her appalling attitude towards my particular grievance is shocking; after all, there is nothing abnormal about me. Okay, so I have a natural magnetism to attract trouble, but who doesn't? I do my best to keep out of Cecelia's way; whereas she's determined to follow me everywhere; making my life a living hell. Where I fail, as you might imagine, she succeeds...and here she is again with her not so friendly lynch mob.

"Pukey Berry, you ain't so scary," she chants, prowling

around me like a wild animal stalking its prey. Her golden, shoulder-length hair glistens under the late afternoon sun. "Appollo would *roar* with laughter if he could see how pathetic you look."

Ba-bum-ba-bum-ba-bum... my heart pounds with each petrified breath, whilst the hairs on the back of my neck quiver. Why does she hate me so much? What have I ever done to her?

Cecelia's friends circle around me.

"What do you want?" My unfamiliar distant voice makes it sound like someone else is asking on my behalf.

I'm yanked backwards. My ringlets tangle in the straps of my fluorescent pink backpack as one girl wrenches it off my shoulders.

"Wonder what's in this tatty old thing," she says, swirling it in the air.

"Give it back." My knees wobble like there's a massive earth tremor, and the more I try to control them, the shakier my legs become. Lunging for my bag, Cecelia tugs at my ponytail, dragging me off balance. *THUMP!* Grit from the road sinks into my arm, leaving little pockmarks over my skin. Pain shoots through my body and my elbow stings as blood oozes onto the road. "Stop it!"

I wipe the spit away from my mouth as tears prick my eyes, and as the girls skip around me chanting, a teardrop escapes and trickles over my cheek. We're in the parking bay outside my block of flats. The girls must have followed me home again.

Cecelia grabs my backpack from her friend. She flips it upside down forcing my InfinityIce tablet to slide onto the floor, followed by my sketchbook and with a final jiggle of the bag, and a squeal from Cecelia, my digital fibre-tip colour pens scramble across the road, and my star-studded purse, left to me by my mother, which despite having nothing much inside surrenders, and bursts open as it bounces off the tarmac.

"Daaaad!" A lump in my throat blocks my cry from

coming out with any real force.

"Aww, she wants Daddy!" one girl says, as she twists her fists into her eyeballs. "Boo-hoo-hoo."

"Look at her hideous puffy face; we'll call you *Cherry Berry* from now on," Cecelia says, and for a split second there's confusion amongst the other girls; they scowl and curl their lips like they're snarling at each other. Still, they soon join in as Cecelia chants.

"Cherry Berry, Cherry Berry."

The thumping in my chest grows as the girls skip around me clapping, shrieking their piercing wailing tune like brawling alley cats. I scramble to my feet, draw in a humongous breath, and fling my arms in the air.

"*Drop dead, the lot of you!*"

Each girl plunges to the floor like synchronised idiots. They're probably playing the most childish game of 'Ring-a-Ring-o'-Roses' or something just as daft.

Ignoring their dramatic performance, I gather my things, stuffing them into my backpack and sprint towards my building, Lowry Height Flats–past the parking-bay lads, and through the automatic foyer doors, racing into, and bouncing squarely off, my dad's chest.

"You, okay?" Gasping for air, he drops his hands to his knees and makes a wheezing sound. Beads of sweat glisten on his forehead. "I flew down the stairs as soon as I heard you."

"Huh... t-they caught me." My voice vibrates as my lower jaw chatters.

Dad peers through the foyer doors at the girls; the radiant caramel colour of his skin transforms into the dullest shade of beige. He grabs my grazed bloody elbow.

"What have you done, Eliza?"

"It's stinging." There's a delicate balance between winning sympathy from Dad, yet not turning him into an overprotective hothead. If he says anything to Cecelia, things will only get worse. "T-they pulled me over."

"No... What have you done to those poor girls? Why are

they lying on the floor?"

"Oh! Um."

Am I reading this right? I've a bloody elbow because a bunch of vicious girls just attacked me, but all he's worried about is how they're feeling? What's going on? I wipe my nose on the back of my hand.

"I d-don't know."

"Eliza!"

"Honestly, Dad, they're just messing about. I told them to *drop dead,* and for some demented reason, they... um."

"W-what?"

He bows his head and raises his eyebrows, making his forehead wrinkle. Is he deranged, or did I just get transported to an alternative reality? Dad surely can't be cross with me. I did nothing compared to what they did.

"Dad, they're being lame. They're not really dead!"

"Sweetheart, I understand, I do, but there are spiteful girls everywhere." He lowers his head. "Wishing them dead isn't the answer." Tilting my chin, he gazes into my eyes. "Just be careful before you think or say mean things in the future. That's all I ask, sweetheart."

Dad is bonkers if he thinks my saying something makes it come true. There'd be bodies piled everywhere if all you had to do was tell someone to *drop dead.* I squidge my nose and hold my breath as my stomach swirls.

"I wasn't being mean." Even by my own poor standards, my voice sounds whiny, but Dad is being so unfair. "Everyone hates me." I wrap my arms around myself and close my eyes. "I've no friends and j-just don't fit in."

"Eliza, don't be silly; I love you." He pulls me towards him. "And when you meet the *right* friends, they'll love you too."

His muscular arms wrap around my shoulders, and he draws me to his chest. A gush of warmth washes over me. The stench of disinfectant and too much aftershave is absolutely perfect.

"Right, come on," he says, kissing the top of my head

before spinning me away. He offers me his arm in a gentlemanly fashion. "Miss Eliza, may I?"

"Why thank you, kind sir." As always, I play along with his crazy games, and as any lady would, I accept his invitation and slip my arm through his; we stumble awkwardly up the stairs towards our flat.

By the time we reach the second floor, the girls are scrambling to their feet, staggering, swaying and knocking into each other like drunken, waddling ducks. Dad smiles as we watch them from the walkway.

"*Creepy Cherry Berry,*" Cecelia screeches, whilst rubbing the side of her head and wobbling peculiarly.

"See, told you they were just being dumb."

Dad nods and squeezes my hand.

"Phew," he puffs, staring at the next flight. He takes a hankie out of his pocket and dabs his forehead, draws in a huge gulp of air, and continues up the stairs. You'd think I'd asked him to scale Everest with the fuss he makes over a few steps.

He knows I'd never ride the lift to the sixth floor. It's not out of order or anything, but there are usually queues of people waiting to use it, which is really odd, because there aren't hordes of people ambling through the corridors or down the stairs. I reckon they all go to a particular flat, like a commune or something. Or the lift is eating them up! Either way, you won't catch me trapped in a poky metal box with a bunch of strangers. Anyway, I keep telling Dad that using the stairs will keep him fit.

"Who's Appollo?"

Dad raises an eyebrow. His pace quickens, which causes him to stumble. "W-what?"

"Well, Cecelia said Appollo would laugh if he saw me. I didn't understand what–"

"Just... um." With a gulp, he places one hand on his chest. "Keep away from her. She's bad news."

"You're kidding, right?" My heart flips. "I t-try... sh-she terrifies me."

We get to our floor. A sweat patch appears on his shirt, sticking it to his chest.

"Eliza, I know things are tough right now..."

"Well, that's an understatement." My head tingles as I untangle my arm from his. "Everyone hates me. Why can't I be more like Cecelia? What's wrong with me?"

"Oh sweetheart," Dad laughs. "To me, you're the most perfect creature in the universe!" He holds my hands, his fingers warm and soft. "We'll leave soon, I promise."

"B-but you've been promising for months..."

"I know, sweetheart. I'm trying."

My forehead throbs. Whenever we talk about moving, all I can imagine is darkness and suffering. Shivers creep down my spine. I snatch my hands away from his and head towards our flat; it's impossible to listen to his fake promises.

"Oh, Eliza, come on..."

Dad's menacing footsteps echo behind me. His arms are outstretched, and with a massive grin and sparkling eyes, it's obvious he's up to something; but before I can work out what it is, he lunges at me. Leaping out of the way, I'm too late. His bony fingers prod into my sides whilst he smothers me with hundreds of wet sloppy kisses.

"Ahh ha ha, s-stop... No more!"

We giggle as I wriggle out of his reach.

"Right," he says, "before we go in, you need to get your story straight." He leans against the wall by our front door. "The school has called again."

"Oh, no way; it wasn't me!"

"I haven't told you what it is yet... but did you tell your maths teacher to 'go chase herself?'"

"No, I wouldn't! Sam sai–"

"Well... apparently she's been darting around searching for her reflection." Dad's eyes widen as he draws in a deep breath. "The last thing she remembers was your voice." He holds his fist to his mouth and makes a grunting sound.

"But–"

"And Ms Sherbetton is keen to find out whether you

know anything about Mr Spruce, your English teacher?"

Snorting snot back up my nostrils, I cross my arms; as usual, it doesn't matter what I say… I get the blame, anyway.

"It appears," he coughs, "that he shaved his hair off during his lunchbreak."

Dad's entire body shudders in waves, like he's trying to stop himself from giggling. Why is he laughing? What's so funny?

"Again, the last thing he remembers was your voice," he says.

"I promise Dad, it wasn't me… he has a terrible comb-over, everyone kno–"

"Eliza, it's unsettling your mother."

"My stepmother, you mean?"

"You know what Daisy's like when she gets flustered."

"I'm sorry, Dad." My bottom lip quivers. "Honestly, I don't know why I always get the blame for stuff."

His soft lips leave a wet and cold patch on my forehead. "I know, sweetheart."

He pulls out his keys. The star keyring twinkles in the setting sunlight, the same motif as the one on my purse.

I touch his arm before he unlocks our front door. "Are you okay?"

"Why?"

"Something feels, well, wrong." He ruffles my hair. "I'm sorry for the trouble I cause."

"It's fine, sweetheart."

He opens the door to our flat. The stench of body odour mixed with warm fermenting cheese bombards my nostrils.

"Wow, ugh gross!"

We stagger backwards. I hold my nose long enough for the stink to escape our flat, or for me to get used to it.

– CHAPTER TWO –

Help!

"Go sort yourself out," Dad says, steering me towards my bedroom.

I dump my backpack on my bed before heading into the bathroom. Dad is draped over the table in our minuscule kitchen. One hand props his head; the other flicks through a pile of ancient scrunched-up papers. He's muttering something to himself, but what is he saying? It's like he regrets what he's done, but what has he done?

The stool scrapes. Collecting the papers together, he barges past me and strides into the lounge.

"I can't live like this," he says, his voice fuming as he flaps the pile of papers in front of Daisy's face. He grabs me by my bad elbow and pulls me into the room. "We can't live like this."

My arm screams as his fingers plunge into my wound. I clench my teeth, wrestling with the urge to howl in pain.

Daisy doesn't care. She doesn't even glance at us.

"You're right, darling; we'll talk as soon as my program finishes."

"No, *now*!" Dad lurches forwards. "Don't you care about her?" He shoves me towards Daisy, like a sacrificial lamb, going to the slaughter.

"Of course I do, darling." She smiles and blindly fumbles,

grabbing my hand. "We all know how *special* she is, and the *chaos* she causes."

Her tedious voice is bitter and expressionless. Her cruelty sends a stabbing pain zapping through my chest. Daisy is so distant and uncaring, and the more I think about what a pathetic parent she makes, the tighter her sweaty hand grips around mine. The agonising pressure stops the natural flow of blood to my fingers, and as they mutate into a weird shape, I snatch my hand away.

"*Special*! You're being spiteful, aren't you? No wonder Dad *hates* you."

If you ever plan on being dramatic, and want to flounce out of a room in style, my only advice is to look where you're going... Pain erupts through my leg like a missile as I whack my thigh on the arm of the sofa. I hold my breath and suppress my squeal long enough to lollop into the hallway.

Dad flings the pile of papers towards Daisy. "Do you have to be so cruel? She goes through enough out there, without getting it from you too." He pivots on one foot and follows me out.

"Darling, I'm starving. Fix me something to eat, will you?" she says.

"What! Is that all you have to say?" Dad spins round. "The museum doesn't pay me enough to feed my daughter, never mind a gannet like you!"

Shrieking at Daisy, he paces around the lounge, foolishly expecting a response from her. Veins pulse in his neck and his hands cling to the side of his head, like he's somehow containing a brain explosion. Daisy doesn't flinch; she's not afraid of him, despite the bubbling anger marching in front of her.

"Dad... Just leave it."

My head is thumping, and as if on cue, my stomach grumbles. It's horrible seeing Dad so sad; he glances over at me. My heart sinks as his eyes brim with tears.

"I can't do this," he says, stomping past me and out the front door, slamming it with such force it vibrates long after he's gone.

I flop into the armchair, thankful for some peace. At this very moment, my life is a war zone; it's like there's no base, nowhere safe to retreat to, and when Dad's so angry I've no one to turn to either. Daisy and I sit and listen to the relative silence. She's probably enjoying the peace of being left alone to watch TV, and I'm relieved the argument didn't get any worse.

"Will you brew me a cup of herbal tea, darling, and see if your dad has left any digestive biscuits?" she asks, chewing at her fingernails. "Check his bedside cabinet. He sometimes hides them there."

"Are you being serious?" My stomach cramps. Catching my breath, I leap from the chair. "Have you no idea how upset he is?"

As usual, she ignores me, but this time I'm not letting her get away with it. I thump the cushion beside her, so hard that it makes her to take me seriously; well, she turns to look at me anyway.

"Brew your own stinking tea!"

Her eyes glaze over as she looks away. I yank my denim jacket nestled behind her, with such force, it makes her jolt forward.

"You're unbelievable." My voice trembles under my breath.

Snaking my way back out through the lounge, I gather the discarded papers, and collect the dirty cups and plates, which have been knocking around for days, and head towards the kitchen. My phone vibrates, pounding my backside like an enthusiastic woodpecker. It's a text from Dad:

Sorry! Got cheesy pizza + cake, home in 20.

He's always sorry after he storms out, but since my mother left eight years ago, it's like he's itching to leave too. On days like this, I'm not sure he'll come back. He says he'll leave Daisy, but he rarely follows anything through. All she has to do is flutter her eyelashes, and he forgives her every time.

"Dad's on his way home; he's bought you a massive cream cake to say he's sorry." Through gritted teeth, and drenched with effort, I hover at the doorway to the lounge. "Maybe if you do the dishes to say you're sorry too, things will be more peaceful around here?"

Her eyes remain fixed on the TV. She mumbles, "Darling, you know I won't be doing them."

A cake of any description usually makes her salivate, but the simple promise of a cake isn't enough to uproot her enormous backside off the sofa.

"Oh... Did you say a *cream* cake?" She rudely interrupts my thoughts. "Yum, it's been weeks since we've had such a treat." She licks her lips; her backside bounces off the sofa. A string of spit predictably crawls out from the corner of her mouth before she wipes it away with the back of her hand; her eyes narrow. "Cakes are my favourite, darling; my absolute favourite!"

She's such a liar; in my pocket, I've still got the screwed-up paper doughnut bag she hid down the side of the sofa yesterday. She devours so much; I doubt she has a clue what she's eaten.

"Darling, I'll need that cup of tea to wash it down." She spins around; her eyes wide. "Do the dishes for your father and pop the kettle on whilst you're at it!"

A stabbing pain shoots through my chest, and as my mouth opens to protest, she adds, "Oh and... um your dad will love a cup of Earl Grey; it'll settle his nerves." She nods knowingly, as though tea is a magical super-liquid. "So, brew us both one, will you, darling, please?"

The window in our kitchen overlooks the front pedestrian walkway, and whilst I'm stacking the dirty dishes into the sink, Mrs Shufflebottom, our neighbour, hobbles past.

The game show presenter on the TV makes a joke, and the audience cheer. I flick the switch, and as the kettle rumbles, I turn on the tap for the dishes. The papers Dad threw at Daisy sit in a puddle of water on the work surface. They say something about "Elek..." but the water has blurred most of the writing.

It's pointless arguing with Daisy. She has a knack for calming both my father and me down, although today she's focused on the TV more than normal.

"What you watching?"

"Oh, it's a classic darling; hopefully a real lifesaver."

The TV dialogue continues:
"A consonant please?"
"A H."
"A vowel?"
"E."
"A consonant?"
"L."
"And another?"
"A P."

– CHAPTER THREE –

Vanished

We moved into flat C6 ten years ago. The block is in the centre of an enormous city with hundreds of similar high-rise buildings. Mayor Franklin Steptoe opened this part of the city in 2033; he renamed the 'City of London' to 'Cresco.' Yeah, I know, it sounds like a name for a shopping centre, but according to my now bald English teacher, Cresco is the Latin word for 'growing and rising.'

The front door clicks behind me as I cross the walkway to the railings. A slight breeze carries dust from the city streets. Licking grit off my lips, I lean over the barrier. This is a perfect place to wait for my dad; he's bound to be home any minute.

Columns of light puncture the dusky sky, like sparkling stars, where people still slave away in their offices. Massive digital screens, which advertise the latest technology, bombard me with flashing images. The shopping centre, in the far distance, with its illuminated glassed-domed roof, reminds me of a moon which has crashed to Earth, and the towering leisure centre, painted the most perfect shade of dreary, makes it difficult to tell where the building ends and the sky begins. The roads, always bustling with taxis, bikes, buses, trains and trams, create a constant familiar hum.

Dad's bike creaks and rattles across the parking bay. He

swerves, missing the stray football a lad overshoots in his direction. One of them sprints across to retrieve it. He ignores my dad. How rude. Those lads are always mooching around outside the flats; pretty sure they're homeless. They sometimes chat with Mrs Shufflebottom, but they never speak to me or my dad.

"Over here lads, come on."

Dad claps, offering to join in their game, but whilst pulling out their mobile phones, they kick the ball to a corner, where no one is standing. I don't get why they hate us so much; we've done nothing to them.

"Whatever," he says, flinging his head back to glance up at me.

My hair dances in the evening breeze as I bend over the barrier and wave frantically at him. He blows me an exaggerated kiss, which makes me smile. Padlocking his bike, he waves once more and with a massive grin, pulls out four bags of shopping from the various carrying containers; although the bike has paint flaking off it, and a dodgy back wheel, he insists it still has years left in it.

Staggering under the weight of the bags, he relies too heavily on his threadbare belt to hold up his cotton-creased trousers; his shirt, pulled out in places, hangs freely, flapping in the evening breeze, and his hair, seldom combed, flops in front of his face.

He disappears out of sight into the tower-block's foyer, and within a few seconds, the lift clunks, as it's called to the ground floor. He always rides the lift when he has shopping.

Rushing through into the flat, the arm of the sofa saves me from skidding off into the TV.

"We'll lie." Hopping from one foot to the other. "We'll say you did the dishes." It's not really a lie; well okay, maybe the tiniest white one. "Daisy?" I waggle her shoulder, trying to get her attention.

"I'm sick of lies." She swivels and slams her hand on the sofa, glaring at me.

"Wow, okay." Flinching, leaping backwards, my eyes fix

on hers; this isn't the response I'm expecting. She normally agrees with most things, if you don't ask her to do anything physical that is... like move. "Fine! Have it your way." My stomach churns. How can anyone be so selfish? She's now too lazy to agree to do nothing. It's impossible to be around her. "You don't help yourself, Daisy." She faces back towards the TV. "*Aaaahhhh...* I've had it with you!" I purposefully slam the front door as I leave.

"You are your father's daughter!" she shrieks.

"Thank God!" Who would ever want to be anything like her?

The lift clunks, the display shows it's stopped on the fourth floor. Leaning over the stairwell, I'm expecting to see frazzled mums, with prams, blocking the doors so they can get their shopping and babies out, but there's no commotion at all; only a mumbling, Mrs Shufflebottom is huffing and puffing as she tries to navigate the stairs, carry her shopping and hold on to her walking cane.

"Is my dad with you?"

She tips her head towards me; her beady eyes narrow through her greasy hair.

"Enjoy watching me struggle, do you? Well, I've seen it all now!"

Her laced-up boots, with flappy soles, and a woollen stained oversized buttoned-up coat is a terrible wardrobe choice for this time of year, and although she dresses like a tramp, who lives on the streets, she acts like she's better than everyone else with her hoity-toity voice.

I leap two steps at a time towards her. "Have you seen him? I'm positive he got in the lift."

"Horrible thing stopping on the fourth floor when he knows I need the sixth." She shakes her head. "He did it out of spite, you know."

It's weird Mrs Shufflebottom refers to the lift as "he" and says things like "he knows to go to the sixth floor," but she's ancient and cranky, and probably isn't quite right in the head. Dad says she's eccentric, but to me she's just grumpy.

We meet one flight up from the fourth floor; she hasn't gone far. She's so bent over she's practically folded in half.

"Those look heavy."

She swings three bags in my direction, bowling me backwards, whilst holding on to the last one herself. Straightening up, she rebalances using her cane.

"Maybe you shouldn't buy so much if it's too heavy for you to carry home."

It would be great if I could just zoom up the stairs and dump her shopping outside her flat, but that would be impolite. Instead, we dawdle at Mrs Shufflebottom's snail-like pace as we climb the next three flights.

"Did you see my dad in the foyer? He has shopping too."

"Ah what? You're muttering child." Her bottom jaw chatters and her false teeth skip out of place. Pausing, she leans towards me, cocking her head to one side. "Speak up. *What*?"

"Did my dad get into the lift with you?" My voice is crackling; there's a fine line between speaking loud enough, so the deaf-old bat can hear me and being accused of shouting at her.

"I'm not an imbecile. The lift is not a Tardis, so stop interrogating me."

This is madness. Why won't she answer the question? It's simple enough. It's obvious he went into the lift. So, what's she hiding? She'll bark my head off if I ask her again; so, we instead shuffle in silence for the next few steps before she comes to a complete standstill. Beads of sweat appear on her face. Her silver rat-tailed hair sticks to her forehead. She holds her chest with her caned hand and snorts, losing her balance for a moment, before righting herself; she grabs the handrail and continues to trundle forwards.

"Have you got your keys ready?"

It's important to treat the elderly in the same way as you would approach a game of chess, but in this game, you always prepare your opponent for their next move. She continues to shuffle forward, muttering to herself.

"Well, you're not coming in!" she says, crushing the silence and causing me to stumble. "You're not invited into my home."

Her pace quickens as we get onto the main walkway, and she pitches her head downwards as if she's in a race.

"No, you don't understand. All I meant was that you need to get your keys out to save you fumbling around for them and getting col–"

"How dare you! I've never fumbled in my life, and I'm not in a rush. What a vulgar child you are."

I'm conveniently dismissed by her front door, so I place the bags on her doorstep. She rummages through her pockets, presumably searching for her keys.

"No problem, you're welcome."

My lesson to teach her some good manners would have paid off if my foot didn't get caught in the handle of one of her bags, causing her shopping to spill out.

"What a mess. Sort it out!" she spits.

As she hisses, an acidic pong wafts over me. Only a few items fall out of the bag, but from her reaction, you'd think I'd emptied all the bags into one enormous pile. I kneel and collect a rolling can of men's shaving foam, a box of chocolate eclairs and a pizza.

"It's fine; nothing's damaged."

I leave her and head down the stairs. The lift is still on the fourth floor; it's empty, with no sign of my dad or his shopping. I go back up; he hasn't come home either.

"Dad, where are you?"

My voice echoes through the stairwell. Miss bleached hair, short skirt, who lives on the ground floor, often distracts him, but she is tottering across the parking bay, towards the flats, with her own shopping. When I dial his number, his phone rings out; he doesn't read or reply to my text message either. From the view up here, nothing's different. His bike is still chained up, and the lads are still on their phones. So, what's happened to him?

I double check the flat, but Dad still isn't home, and as I

enter the lounge, Daisy is watching the exact point, in the same TV show, she was watching earlier.

"A consonant please?"
"A H."
"A vowel?"
"E."
"A consonant?"
"L."
"And another?"
"A P."

"This program is going in circles." I whack the cushion on the back of the sofa to get her immediate attention. "Daisy!"

She sighs, rotating her back towards me. I shake her shoulder. Spinning round, she purses her lips and shuffles her backside to the edge of the sofa; the frame groans a sigh of relief. She tips her head to one side. I'm sure it clicked. A shiver tracks down my spine; my eyes fix on hers. Her mouth is down-turned. She shudders.

"It amazes me you've noticed; I'm sure it'll right itself soon enough," she says.

Pretty sure she's lying, and why is she getting ready to leap up? The tone of her voice is daring me to mutter another word. Daisy rarely gets irritated, it's practically impossible to wind her up, so what's made her so uptight? It can't be Dad; she doesn't give two hoots about him.

"Don't let it concern you," she says as she wiggles backwards.

Her voice softens, and a sense of peace washes over me.

The lift clunks, drawing me outside. The down arrow is flashing. I leap three or four steps at a time, catching up with it on the ground floor, but what's really odd is no one is waiting to get in. The doors open, and even odder, no one is trying to get out either!

I dart outside. "*Daaad*!" I distract the parking-bay lads from their phones, as they glare at me; blood rushes to my face. "Have you seen my dad? Did he come back out?"

They're so ignorant. I bet they know what's happened to him, but what should I do? This is ridiculous. He can't just disappear. Should I wait in the flat for him to come home? He'll be furious if he knows I'm out searching for him, but something isn't right.

The lights in the foyer flicker on. The lift opens and closes its doors as though it's applauding me. Is that metal box inviting me in? My skin tingles at the thought of riding the lift. Dad says I should never use it without him, but what would Cecelia do? Well, it's pretty obvious; she wouldn't stand here messing around. It's not the time to be feeble and pathetic. I accept its invitation and dive in.

– CHAPTER FOUR –

Hello?

BANG! The doors to the lift slam behind me. My heart leaps into my throat.

There's no doubt about it, Mrs Shufflebottom stinks, but this odour is a mixture of rotten eggs, combined with someone's ancient, musty, cheesy socks. Holding my nose, I try to breathe through my mouth, but the acidic air burns the back of my throat. The lift must've been fanning this stench out. It's malfunctioning!

I strike the button for the sixth floor, but the lift isn't moving; it won't let me out either.

"Hello?" My voice is barely a whimper.

I press the number six, G for Ground and the number four and then press them all over again, several times, but nothing. Covering my mouth, I close my eyes and lean on the graffitied wall. A gentle buzzing in my ears searches for any sounds, a clue to what's going on, but there's silence. I whack the console squarely with one sharp blow. All at once, a series of buttons light up.

The lift bursts into life, jolting so fiercely it sends me tumbling into a sitting position on the filthy, urine-stained floor.

"Ow! That hurt!"

The lights flicker.

"Sorry!"

"Hey! Who's there?"

I'm not an idiot. Someone's here, well at the very least, someone is watching me. Peeling my hand off the sticky floor, bits of dirt and grit cling to my skin. A yellow slimy substance bridges the gaps between my fingers.

"Yuck... that's disgusting."

Something's not right with this lift. You know, the feeling you get when you enter a room and everyone suddenly goes quiet, that feeling. Terrible thoughts that a lunatic might have trapped me here dramatically creep through my mind. Scrambling to my feet, I smear the gluey substance across my school trousers. Sorry Dad!

The lift is moving, but the floor lights aren't changing. I bang each wall in order. It wouldn't surprise me if there's a secret door or another way out. Squaring up to the main doors, I examine them like a curious scientist. The rubber buffers seal them closed; squeezing my fingers through the join, I prise them apart and then pull at the steel edges of the main doors, forcing them open.

"Help... Is anyone out there? I'm stuck in the lift."

Freezing air pounds in through the tiny gap, forcing it to widen. Maybe I should have waited until the lift stopped. I can no longer feel the tips of my fingers; they're being crushed as the doors wrestle with me to close.

"Hellooo, Daaad? I'm stuck, hellooo..."

"Nooo!"

The voice crackles like a broken loud speaker and the doors slam shut, forcing my fingers out.

"Who's there?" My head spins as the light flickers. Is the lift winking at me? "Show yourself!"

It's probably some idiot security guard sat in an office somewhere trying to scare me. There's bound to be cameras peppered all over this place.

"Let me out, you moron!"

Insulted, the lift jerks again and knocks me off balance. As it shudders, my stomach lifts into my throat.

I saw a movie once where a lift shook because the cogs were all rusty and bent, with frayed cables and ... and it plunged out of control. My heart flips. Taking in a huge breath, the thought of plummeting to my death makes me want to pee.

Am I seeing this right? I rub my eyes, but there's no denying it; the floor is swaying, but that's impossible. I stretch out my arms to stabilise myself. My body swings with the movement of the lift, like the pendulum on our mantelpiece clock. As I wedge myself into the cleanest corner, I blow into my cupped hands and sink to the floor. I wrap my jacket around me and track my warm escaping breath.

It feels like I am trapped on a roller coaster ride. It can't still be at Lowry Heights Flats, can it? I can hear Cecelia's voice now, squawking like a vicious crow... '*Pukey Berry*'. Well, the way my stomach is churning, she's right.

The icy air stings my eyes, causing them to water and a tear rolls across my bottom lid. Wrapping my arms over my knees, I bury my head in my lap. Am I going to freeze to death?

It's possible that I'll end up like one of those teenagers on the news, the kidnapped or murdered ones. What if the lift goes somewhere where there are terrible people? What if it doesn't open for days? What if I die right here on the floor? Why did I ever get into this stupid lift? Dad will definitely be back in the flat by now, and I've made things worse, and yes, they're worse, because nobody knows where I am.

My icy hands wipe the rolling tears away from my face, which only encourages more to come. My chest flutters as a solid lump of air blocks my throat. Gulping, I try to relax. I'll just have to wait it out. The lift seems smoother, gently humming to wherever it's going.

"Do not worry.
Do not fear.
You are safe.
With me in here!"

Scrambling to my feet, my stomach leaps to my throat.

"W-what!"

My heart, which has only just settled into a gentle rhythmic beat, builds within seconds into a huge crescendo, like an orchestra pounding through every part of my being.

"W-who are you? W-why've you trapped me here?"

Tremors smother my body. I gasp for air as a cold sweat trickles down my spine. I can't breathe; rasping, I try to draw in air and call out for help all at the same time, but nothing's working. I'm suffocating. My lungs scream for oxygen like they once did when a rat ran across our lounge. I remember, I nearly fainted then too, but Dad saved me with a paper bag... Dad?

"Doughnuts!"

I rummage through my jacket pocket for the crumpled paper bag salvaged from the sofa yesterday. Wheezing deeply into it, my heart, thumping through my head, settles as I inhale the delicious sweetness of the sugar dregs from the bottom. Thank you. I slump to the floor, my body exhausted and crumpled as though a juggernaut has just run over me. Sitting back against the wall, I close my eyes and listen to the gentle hum of the lift.

Cecelia wouldn't just sit here doing nothing, wheezing and complaining. No, she would sort this mess out; she'd be out of here by now, not howling like a baby, but what's freaking me out is the voice, the rhyming voice.

The lift console is like a useless, archaic calculator, but I press every button anyway. The digits all light up, and then, by pressing them all over again, they all go out. Even by my dismal standards, this isn't a brilliant plan. But maybe Dad did the same thing. The timing is perfect; he went through the foyer doors and within seconds called the lift, and I reckon that when this thing stops, he'll be waiting for me at the other end.

It says on a notice on the graffitied wall you shouldn't–obviously–use the lift if the building is on fire, it doesn't say–obviously–I made that bit up. There's an advert on how to report domestic violence, an obscenely disgusting message scribbled over a local takeaway menu, a bus timetable and a telephone number for the local CabCars.

"Oh, tut what a dimwit!" Pulling out my phone, I'll tell Daisy what's happened and where I am, and she can tell my dad if he's there. "Damn, no blinking signal."

I dial anyway, in the random hope something incredible is about to happen. I swing the phone through every angle, launching it into every corner, but nothing.

Whilst pirouetting, like the ballerina I've always wanted to be, the lift comes to an abrupt halt, causing me to stumble backwards. The far mirrored wall saves me from toppling over again.

"Let me out pleeeease!" I hammer on the console with both fists. I'll punch my way out of this box if I have to.

Was I blinded by panic? What's right in front of me, above the R button for Roof, is an oversized red button, with worn-out writing. Does it say *EMERGENCY*? Just as I'm about to press it–as being trapped in an unreliable lift must be, by anyone's standards, an EMERGENCY–there's a hissing squeaky screech, like a tannoy being tested.

"The red button is only for emergencies.
Should only be pressed if there's an urgency.
If you think you will end up dead.
That's the time you should press red.
Other times, use your brain.
And try your hardest to refrain.
Cause if no danger does exist.
Then please make sure you resist."

My heart skips.

Is it a puzzle? Is this a test? If this is an actual person, he must understand how stressful this is.

"C-can you help, please?" A tingle washes over me; this nightmare might be over. "I'm stuck in the lift."

Is this mirror two-way? Shading my eyes from the light, I misjudge the mirrored wall and accidentally head-butt it.

"Hello? Anyone in there?"

My finger hovers over the red button. Should I press it? The message vibrates again through the lift space, but this time the voice is more agitated.

"The red button is only for eeeemergencies.
Should only be pressed if there's an uuuurgency.
If you think you will end up dead.
That's the time you should press red.
Other times, use your brain.
And try your hardest to refrain.
Cause if no danger does exist.
Then please make sure you resist."

"Are you saying this isn't an emergency?" It's important to weigh-up my options before I make another dumb decision. "I know you're not a recording. Answer me!"

Is it more dangerous out there than in here? Logically, I'm still at the flats, but the lift's been travelling for ages, so it might have gone to a commune, or maybe a penthouse or something. Mrs Shufflebottom said it isn't a Tardis, but was she actually trying to tell me it is? What if I'm nowhere near home at all?

The fact I'm stuck in a lift at thirteen-years-old, with only a weird lift attendant or security guard knowing where I am, must be an emergency. I'll get the blame for it, anyway. Within a split second, the fear of being scolded is worth it and... I press the red button.

– CHAPTER FIVE –

TrueBias

The doors open into an eerie, unwelcoming darkness. My chest tightens as I inhale a huge breath of damp air. I wipe my clammy, sticky hands over my trousers.

"Hello?"

I press the red button again, but there are no police sirens, no swat teams nor the fire brigade; not even the lousy rhyming lift attendant has anything to say. No one is coming.

Using the light from the lift, I lean out into the room. The air outside is warmer than in the lift, but it's still bitter.

In front of me is a grubby dented washing machine; a tower of black plastic bags and an enormous stack of old-style newspapers, all connected by a network of undisturbed, silky, glistening cobwebs.

The room, beyond what's being illuminated by the light of the lift, is in darkness. Sliding to the floor, my legs straggle across the threshold, and support my back against the doorframe. What am I supposed to do now? Gently, I tap my phone on my thigh; it's tempting to leave the safety of the lift, but without light that would be dumb. The warm air from my lungs spirals into the darkness as the screen on my phone flashes, momentarily lighting up the room as it searches for a signal.

"Flashlight!"

I switch on the built-in torch app. My immediate world expands, admittedly in sections. I dart my phone around in every direction; the shadows seem less threatening somehow.

There are no obvious piles of bodies or, worse, human skeletons or evidence of evil sacrifices of animals or children. It's important to consider these things, as it might be a place where kidnappers torture people and hold them for ransom. Shuddering, I hope I'm wrong, but let's be honest; this may be the last place I'll ever see. My dad's broke, so I've no idea what ransom they could try to extort out of him.

It makes sense he's here, but where? I tiptoe out of the lift and scan the surrounding area. I hope I'm not about to be ambushed. I'm not sure my heart can take any more surprises. The room appears empty of anything really, certainly anything threatening; there are just piles of discarded junk and old bits of furniture.

"Dad, are you here?"

The cobwebs cling to me, sticking to my skin and crackling as I sneak through them. I rub my hands over my face, destroying the spider's intricate work within seconds. This place seems familiar. I'm getting a serious case of *déjà vu*. You know, when you think you've done the same thing before, but you can't remember when.

I creep further into the room, just as a shadow dashes between the wide concrete pillars. My heart leaps. A chattering warble, from the far side, echoes through the darkness. I spin around, falling onto a pile of old newspapers as they rugby-tackle me to the ground. I slam headfirst onto the filthy concrete. My phone shoots out in front of me as the papers topple, gracefully sliding across one another, creating a perfectly carpeted floor. From the corner of my eye, something glints.

"Show yourself!"

It can't be my dad; he wouldn't be lurking around in the shadows like a creep. Scrambling for my phone, I clamber to my feet and sprint towards the lift. Are footsteps tapping behind me? Is someone chasing me?

WHACK!

I slam into the lift doors as they shut, forcing me outside. Tumbling, I land on my backside. I pivot, pressing my back firmly against the rusty washing machine as I swallow a dry lump of air. Is this my time? Will it be torture or murder? If it's a trap, they've caught me!

My phone bleeps to tell me it's switching to 'power-saving mode.' Typical. As the light fades, my hopes of getting out of here fade with it, leaving me in absolute darkness. I drag my knees to my chest and hug myself; as I close my eyes, tears again roll over my cheeks.

"She's afraid of the dark.
She's afraid of the light.
Even a shadow gives her a fright.
She's making a mess all over the floor.
We need TrueBias' help for sure."

THUMP!

The back of my head bounces off the washing machine.

"Who's there?" Adjusting my eyes to the darkness, there are no fresh shapes or objects. "Are you watching me?" The rhyming voice came from inside the lift, but that's impossible; the lift has gone nowhere, unless it is a Tardis of course, but that's pretty unlikely! "Come out and show yourself."

The silence seems endless, allowing my mind to sink into a numb fear; my bottom is frozen to the floor, my back firmly pressed against the machine. I'm not moving anywhere, not whilst it's pitch black, nor whilst I don't know who, or what, is out there.

"It's truly fear, for that is clear.
But you're not really stuck down here.
Eliza, be brave and you will see.
There's no need to be afraid of me."

"What's happening? W-where are you? H-how do you know my name? Why the silly rhymes?"

I'm now in real trouble. A few moments ago, it was only me and a lousy broken lift with a dodgy recording and my incredibly stupid imagination. Now someone is definitely here. He knows my name; he's tormenting me with specific riddles whilst watching me suffer. No kind person would do that. Would they? Maybe he knows my name because he overheard the kidnapper's plans. The voice said, 'Be brave... no need to be afraid'. Is it a riddle, a secret clue or password?

"Are you h-hurt? Tell me w-where you are, and I'll try to find you."

My trembling voice matches the increasing thumps in my head... Something scampers through the shadows.

POOF!

The washing machine, my only piece of security, disappears. Where's it gone? Washing machines weigh a ton, they don't just vanish. Rolling backwards, I instantly leap to my feet. The doors of the lift open and light floods into the room. I raise my hands to shield my eyes from the blinding brightness.

"TrueBias is here.
So give out a cheer.
For he's our friend.
No need to pretend.
He'll help you out.
So please don't shout."

A piece of material is flung over my head.

"Aaaahhhh, wh-hat!"

Rodents dash past me as they reconsider their hiding places. I swing my arms and kick-out my feet, trying to defend myself from my attacker. The material, which has now slipped onto my shoulder, slides to the ground and scurries away on the back of a distraught rat. My knees buckle as tiny, clawed footsteps clamber over my feet. I gasp for air, but there's nothing here, nobody is attacking me. There's silence. I stand still. My chest heaves as my heart pounds in my throat like a deafening drum.

"Hi Eliza, I'm TrueBias, capital T capital B, so pleased to make your acquaintance."

I spin round. "Wow."

A guy, a little older than me, perches himself on the arm of a tatty armchair; he is leaning forward and holding out an unshaken hand. He smiles, his perfect set of teeth like a Cheshire cat, dazzle in the lift's light. I keep one eye on him whilst scanning for a weapon to defend myself.

"I understand it's all been a bit of an ordeal for you; well, it's been deplorable for Jack too."

My eyes try to absorb as much information as they can; I swallow a fresh wave of panic. This guy is from America. His voice hangs oddly on every word.

"A-am I in America?"

Okay, I agree; it seems a dumb question when I say it out loud; well, considering all the other things I could ask, such as whether he has kidnapped me, or whether he is trapped here too, but somehow, above everything else, it's important for me to know where I am.

"What? How ridiculous! Of course not." The guy flaps his hands downwards, a frown furrows his forehead, and he chatters his teeth as though my suggestion is the most ridiculous thing he's ever heard. "You're in the basement!" He slides off the arm of the chair into the seat. "You've gone an odd colour. You okay?"

The lift displays G to R; Ground to Roof, no B for Basement. How dumb does he think I am? Although he doesn't strike me as a typical kidnapper, it's difficult to be sure, because I don't actually know what a kidnapper looks like. A massive wave of peace washes over me all the same; I'm relieved someone else is here with me.

"What did you say your name was again?"

He frowns and wrinkles his forehead. "You seem a little

discombobulated. Are you okay?" His voice softens. "Oh sorry, you seem a little bewildered. That's what I'm trying to say." He leans towards me and holds out his hand. "Let's start again, shall we? I'm TrueBias, capital T capital B, it makes sense that way. My friends call me 'True.'"

My hand remains firmly by my side. He withdraws his and rubs the back of his neck as though he's deep in thought. His steel-grey eyes don't falter from mine.

My intense breathing and the gentle drip of the overhead pipes spoil the silence. The hairs on the back of my neck stand to attention as the staring makes me uneasy. The temperature has dropped, and my sweaty clothes are cold and uncomfortable. I shudder and wipe snot off my face with the back of my hand.

"That's what the hankie is for." Raising his eyebrows, he reclines back into the chair. "Your nose is bleeding." He points to his own nose. "Maybe you should squash the top of it, or something, to see if you can suppress it."

The handkerchief is probably now a cosy rodent's blanket. I snort again and, as instructed, pinch the bridge of my nose.

"T-the lift." Nodding towards the direction of the lights, I lean forward so 'the lift' can't hear me. "T-there's somebody in there, a p-poet or something."

"Oh, are you referring to Jack? You're so generous, suggesting he's a poet. Be careful, flattery will get you everywhere!"

TrueBias stands and paces the narrow space in front of the chair; the corners of his mouth curl upwards. Snorting gently, he draws a design on the grime-covered floor with his trainers.

"I can't see anyon–"

"Now personally," he says, "I would consider him more of a rambling freestyler than a poet, but you gave the compliment, and it's not for me to retract it."

The doors of the lift open and close like a clapping seal waiting for its fish supper.

"Well, w-where is he?"

Is the lift operated remotely by someone spying on us?

"Tut... umm... Eliza; I'm sure you're not ready for this."

"Ready f-for what?" I catch my breath.

"The truth..."

"You know where my dad is, don't you?"

"Jack, the voice in the lift," TrueBias says, scratching his head; his face hardens and his eyes pierce through mine. "...is an empath; he's a conscious entity who travels through space and time. He reads the emotions of others... Your powerful emotions of being trapped in the lift and your incredible finger work sent him here."

"W-what?" I bite down on the side of my finger. "Y-you're joking!"

TrueBias collapses back into the armchair.

"I understand this doesn't fit into your conventional perceptions of how life should be, but if you listen and allow yourself to be receptive to, umm, open you mind to other possibilities–"

"Okay." I smother a snigger slapping my hand across my mouth; it might just be nerves. "If, huh, I could see him, it would help."

I trot towards the lift, kicking a black bag out of my path; although it's obvious the lift's empty, I try to show willing by peering around the doors.

"Jack neither reflects nor absorbs light, in this realm, he's invisible."

TrueBias' face is intense; I'm waiting for him to say 'gotcha' or something.

"Oh, how very convenient!" A giggle tries to escape. "Am I on some sort of game show?"

"I realise this may be difficult for you to appreciate, but the lift... it's not *just* a lift. At Lowry Heights Flats, it's used to disguise the wormhole to Conexus."

I almost laugh out loud, but he seems perfectly serious.

"Okay, let's assume I buy your story. What's Conexus?"

"It's a station in space between wormholes... much like a

human airport. Jack, Daisy and even Rose Shufflebottom, to a degree, monitor all movement through the wormhole to prevent any 'undesirables' coming to Earth, any aliens without valid papers, that is."

"Humph." Trying to hold down a chuckle, the sound comes out more like a snort. "Now I know you're joking. All Daisy does is watch TV and eat us out of house and home. She can't even do the dishes!"

TrueBias leaps up; his sudden movement causes my heart and me to leap as high as he does.

"Well, we haven't got time to deliberate. Are you ready to go home?" He strides past me and into the lift. "Eliza?"

I have little choice, and although he knows both Daisy and Mrs Shufflebottom, he could still be a kidnapper. TrueBias scrutinises his reflection in the mirrored wall of the lift as I step in. He pulls a face as the doors shut... I gulp.

TrueBias spins around and holds out his hand. My heart leaps into my throat; the wall of the lift traps me as I step back. There's no escape. He stares intently into my eyes as his icy hands grab mine.

"Eliza, I'm being sincere. The TV Daisy watches all day monitors wormhole activity. Consider her a security guard of sorts; she helps protect Earth from criminals trying to come through, just like your mother once did many years ago."

I snatch my hand away from his, suddenly chilled through to the bone, and not just because of my damp clothes. How dare he talk about my mum. "What do you know about my mother?" My voice is barely audible.

"Poppy, your mother, like Daisy and Rose, are Dolces." TrueBias flings his arms in the air, his voice excitable. "They're aliens from a far-off galaxy, the Flos Region. I consider Dolces to be one of the most formidable beings in the universe thanks to their unique abilities; abilities which *you* may have inherited–"

"Yeah, right!" In contrast to his, my voice is bitter. He's teasing me. "The only ability I have is running! I can run away from anything. I'm brilliant at it!"

"Are you ready, Jack?"

"I am ready, but you should know.
Eliza is confused and wants to go.
She's frightened by what you've said.
A lot is running through her head.
Please be kind and give her time.
She will turn out pretty fine."

"That's awful Jack." TrueBias says as he stares up into the lights. "Six out of ten, and I'm being generous."

Well, Jack's right, I am confused. TrueBias is punching numbers into the console. Surely, he only needs to push number six.

"It's odd that I've never heard Jack before. I'd know if we had a rhyming lift at Lowry Heights Flats!"

"Well, that's easy." TrueBias faces me and leans against the console wall. "Humans would go absolutely insane if they could hear empaths."

"Oh, so humans can't hear Jack?"

"Spot on..." He punches in a few more numbers, twists his head and peers at me over his shoulder. He winks. "Hold on!"

"I'm human!" I've a smugness in my voice that I don't even like.

Jack makes a gentle clunk as if he's releasing his brakes. A massive downward pressure on my shoulders forces my knees to buckle. We're moving. I grab the walls, wedging myself into a corner. The pressure eases and my ears pop before the lift stabilises. TrueBias raises his foot against the wall, and fiddles with his fluorescent-coloured laces.

"Eliza, the fact you can hear Jack proves you're not entirely human."

— CHAPTER SIX —

Alien!

Has TrueBias kidnapped me? Is he going to kill me? Or is he telling the truth? Let's be honest, I'm more likely to be murdered than be an alien!

"Where's my mum?"

My dad refuses to tell me anything about her, yet I'm desperate to understand why she left.

"Poppy?" TrueBias' eyes sparkle. He scrunches his nose and smiles. "She's an incredible Dolce, back in the Flos Region now, of course, teaching 'Intergalactic Ethics.' The Federation frowns on inter-species breeding," he says. "You can never predict the offspring. After all, it could be a hybrid of freakiness!" His bottom jaw vibrates, making a chattering sound, and his wide excited eyes fix on mine.

My heart leaps. "Are you saying I'm a freak?" It seems TrueBias is the same as everyone else. "Cause if I am, as you say, both human and a Dolce, that's *exactly* what you're calling me."

"Oh, come on, don't be so sensitive. I said, 'could be,' not 'is' a freak; it's not guaranteed, 'could be.'" TrueBias rubs his forehead. It's like I've deflated him somehow. His stare penetrates right through me before he turns away and admires his feet. "If a species feels the inclination to breed, it's best done within the same species group; that's all I'm saying."

If I am part alien, it would explain why people don't like me; they must sense something odd about me.

"Okay, well tell me about Dolces... Tell me about my mum... Tell me about me! *Make me understand*."

TrueBias shrugs. "Dolces are an incredible species. They're kind, non-confrontational and they work extremely diligently."

"Well, that's definitely not Daisy." I swallow a snigger, which transforms into a hiccup. "She's none of those things."

"And an adult Dolce is telepathic; they can mind-map. They know what's running through your brain, and if they choose to, they can alter your thoughts and behaviour."

"W-what! Don't be stupid!" I feel my head shaking in disbelief, but equally, I'm disappointed in myself for being so dismissive.

"Why is that any more unbelievable than Jack being an empath or you being a mutant?"

As much as I'd like to think Daisy is just a complete waste of space, he has a point.

"Let's get this straight; are you saying Daisy can read my mind?" A jagged spasm shoots across my forehead as though my brain suddenly realises Daisy has been wandering through my head all this time. "And she can control my thoughts?"

"Yep, that's exactly what she can do." TrueBias uses the mirror to tie his shoulder-length chestnut hair into a tidy knot on top of his head. He's acting as though mind control is the most normal thing in the world. "Poppy, your mum is a fantastic Dolce; Earth lost an amazing asset when The Federation forced her back to the Flos Region."

"Forced?"

"Well, with a daughter as special as you, The Federation questioned her impartiality, and whether she'd protect the Earth over you."

"So that's why Daisy came to live with us?"

"Yeah, the day they dragged your mum away from you

was the day of reckoning for planet Earth. Poppy, with her incredible powers, put up an enormous fight. They revised the laws after that; now The Federation carefully monitors all known Dolces throughout the universe."

TrueBias sounds so unbelievably convincing that it makes me especially suspicious. But what if he's telling the truth about my real mum? Wiping the moisture from my eyes, I heave an enormous sigh of relief as a warm, cuddly feeling smothers me.

Jack hums as the lift moves in an upward direction.

If TrueBias is being honest, then a lot of stuff makes sense. My mum, Poppy, didn't abandon me; she fought for me and... if Daisy can read minds; it explains why she always catches me out when I'm lying, and why she nearly popped my hand earlier when I was thinking about what a useless parent she makes. Wow, she must know what Dad and I have thought about her all these years, too. A lead weight drops from my chest to my stomach. If all this is true, it must be hell for *her* to live with *us*, not for *us* to live with *her*! We pick on her every day.

"Does Dad know?"

"Does your dad know what?"

"That Mum and Daisy are Dolces?"

"Yeah, he knows, and he knows you may have some of the mind powers of a Dolce too." TrueBias smiles. "He loves your mum and you very much."

Tears bubble in the corner of my eyes. Somehow, knowing my mum loves me fills a vacant space inside. This entire time, Dad would have found it impossible to explain any of this to me. How could he? I would have just made fun of him. I'd never believe him if he'd told me mum and Daisy were aliens. It still sounds mad, but maybe being shut in this lift is warping my brain. Can I trust TrueBias? It would be great if what he says is true; it would definitely explain a lot, particularly why people treat me differently. Or is it I just want to believe him as a reason to justify my weirdness?

"Well, I can't control anyone's mind, so I can't be a Dolce.

I've tried loads of times to stop a girl at my school from picking on me, but she doesn't."

"You have to appreciate, Eliza, that your abilities are still developing, but equally, you're not a pure Dolce, so it's impossible to know what your unique talents are. There may be species over which you have only partial or temporary control, or others where you have no mind control at all. Have you ever thought of something, and it's happened?"

Every day, something odd seems to happen. I'm not entirely sure it has anything to do with me, though.

"Maybe you said something casually to somebody?" he adds.

"Hmm... I told a group of girls to drop dead. Does that count?"

TrueBias' eyes widen and his mouth drops open. "Well, did they?"

"No!" What a dumb thing for TrueBias to ask. "Course they didn't!"

Like I said earlier, I'm pretty sure it's impossible to *will* someone to die just by telling them to, but Dad seemed frightened when he saw the girls lying on the tarmac. It makes sense now; he thought I'd killed them, too.

"Well, it's reassuring to know," TrueBias says, "phew." Grinning, he wipes his hand across his forehead and flicks imaginary sweat onto the floor.

He reminds me of Dad.

"My teacher shaved his hair off because I thought his comb-over was terrible, but I didn't say it out loud."

"Maybe you have more abilities than you realise. Just be careful what you think and say."

"Yeah... that's sort of what Dad said."

The lift jerks, thrusting my stomach into my throat. I lean onto the wall to regain my balance.

"Turbulence," TrueBias says.

"How can we have turbulence going from the basement to level six?"

TrueBias wipes his hand across his trousers. "I didn't

say whose basement we were in!"

"So, the lift is a Tardis?"

"Well... They popularised the word Tardis many years ago, but..." He purses his lips and looks at me. "In essence, I guess it is."

"So, can people use the lift in Lowry Heights right now?"

"It'll be out of order; it can't be in two places at once. I'm hoping we can get back in a minute or two."

"There's an issue, that I'm sure.
Please listen, I do implore.
We're heading towards a place of trouble.
It will turn you into a muddle.
Hold on! I'll do my best.
It's up to you to do the rest."

The lift jolts; my feet leave the floor and, for a second, I'm floating in mid-air before plunging to the ground with a thump. My head bounces off the mirrored wall whilst my elbow screams as it pounds the floor of the lift.

"Ow!"

My neck throbs. It cracks as I twist it. Everything is blurry. A shadow crouches before me, and a faint voice buzzes.

"Eliza... Eliza..." My cheek is being patted by an icy hand. "Are you alright?"

"Yeah, I tripped. I'm okay."

Pulling my legs towards me and using the wall of the lift as support, I clamber to my feet. The reflection in the mirrored wall shows a battered version of me. My eyes are bloodshot and sore and my skin is cut and swollen. My curly, raven-coloured hair sticks out in every direction. I pull out my ponytail, and tease a strand out from the gash across my forehead, and another, a stubborn lock caked into the blood clogged around my nose. My reflection doesn't reveal the aching sensation surging through my body. I lean against the wall, fasten my hair and pull my jacket tighter around me, whilst closing my eyes.

"You okay, Eliza?"

"Yes, just feels like we've been on a terrible rollercoaster ride."

My stomach churns; I'm unsure whether I'm dizzy, sick or screaming for food.

"We're travelling at high speed. There will be some bumps and issues with gravity, although Jack should stabilise everything inside the lift, it'll be a little uncomfortable for a bit."

"I can't believe I've caused all of this."

"It's not all you. Jack has had a terrible day, haven't you, Jack?"

"It's been a day of strife and trouble.
I just seem to be in a muddle.
When a Menax and a Viscorpus came in.
Mrs Rose Shufflebottom went into a spin.
Eliza Berry's father fell back in error.
The Viscorpus caused a lot of terror.
Whilst they knocked the Dolce out cold.
The power of the Viscorpus took a hold.
With old-style Terminator, they took control.
And I had no choice but to let them go.
He forced me to open up my door.
Whilst Rose lay flat, dead on the floo–"

"Jack!"

"He hasn't finished. What did he say about my dad? Mrs Shufflebottom, is she dead? I only spoke to her a while ago."

"Let's say it's an unwelcome artistic flair Jack has unfortunately developed. Rose Shufflebottom isn't dead." He hurls a sharp sideways glance towards the lights of the lift.

"Yes, your dad, we need to talk–"

"All I care about is my dad. What do you know?"

My heart races in excitement as shockwaves pound through my body, causing a sharp stabbing sensation to pierce through to the back of my head.

"It's not normal to change colour like that. You sure you're alright?" he asks.

"My daaad?"

"A great deal has happened." TrueBias' face glazes over. He steps towards me; I hold my breath, easing myself back further into the corner of the lift. "The Federation of Nobles, who form part of the Universal Federation of Planets, employs me, Jack, Daisy and many others to protect this galaxy. Daisy called me here because an illegal and highly dangerous alien, a Viscorpus, made his way through to planet Earth."

"What's this got to do with my dad?"

"I'm not sure it has anything to do with him, but your dad has got himself caught up in this mess." TrueBias looks away, twists his head robotically and steps back. "The Viscorpus has the potential power to destroy the Earth and this galaxy, and it's my job to stop him."

Has TrueBias just recited a paragraph out of a superhero magazine? I'm not entirely buying it.

"Where's my dad?"

TrueBias is unnaturally perfect, like Cecelia Latimer. He grabs my hand and squeezes it, causing my fingers to bulge and my heart to leap.

"I understand how important your father is to you, and hopefully we can find out what's happened to him, but in the meantime, I'll need your help to save the galaxy, that's trillions of fathers... Can I count on you, Eliza?"

Why would he need my help? Only a lunatic could create such a story and expect people to believe it. He seems to know more about my dad than he is letting on. Surely, it's me who needs his help.

TrueBias again admires his reflection, but out of the corner of his eye, he's watching me in the mirror. Does he know I don't entirely believe him? I'm pretty sure he's trying to rile me. Is there a camera behind the mirror filming us? It's the type of thing Cecelia Latimer would do; she's bound to be behind all of this. She's obsessed with me. Why else would anyone keep checking themselves out in a mirror? No one is that vain! I bet they're relying on me to buy into this story, and then they'll spread the clip around school, making my life a living nightmare.

"How's Cecelia?"

"Who?" TrueBias frowns, tilting his head towards me.

"Cecelia Latimer, you know the girl? She's about your age, goes to my school–the one who's so blinking perfect she squeaks."

His eyes are piercing. "I have no idea what you're talking about; I don't know a Cecelia Latimer." He places his hands together in front of him as though he is about to prey. "I'm not sure what or whom you're referring to, but you need to remain focused. You're an alien, a combination of different species. Your skills and powers are developing; you need to learn to control them, and if your abilities are developing, as Daisy says they are, then I'll need your help to save the galaxy."

The lift has been stationary for the past few moments. The doors open to level six. I puff an enormous sigh of relief as we head towards flat C. Mrs Shufflebottom, referring to the lift as 'he' and Daisy, being so great at pacifying me and my dad, is making more sense. I've no choice; it's up to me to do everything and anything I can to save my dad from whatever trouble he's in.

"If I'm honest, the only thing I'm bothered about is finding my dad."

TrueBias' jaw drops.

"So, can you please point me in the right direction so I can find him? I'm sure he'll help you save the galaxy."

"Have you understood anything I've told you?"

"Yeah, all of it, But I'm my mother's daughter, and I will do everything I can to keep my family together."

As we enter my flat, Daisy bolts upright, her eyes wide and swollen, her fists clenched.

— CHAPTER SEVEN —

Black-Rimmed Spectacles

"You saw my message then?" She stares at TrueBias, but I'm not sure her question needs an answer. "They've disrupted the communication links. The game show was the only route I had."

So that's why she was repeatedly watching the same show. She was spelling out *help*! A cold prickle smothers me. Daisy was calling for help, and in my anger and frustration, I didn't even notice.

"You could have called," TrueBias says.

"Nothing was working." Daisy shakes her head. "That's the first thing I tried."

"Dad back?"

"No, darling."

I dock my phone; the screen is blank. "Where is he?"

"Darling, I need to speak with TrueBias first."

The urgency of needing to know what's happened to my dad somehow seems less important. Well, for now, anyway.

"I'll get out of these things."

Daisy doesn't mention the blood plastered over my face and clothes; she may be an incredible Dolce, but she's not much of a mother. As I sort out fresh clothes and wash my stinging face and hands, the conversation from the lounge distracts me.

"She's immature, an emotional wreck. She understands nothing I've told her. All she cares about is her father," TrueBias says. "She'll fry my brain, Daisy."

"He's everything to her."

"She has absolutely no idea about her capabilities, and you know I hate surprises. She would be a reckless nuisance on such a sensitive mission. I just can't do it," TrueBias says.

"Agreed, she's a little head-strong, but all she needs is to think before she says anything." There's silence. "She's only thirteen; Dolces mature around this time and as a hybrid, there's no telling what she is capable of. Let her go with you; you know I can't. She'll be an asset, I promise."

Hybrid! How typical 'lazy Daisy' trying to wriggle out of doing anything, as usual.

"You're joking, right? It's way too risky. I found her and Jack in 2020." TrueBias makes the same chattering sound he made earlier. "Our usual jolly Jack was joyless as she forced him to follow her coordinates. Fortunately, he had the excellent sense to land in a basement until I could get there."

"Unless she knows what she is capable of, she will only cause more problems for herself and everyone around her. Every day I hear of things she's inadvertently done. Her abilities are getting stronger and there are things you can't do."

"Can't we get any help from Conexus?" TrueBias says.

"No, not with the communications disrupted and the wormhole rebooting."

"The union would be fundamentally flawed, Daisy. You know you can't force me. Neither a Dolce, nor anyone else, will change my mind!"

"I'll go through some bits with her," Daisy says, her voice pleading. "I'll get her to focus her mind, which will help."

"You can try." With a sigh, TrueBias makes a clucking sound and adds, "What's her father's involvement in all of this?"

"What about my dad?" Both Daisy and TrueBias flinch as I sneak back into the lounge. The TV is on, the sound down. I disconnect my now charged phone. "What's happening? Will someone tell me about Dad?"

Are Daisy and TrueBias colluding to get rid of my dad to steal his identity? He has nothing else of any value. They may plan on getting rid of me, too. Is 2020 a code? Why do they need me? Maybe they're body-snatchers planning to replace me with a machine. Questions explode in my head like fireworks, but I've no answers.

"You have the funniest imagination," Daisy smiles.

Is she reading my mind? She pats the sofa, inviting me to squeeze in beside her, like there's room!

"We will never do such terrible things. Please trust us, Eliza darling."

Crossing her chest with one hand doesn't reassure me because she has her other hand behind her back, probably with her fingers crossed. As I speculate on her true motives, she draws her hand from behind her and waves both hands at me, smiling.

"I promise you. You're safe."

A wave of peace washes over me.

"Right Daisy, what do I need to know? I've got Jack's version, although I'm not sure how much of it is his artistic flair!" TrueBias says.

TrueBias sits on the arm of the chair and flicks through the TV programmes.

Is this all a cosmic joke? I don't have to be a genius to work out that scanning through the TV shows is hardly the actions of a superhero, or someone whose mission is to save the galaxy.

"TrueBias darling," Daisy says. "Give Eliza the spectacles."

Is she reading my mind? TrueBias rummages through his pockets and pulls out a pair of black, heavy-framed spectacles and gestures for me to put them on.

"There's nothing wrong with my eyesight! Are you going to trick me into wearing a squeaky red nose and spinning bow tie, by any chance?" They both chuckle. Well, TrueBias chatters in the same way as those plastic wind-up teeth do. "I'm not joking!" Has Cecelia roped them both into playing this massive, cruel joke on me? As I storm out of the room, I kick at the open door, forcing it to bounce off the wall. "I need to pee!" How much more of this can I take? I stand just outside in the hallway.

"You're right, she may not be ready," Daisy says. Her voice quietens to a whisper, causing me to creep further into the room. She leans towards TrueBias, shaking her head. "But you really have little choice."

"Look, it's not a problem. To be succinct, she will be a right pain in the backside." TrueBias is still searching through the channels. "We need to concentrate on stopping the Luxlumen leaving the planet, not on supervising a thirteen-year-old."

"Yeah, we're all in real trouble," Daisy says.

"Don't stress; I'll do my best... Eliza, can you come here?" TrueBias calls me; he quivers as I swing my legs over the arm of the sofa. "Don't creep up on me like that, very uncongenial. That means–"

"Uncool, I know." I put on the spectacles and stick my tongue out at him; he smiles.

My mind whizzes. Spluttering, I shower myself with my own spit. The TV isn't a TV but a huge dashboard of switches, buttons and flashing lights like a flight-deck of an aeroplane. My mouth dries as a hundred questions pop into my head.

"Uh... W-whaaa–"

"This is what Jack recorded," Daisy says.

On the screen, my father, who looks rather hot and flustered, steps into the lift and places his shopping bags on the floor. Mrs Shufflebottom is already in the lift and is facing the mirrored wall; her head is down. It's like she's intentionally hiding from the cameras. I know it's her because I recognise the battered clothes and scrawny hair.

"Hello Rose, are you getting out?" Dad asks.

She lifts her cane and waggles it at my dad. "Nobody else is here," she says.

As the doors close, my dad says nothing else. He presses a button on the console and the lift jerks into action before it stops. The mirror on the back wall transforms into a black pulsating hole and swirls of dancing mist judder with each beat.

"I knew it, a two-way mirror!"

My dad weirdly notices nothing going on around him. A man appears through the hole, a stumpy man, shorter than the bent-over Mrs Shufflebottom. He has huge ears, a bulbous nose and a pointy chin. He reminds me of a chubby troll from a fantasy movie. His creamy hair blends with his beard, which grows only from his cheeks, and the straps on his chocolate-leather dungarees drape freely around his waist.

"How dare you!" Mrs Shufflebottom says, whacking the man with her cane. She is trying to shove him back him into the hole, but despite his size, he isn't moving and raises his arms to defend himself. "Get back!" she shouts. "Go back; you've tricked me!"

My dad isn't paying any attention at all to what's going on right beside him. Mrs Shufflebottom strikes the man right on top of his head and he stumbles.

"Get off me," he says. "You go back, you slithering lizard."

He knocks Mrs Shufflebottom sideways, and she topples over her cane into my dad, who stumbles backwards through the hole. He disappears as the wall transforms back into a mirror.

"*Daaaaad.*" Leaning forward, tears sting my already sore eyes.

"Open it or I'll kill her," the man is banging on the lift doors as Mrs Shufflebottom lies face down on the floor.

"That's a Menax, Eliza; they are relatively harmless creatures, more useless than anything else. The problem here is that one has smuggled a Viscorpus through the wormhole with him," TrueBias says. "Viscorpus are the most dangerous 'beings' in the universe; they're not allowed to travel to planet Earth because they are so ruthless. Jack did a splendid job trying to keep them trapped in the–"

"Watch," Daisy says.

"Why didn't my dad help her? Why did he ignore Mrs Shufflebottom?"

"Rose told him he was on his own in the lift. He couldn't see any of this," Daisy says as she squeezes my hand.

The Menax draws a silver spoon-shaped object from his pocket. TrueBias' head jerks, leaning closer to the TV.

"Jeez, you're so kidding me. How did he get his hands on one of them?" he says.

"What is it?"

There is urgency in my voice as an overwhelming wave of fear erupts inside of me. Am I sensing TrueBias' emotions, or am I petrified that this unimaginable world might actually be real? I'm pretty sure that what I've just seen on TV is a new reality show. You know the sort where you can create real-life experiences. It didn't actually look much like my dad, or in fact, Mrs Shufflebottom when I think about it.

TrueBias shudders. He pulls the band out from his hair and twangs it across his fingers.

"It's a Terminator, Eliza. I thought Jack was kidding. It's like a gun, which doesn't run out of bullets, but sends you into millions of pieces." The doors of the lift open, and the Menax leaves. "The Viscorpus will vaporise him; he's served his purpose."

Mrs Shufflebottom clambers to her feet. She presses several buttons on the lift console. I can't see her clearly, as her hair smothers her face, but she looks odd and pale. She gathers my dad's shopping and her cane, and shuffles out of the lift.

"I didn't see the Viscorpus. Where's the Viscorpus?"

TrueBias looks at me.

"Eliza, he's gone. The Viscorpus cloaked himself and held on to the Menax through the wormhole. Only Dolces can accurately sense a cloaked being. That's why they jammed the communication links before he travelled to Earth." TrueBias grabs my arm. "It's an ingenious plan." He frowns, his forehead creases, and his eyes squint. "Viscorpus are from the planet Elekron. They draw on energy to stay alive; he's here for the Luxlumen; they want to destroy everything–"

"Tried to call you as they entered the wormhole," Daisy interrupts. "They blocked the entire system at exactly the same time, so I couldn't communicate with customs in Conexus. Can't understand why Rose didn't detect the Viscorpus. He's definitely here for the Luxlumen, isn't he?"

"What's a Luxlu–?" My jaw drops. "Uhhh… umm."

Daisy is not the Daisy I know. Her voice is the same, her hair identical, and she is the same height, but otherwise she is completely different. She's human shaped, but one who's starved of nutrition. Her skin is a dull grey, scaly, fishlike, and taut against her bones. Her owl-like eyes sunken into their sockets. Her skull and forehead are much bigger than a human's and much too big for her body. Her legs and arms are short and thin and there's little, if any, muscle. She is literally skin and bones. Has TrueBias been telling the truth all along, and aliens really do exist, or is it more likely that I'm wearing some pretty incredible spectacles?

"The Universal Federation of Planets took Elekron's sun, the Luxlumen stone, which placed their entire world into darkness. They hid the stone on planet Earth. It…"

As TrueBias is chatting, Daisy glances at me and towards her hands nestled on her lap.

"Can you remove your spectacles, Eliza darling?" she says.

Racing into the bathroom, I'm desperate to check, with the spectacles on, whether I take after my mum or my dad. If my mum, Poppy, is a Dolce, like Daisy, then I may be grey and starving looking, with a massive head.

"Phew!"

Although my reflection is different, I'm obviously my dad's daughter. I pull out my ponytail and my hair cascades over my shoulders. The only thing which is different is the colour of my skin. These spectacles must have a colour filter on them or something. They're probably magical, like those funny mirrors at the fairground, you know, the ones which change your shape when you peer into them.

Placing the spectacles into my pocket, I glance once more into the mirror, and my normal reflection smiles back at me. "Wow! They are magic." I head back into the lounge. "TrueBias, what were you saying?"

"We have to prevent the Viscorpus from leaving Earth with the Luxlumen; if we don't... *you* are all dead!"

"Yeah, okay, but what about Dad?"

"Did you not understand Eliza? Everyone will die if we don't stop the Viscorpus."

"Okay, but where is he?"

"Oh, he'll be in Conexus, the space station, the Galactic Hub."

"Can't we get him first?"

"Eliza, Rose, before she left the lift, froze the wormhole; it is protocol in such emergency situations, which means it's recalibrating. No one can travel through it at the moment, but in six hours it will reboot. If we don't stop the Viscorpus from stealing the Luxlumen, then Earth and everything on it, plus every species living on every planet in this galaxy, will eventually perish. Your dad is the least of our worries."

Yeah, my dad might be the least of his worries, but he's my biggest. The problem I've got is that I need TrueBias' help to find him.

"Right, well what do I have to do?"

Focus, Daisy says. *Listen to what I am saying.* She stares directly at me. *Clap your hands.*

"Why?"

"Why, what?" TrueBias says.

"Why clap my hands?"

"What's going on?" TrueBias raises his hands. "I'm perplexed."

"Eliza, I just spoke to you telepathically. I told you to listen and to clap your hands." *Answer me telepathically; focus your mind and focus your thoughts.*

Daisy, where... is... my... dad?

Go with TrueBias and you might find him!

Are you brain washing me?

No, follow your heart, Eliza. Don't let fear block your way. Be brave and believe in yourself.

Daisy flutters her eyelashes. She wipes away a tear. A wave of sadness washes over me. It's horrible seeing Daisy like this.

"TrueBias, I'm sorry about earlier. I was being dense. Of course, I will help if I can."

"Great to have you on board." He grips my shoulder. "The first thing we need to do is interrogate Rose." He hops from one foot to the other. "And then find the Viscorpus, of course." His neck twitch's and clicks oddly. "None of this will be straightforward." He swings round and heads towards the front door. "Let's see what feeble explanation Rose has."

Smiling at my stepmother, I send her a telepathic message. *I love you, Daisy.*

Heart rendering sobs come from the lounge as I shut the front door behind me.

— CHAPTER EIGHT —

The Mission

TrueBias has already left the flat and is heading towards Mrs Shufflebottom's next door. Without knocking, he pauses for a moment, and stares at the closed front door; he then steps straight through it. It's an incredible sight. If he can do it, with my superpowers, surely so can I! Squaring myself up in front of her door, I tap it gently with my foot; it seems solid enough, but maybe this is all about confidence, and has nothing to do with physics. Taking in a huge deep breath, with my arms beside me, I step face-on into Mrs Shufflebottom's door.

WHACK!

My nose splats on the toughened safety glass panel and the world spins around me as I tumble backwards.

"Ouch! That hurt."

The front door opens. TrueBias stares at me, as though I'm a complete idiot.

"Why did you do that?"

"I dunno!"

The stench of Mrs Shufflebottom's flat wafts around us, and it burns the back of my throat as we parade through her hallway into the lounge. Mrs Shufflebottom is wedged in a velour-stained crimson armchair, mumbling. Her bottom jaw is shaking and her false teeth are chattering. I've never been to her flat before. The layout is identical to mine. Food cartons, dirty plates and cups sprawl across every surface.

"Rose," TrueBias says, as he twists his head and cracks his knuckles.

Is he preparing for a fight? Surely, he will not hurt a fragile old lady. He freezes, his eyes are expressionless, and he stares blankly into the distance. Is she controlling his mind? My chest heaves. I'm sure I'd feel more comfortable if someone said something.

She flings her arms in the air, causing me to flinch.

"It's usual to knock first," she says, as if she's reading my mind.

"I did with my face!"

Mrs Shufflebottom shoots me a sharp threatening stare, her eyebrows knit together into a perfect V shape.

Quiet!

Did I just hear her thoughts, or did the deathly look tell me to be silent? Whatever, trying to joke to ease the growing tension building in this room is failing dismally.

TrueBias' stare changes as he faces Mrs Shufflebottom; his forehead wrinkles, and although it has only been a few seconds, it feels more like minutes have ticked by. No one in the room dares to move or utter a word; it's like playing the dullest game of musical statues, with no music!

I hop from one foot to the other to crack the stand-off. Mrs Shufflebottom's beady eyes glare at me and her mouth twists into a sneer before an enormous black cat, which has just scurried across the back of the sofa, draws her attention. It's heading straight for an abandoned chocolate éclair cream cake carton. We watch it slobber over the creamy remains left in the corners of the packaging.

"What's that flea-bitten thing doing in here? Get it out. I hate cats!" she shrieks.

"Is that my dad's shopping you stole?"

Her eyes dart towards her lap, scrutinising her fingernails. TrueBias paces the room.

"I've seen the recording, so don't play the innocent victim, Rose!" TrueBias' aggressive voice is threatening; I'm relieved he didn't have the same tone with me when we first met. "A Viscorpus! What was going through your stupid head? A*re you crazy*?"

"They tricked me. I-I'd never let a Viscorpus in, y-you know that." Her voice is spluttering as if she's eaten a mouthful of feathers. "I froze the wormhole as soon as I could." TrueBias is thundering around the lounge. "It was a harmless Menax I was smuggling; I didn't sense the Viscorpus. I–I didn't know he was there until it was too late. I–I."

"Harmless... smuggling? Rose, those words don't belong in the same sentence! You've broken Intergalactic Law."

TrueBias is terrorising Mrs Shufflebottom. Well, to be honest, he's scaring me a bit, but I can only see her fear. I can't sense it; it's impossible to decipher specifically what she's thinking, as her thoughts are more complicated than Daisy's. I'm sure she's being honest, but she's so petrified, it's difficult to tell.

"It's not my faul–"

"Not another single word!" TrueBias bellows, the windows rattle and the doors slam. "I can't trust anything you say!"

Searching through his coat pocket, he pulls out what appears to be an oversized marker pen. Is he going to draw on her, or issue her with a ticket?

"This is an Insync Harmoniser, a brilliant invention, but not of this galaxy or time."

He points the Insync Harmoniser at Mrs Shufflebottom. Beads of sweat appear on her forehead. She's struggling to breathe, and she shuffles from one butt cheek to the other; ironic really considering her name.

"Please don't send me back, they'll punish or vaporise me, pleeease, TrueBias pleeeeease."

She's gone.

TrueBias replaces the Insync Harmoniser back into his coat pocket as though he is replacing a pistol in a holster and glances at me. My eyes focus on the chair where Mrs

Shufflebottom *was* sitting. My feet, now frozen to her sticky carpeted floor, are like lead weights. A clammy sensation smothers my entire body. I catch my breath, as though somehow, if I'm still and silent, TrueBias will forget I'm here.

"Eliza, we need to go."

I gulp, and like a rabbit trapped in the headlights of a car, I continue to stare forwards. I focus on one spot. TrueBias grips my shoulder.

"Eliza, you okay?"

"W-what just happened? What sort of person does that?"

Stepping backwards, my eyes lock on TrueBias. My back butts up against the doorframe, preventing me from escaping. I didn't particularly like Mrs Shufflebottom, but how could he vaporise her? How can he be so brutal and uncaring?

"Eliza, we've things to do."

"No, I'm not going; y-you've m-murdered a defenceless and frail lady begging for your forgiveness. You d-didn't listen to what s-she had to say. You didn't give her a c-chance."

The little trust I had in TrueBias has vanished as quickly as Mrs Shufflebottom did.

"She's fine; don't be so silly! She's gone to a holding cell in Conexus. It's an appalling crime, smuggling, and smuggling a Viscorpus, well!"

"She didn't know it was a Viscorpus, she said as much."

"You're missing the point." TrueBias frowns as his tone deepens.

"Okay," I sniff, "so yeah she did something really wrong. She admitted it, but you didn't even listen to her."

"I listened to everything I needed to hear." TrueBias steps towards me and holds my hand. "Can we discuss this later? The wormhole will reboot itself by 3 am, so we've little time."

"Be honest, is she dead? Did you kill her? Is my dad dead?" Although I ask the questions, I'm not sure I'm ready for, or will believe, the answers.

"We've shut down our link to Conexus. Nobody is going anywhere until Earth's wormhole reboots. Come on, we need to get going." He strides past me towards the front door. "You can, of course, stay here with Daisy."

"You said no one can travel through the wormhole, but you've just sent Mrs Shufflebottom." My neck clicks; I've been holding it so rigidly it aches. "It just doesn't add up!"

"That's not quite accurate. The Harmoniser turned her into a trillion pieces, and hopefully reassembled her in the coordinates of a holding cell in Conexus."

"Hopefully? What you don't know?"

"Well, no, not until I can get back to Conexus. It's not an exact science."

"Well, as a Dolce, why didn't she just use her mind to control you? Surely she can stop anyone if she chose to?"

My head is throbbing; things aren't making sense. The cat snakes between my legs; it glances upwards and winks.

"You will understand in time, but the constant drone and chatter of everyone's mind is enough to send any Dolce insane. Rose was out of her depth. The collective minds of your dad, the Menax and Viscorpus were overwhelming for her. She wasn't expecting the Viscorpus." TrueBias smiles. "It's tremendous that you have so many questions, but you need to trust me. We need to find the Viscorpus." With his hand about to open the door, he stares at me, and with a sigh, says, "Can we please go?"

I usher the black cat out of Mrs Shufflebottom's flat as we leave.

"What's the Luxyeman like?"

I skip beside TrueBias, partly trying to keep up and partly trying to avoid the cracks in the walkway.

"The Luxlumen?" he corrects me. "It's Elekron's planetary heart, sort of their sun. An exquisite translucent white stone that's not much bigger than my hand." TrueBias clenches and examines his fist. "It's said that the chosen one, who harnesses the entire power of the stone, will lead the Viscorpus race to utopia."

"Utopia?" We pass a neighbour's window and TrueBias briefly stops to check his reflection. "Where's that?"

TrueBias chatters and peers at me from the corner of his eye.

"It means the chosen one will lead their people to a place of peace and tranquillity."

"Well, no wonder they need it back, if it's their sun and it will bring their race peace. Where is it?"

"It's, um, at the museum."

Stumbling forward, I grab the railings to steady myself.

"What, here in Cresco, where my dad works?"

"Yep, the museum."

"Well, whoever put it there must be a dimwit; it will not be hard to find at the museum."

"You're right; but it was hidden. Well, until humans uncovered it by building on every available piece of land!" TrueBias nods his head. "This planet is being devastated by humans."

"Well, if they found it, why didn't they hide it again?"

"They didn't appreciate what they'd found; they saw it for the incredible stone it is." TrueBias twitches. "The Federation makes sure it's heavily guarded at all times." He stands and stares at the floor with a blank expression on his face before snapping out of it. "News soon got back to Elekron that the Luxlumen was on planet Earth."

"You okay? You keep twitching."

"Yeah, don't worry; I'm fine."

TrueBias leans on the railings overlooking the parking bay. He grips the handrail, blinking rapidly.

"Why don't we just give it back?"

"We can't." He shakes his head like I'm asking the dumbest question. "It's written in the *Chronicles of Elekron* that once the Luxlumen is returned to its rightful place, the punishment will be to use its power to drain the energy of every sun in the galaxy which hid its light. This will destroy life as we know it. It took them years to discover where it is and–"

"So, Elekron will give us a piece of our own medicine?"

"Yes, sort of, but it's not quite that straightforward.

Elekron's Luxlumen stone, although their sun, is not the same as your sun." We continue towards the lift. "When they lost the Luxlumen 200 years ago, it was like switching off a light, but if they drain and destroy the millions of suns within your galaxy, most species will die." TrueBias quickens his pace, probably because I'm bombarding him with questions; well, it's that, or he has just raced me to the lift. He knocks on Jack's doors. "We need to protect the billions if not trillions of lives this one act may destroy."

"If I was left in the dark for 200 years, I'd be pretty mad too." All I need to do is find my dad; he's bound to know what to do. "Do you have a plan?"

"We need to find the Viscorpus."

"Well, I'm guessing he's gone to the museum."

Isn't it obvious? Is TrueBias being dense on purpose?

"He can't get into the museum on his own, nor back through the wormhole; he'll need help," he says.

Jack opens the doors to the lift and we head to the ground floor.

"So, what's the plan?" I tap the mirrored wormhole wall. "Can we open it?"

"Daisy is keen for you to tag along, but now I've seen how you've reacted to Rose being sent to Conexus, I'm not so sure it's such a marvellous idea. On this journey, you will experience things you will not be ready for. You're not obliged to come. It's not a problem; I can sort all this out by myself."

My questions must really be annoying him. We haven't even got to the foyer yet, and this is at least the third time he's tried to get rid of me. The last thing Daisy said to me echoes through my head.

Follow your heart. Don't let fear block your way. Be brave, and believe in yourself.

I need to find my dad and TrueBias is my best chance of doing that.

"I'll keep out of your way." I cross my chest with my fingers. "Promise."

The doors of the lift open on the ground floor. TrueBias

glances in the mirror as he picks at his teeth with his perfectly manicured nails and grins.

"Shall we?" he says.

He encourages me out; clearly, he doesn't trust me in the lift, on my own.

"Where to?"

"Let's walk and think." TrueBias watches the doors to the lift shut.

"You mean walk and talk?"

"No, really I don't," he says.

"Why can't the Viscorpus transport himself back with his Insync Harmoniser the same way you sent Mrs Shufflebottom whilst the wormhole is rebooting?"

"The Terminator is an ancient weapon. It can only vaporise; it can't transport you." TrueBias smiles. "Let's get going, shall we? Enough of all these questions, I need to think."

– CHAPTER NINE –

The Parking-Bay Lads

We stroll out through the double doors into the parking bay. One lad holds up his hand and waves at me. Oh, now they want to be friends; it's probably because I'm with TrueBias. I wave back.

"Hello Misster, it'ss great to ssee you, we ssaw what happened. The Visscorpuss uncloaked himsself ass he came out." The lad glares at me. "Keep an eye on her," he says. "Here if you need uss."

TrueBias nods his head in appreciation towards him. Oh no, he wasn't waving at me at all; my cheeks burn. He must think I'm a right, idiot. I lift my hands in a swaying motion, spinning them around, trying to conceal my mistake, but I'm not sure whether I've made an even bigger fool of myself. TrueBias raises an eyebrow and increases his stride. It's obvious he's embarrassed. I guess it's not *cool* to hang out with me.

"What does he mean by 'keep an eye on her?'"

"It's complicated," he says.

TrueBias' pace quickens as he hurtles across the parking bay.

"Are you trying to get away from me?"

He's about three metres in front, causing me to combine

a mixture of skipping, walking and running to keep up.

"Walk faster," he says.

"Have you ever met those lads before? They're always loitering about."

"Use your spectacles."

I take them from my jacket pocket. TrueBias strides back and grabs me by my bad elbow and tugs me towards him.

"Hey, you're hurting me."

"Come on, we need to go."

"Where?"

It seems odd TrueBias is in such a hurry to go nowhere.

"Away from here. Quick, come on."

He's acting really oddly, and why does he keep peering back at the lads? Is he frightened of them? I put on the spectacles.

"Those lads, Eliza, are the Reus, the human equivalent to the military. We use them for security on planet Earth and they protect the wormhole. My recommendation is to keep away from them."

My jaw drops. Incredible athletic creatures prowl outside the flats, towering lizards with red shiny snake-like skin. Their hands are enormous, multi-jointed claws which take up half their arms, as do their flexible feet, forming a huge proportion of their legs.

"Don't stare at them. They're an aggressive race."

It's impossible to draw my eyes away.

"Why are their claws so enormous?"

"They use their claws to rip into their prey and climb sides of buildings."

"Their skin's so shiny and silky smooth."

As I scrutinise the magnificent Reus, an overwhelming wave of excitement engulfs my whole body. This is an incredible experience. I step towards them.

"Have they got ears or noses? Can they hear and smell?"

"Yeah, of course; you've just heard me talk to them. They have holes for those senses. Other than their tail, nothing protrudes, which makes it difficult for predators to catch hold of them."

TrueBias grabs the back of my jacket, and as I'm being dragged backwards, he says, "Come on, we've got to leave."

"They're amaaaazing; these spectacles are incredible."

"It's not the spectacles. All they're doing is removing the filters. You could hear Jack in the lift without them, because you were so desperate to be saved. With them, you can see Daisy, and the world as it truly is. Humans live in a filtered environment, where they only see what they're trained to see, or what they understand. The spectacles remove the filters for you, that all."

As I lift the spectacles onto my forehead, the Reus miraculously transform back into the parking-bay lads. "Yeah, they're really cool." I drop the spectacles back down.

"Eliza the Reus are dangerous and extremely sensitive." TrueBias yanks me sharply, pulling me off balance. "Stop staring at them."

As TrueBias warns me, a Reus has clocked the unwanted attention. A massive lump of air catches my breath. I release it as though I'm blowing out a huge candle. He pops his phone into his pouch; it's like a kangaroo's pouch, hidden in his belly, and he lollops tentatively towards us, dragging his several knuckles on the floor.

"They can be very violent and territorial. This situation isn't good."

The Reus speeds up, bouncing towards us and makes a beeline for me. He's now only a few metres away. His fishy body odour reaches me way before he does. I crush the urge to bolt. Instead, I try to grab TrueBias' hand, but he's gone. The Reus raises his claws to swipe me. Collapsing to my knees, I close my eyes.

"Please forgive my friend, dear fellow." I lift one eyelid. "She's a foolish juvenile."

TrueBias is blocking the Reus' claw from whacking me.

"No excusse to sstare at a Reuss, esspecially her. Sshe'ss ssearching for trouble that one and sshe'ss found it."

The Reus jerks his head towards me and back the other way, as if he is loosening bolts in his neck. Each one clicks rhythmically.

"Accepted and there is absolutely no excuse to be so discourteous. Please accept my apologies and that of my dear friend."

TrueBias grabs the collar of my jacket and yanks me to my feet, thrusting me towards the Reus, to apologise, I guess. I wipe my mouth with the back of my trembling hand.

"S-sorry, ealy orry."

"No one challengess the Reuss." The Reus stares.

He isn't accepting my apology.

"Not the most forgiving breed," TrueBias mutters. "I understand, my splendid fellow. Just, it's also important for you to appreciate, my excellent friend, this naïve and arguably insensitive child, is also a Dolce." He raises me higher; I'm standing on the points of my toes. "Inconceivable but true." TrueBias' voice is practically a squeal as he hovers me in front of the Reus.

Naïve, yes, insensitive, maybe, but why is it inconceivable I'm a Dolce? Is TrueBias saying that me being a Dolce is universally unimaginable? Pulling from his grip, I stand on my own two feet. Plus, these Reus know who I am; they've seen me go in and out of the flats hundreds of times. I don't know why, but they've always hated me and my dad. Still, it's crazy to create enemies, not that I'd be successful in challenging one of these things, and although I'm focusing on his mind, as Daisy taught me, nothing is zooming through his head, which is pretty obvious: they're thugs after all.

"I'm a Dolce, believe it or not. You're an incredible-looking species and that's why it may seem like I was staring. It's not my intention to be disrespectful. Please accept my apologies."

This Reus, either from being told he is incredible, or I'm a Dolce, reconsiders his position. His beady beetle-glazed eyes turn away, and without further comment, he spins towards his friends. His lizard-like tail whips the air, the tip flicks my face.

"Aaaahhhh."

I bite on my lip as my face stings. I grab my cheek as blood spills over the palm of my hand and through the gaps in my fingers. The Reus plods back to his group. I wipe my snotty nose with my sleeve whilst keeping my hand over my cheek.

"Have you got a tissue?"

TrueBias has already stormed off. I jog to keep up with him, one hand on my face, trying to curb the bleeding. I open my mouth to shout after him, but the wind blows my words back. He doesn't even check if I'm okay.

Within minutes, we arrive at the main highway, which links every part of the city. The rumbles of vehicles hum as drivers beep their horns and shout impatiently at others. A sudden gust of wind swirls dust up from the road, and the familiar taste of the city's gritty air lands on my tongue. TrueBias stops, allowing me to catch up. His eyes are narrow and his lips are pressed firmly together. He nods his head; I'm sure he thinks I'm an idiot. I bet he regrets letting me tag along now.

"There's a lot for you to learn," he says.

I sniff, wiping my nose with the palm of my hand. He rifles through his pocket and pulls out his Insync Harmoniser and points it at my head.

"You subjected yourself and me to unnecessary danger, Eliza."

"I knew it! You're determined to get rid of me!"

Skidding sideways with one hand on the pavement, I'm off. As I cross over the lanes of traffic, a harmony of cabs blow their horns and drivers shout out of their windows. I'm causing them to break and swerve. I leap back, dodging the bonnet of a taxi, and catch my foot in the spokes of a passing bicycle, sending the cyclist to the floor and others into the air as they collide into each other.

I yank my foot free and sprint across the road, darting and diving, tormenting the already frustrated drivers.

TrueBias is no longer behind me; he's vanished.

"Aaaahhhh."

I trip over a tram line, tumbling. I fall headfirst, flat on my face, right in front of an oncoming bus. Its horn screams as the hydraulic breaks hiss. I move my head out of its path as it thunders by. Clambering to my feet, I make it across the final lane and lean against the railings, placing my hands on my knees. I'm going to be sick. My head is pounding, and my chest heaves. I swallow, trying to moisten my dry mouth. I roll my neck backwards and open my eyes. TrueBias is standing right in front of me.

"You've caused chaos. You could have killed yourself." My heart crawls out of my throat. It's impossible to get away from this guy. "The Harmoniser was to heal the gash, the one across your cheek. Well, your entire face. It's a mess! What were you thinking?"

Sweat rolls off my forehead and stings my eyes, and although I open my mouth to speak, no real sound comes out. TrueBias' voice softens, probably because I've nearly killed myself and I bet he's not too keen on returning me to Daisy in a body bag.

"You're trembling. This is too much for you, isn't it?" He smiles and scans over my face with his gadget. "You've changed colour again. You sure you're alright?" He tosses the Harmoniser in the air. "There you go," he says, "all done." He slips the Insync Harmoniser back into his coat pocket.

My entire face and cheek are smooth, no bleeding, scabs or soreness.

"Thanks."

I collapse on the pavement whilst waiting for my heart thumps to settle.

"Eliza, you need to trust me."

He squats down beside me, wraps his arm around my shoulders, and hugs me.

"Will you show me how to use the Harmoniser?"

TrueBias takes it out of his pocket.

"It's not a toy. Maybe when you become a little more

familiar with this world." The casing is squidgy, rubbery and a tiny blue light on the tip is flashing. "All you have to do is focus on your intention, and it should harmonise with you."

"What? Can you do anything with it?"

"Like I've said; it's not a toy." He pops the Harmoniser back in his pocket. "Come on, let's go!" he says.

As he scrambles to his feet, he holds out his hand and pulls me up.

The cab drivers are all aliens, happily escorting their alien and human passengers. There are alien shoppers served by human assistants, and humans and aliens mingling and yapping amongst themselves, waiting for buses and queuing inside takeaways. The humans can't see the alien form; they only see them as other humans. This can't be right, can it?

Basically, every human is being tricked. A shudder shoots down my spine; a few hours ago, I was living a lie too.

"Some of these aliens look p-pretty scary!"

TrueBias isn't listening; he's breathing in the city's hustle and bustle; his head is high, surveying every direction, like a meerkat on sentry duty. The noise is deafening. We stroll past a Reus who is guarding the entrance to a jewellery store; he glances at me but, even though I concentrate and focus on his mind, it's blank. I'm not sure I have any skills of a Dolce; it's that, or the Reus' have no thoughts at all, and are just knuckleheads.

"Yes, I agree; some aliens look monstrous, whilst others, not so much," he says. "It's like everything; it really depends on who's looking."

He points to a wide-eyed species with an enormous head and flowing pink hair which gathers on the floor.

"She's handsome," he says. The creature spots TrueBias talking about her, curls her lips and opens her mouth so wide, it turns her face in-side out! "Not so keen on the needled teeth though." He winks and nudges me, knocking me off balance.

I grab his arm and pull myself closer to him. Trying to be

calm and absorb everything going on around me isn't easy. It's taking an enormous amount of willpower to stop myself from screaming and running hysterically down the road. My brain is being bombarded with unanswered questions. It's like I'm creeping through a horror movie, and I'm not sure which creature is the monster. Instinctively, I'm terrified of them all. Cecelia Latimer would easily fit in here. If only I could be as fearless as she is.

The cyclist I collided with is limping along the opposite pavement next to his bicycle, which now has a buckled front wheel. He glares at me and shouts, *You're an idiot,* yet he is not opening his mouth. I guess I might be reading his mind, but let's be honest, it's highly unlikely. Maybe he's a ventriloquist alien and projecting his voice. Or someone else is saying it, and it has nothing to do with me. Well, if I am reading his mind, I hope he can hear this. Staring back across at him, I focus on his brain.

I'm not an idiot for your information, you ghastly thing. But I'm sorry.

The other cyclists don't appear bothered; they are standing and chatting to one another, maybe comparing injuries. All of them remind me of enormous stick insects, skinny long bodies and legs, but with eyeballs at the end of their tentacles. A rather round lady is bashing an equally rounder man with her handbag. Each blow is denting his arm in further. He doesn't appear worried that she is whacking him; he's acting like it's the most normal thing in the world.

"Don't be perturbed," TrueBias says, looking at them. "Those are Urbes, malleable creatures like play dough."

"Aren't they too old for play dough?"

"I'm referring to their form; they're malleable like play dough, which means they're flexible, or stretchy, bendy, able to alter their shape."

"What, like a shapeshifter?"

"No, shapeshifters are a species called *Simulos*; Urbes are bendy."

Cresco is never truly dark; streetlights illuminate the

sky, electronic back-lit display boards cover the sides of buildings and speckled office lights puncture the dark skies as people work long into the night, and the shops, well, they never close.

— CHAPTER TEN —
The CabCar

My mum, my *real* mum, is out there somewhere, somewhere far away. I bet she thinks about me as much as I think about her. When I find Dad, I'll tell him, I'll tell him we need to find mum.

"Are we going to the museum, then?"

"No." TrueBias smiles as he unravels my arm from his. "The Viscorpus won't be able to get into the museum; it's like a fortress. He can't travel back through the wormhole without a host either." TrueBias' eyelids flicker as he stares out into the distance. "We need to find out who's helping him; if we do that, then we can stop him. Now, who would be his host?"

We've been dawdling around a pedestrianised area for the past few moments without actually going anywhere.

"Needs a host? It sounds like the Viscorpus is a parasite!"

"Yes, quite an accurate inference."

"Wait!" Standing still, I catch hold of the back of TrueBias' coat. "Aren't there millions of aliens on Earth? It'll be impossible to work out who's helping him."

"Maybe, but I reckon his host is going to be a species that travels a lot, like a trader." TrueBias tugs at my hand. "Let's go."

He marches me back through the pedestrianised street;

well, he's dragging me. Aliens dodge and leap out of our way.

"Everyone's avoiding you." I pull at his sleeve. "Slow down." He's in a trance, striding towards the highway. "Can't we just wait at the wormhole?"

"No, even though it reboots in a few hours, they may not travel back immediately. Or they may try to smuggle another Viscorpus in. Jack will keep me informed of what's going on outside Lowry Heights." He twitches, his eyes flicker. "Conexus may, in time, increase security, but the Viscorpus are an old, advanced race. There's no telling what they're capable of."

"Advanced?"

"Shush! I'm thinking, Eliza."

TrueBias stops so abruptly he nearly yanks my arm out of its socket, and although he's staring at me, he's whispering something to himself, as if he's having a conversation with someone in his own head. It's impossible to read his mind. Like the Reus, it's completely blank. I'm pretty sure I don't have any powers. It's probably Daisy trying to be nice to me, trying to make me feel *special*.

"Are the Viscorpus friendly with another race?"

"We need to catch a cab."

"Where are we going?"

"Hopefully, the cab driver will tell us that!" TrueBias spins round and dashes into the road. "We need a Garrae driver," he says. "They're the biggest gossips in the universe."

It's fascinating to watch TrueBias hail a cab. Most normal people would wait on the pavement and patiently lift their arm as an available cab drives by. I'm on the pavement, but TrueBias is acting like a lunatic; he's dancing in the middle of the highway trying to hail a specific type of cab, but each one he waves down, swerves and drives straight past him. He's ignored several more times, and as each cab passes, TrueBias flings his arms in the air in an exaggerated disbelief fashion. The cabs speed up and cross four lanes of traffic to avoid him. Not wanting to state the obvious, I can't help myself.

"They're not stopping." He's been suicidally hailing a cab for ten minutes. "I'm starving."

TrueBias disappears. He was there one minute and now he's gone. He's left me standing in the middle of the pavement on my own. Has he abandoned me? Is he coming back? Which way's home? I'm still standing where he's left me when a cab reverses in front of me. The back door swings open, a powerful stench of fresh sick bombards my nostrils, and for a split second I hold my breath. TrueBias grins as I skid into the back of the cab and scoot across the sticky leather seats next to him. He's fiddling with his face; he has a crisscross pattern indented across his cheek.

"Where's that mark from?"

"There." He points to the metal mesh screen between us and the driver. "My excellent friend was reluctant to stop. Well, until I jumped in, of course. Then he decided an emergency stop was the most appropriate course of action, before he'd allow me to fasten my seatbelt."

"You gave me a right old fright Squire! Wasn't expectin' it was I?"

"No, me and you both," TrueBias says.

"Sorry Squire didn't fink."

"Well, well, it's done now. I'm sure my face will repair itself."

"Where to Squire?"

TrueBias' face is healing itself as he talks. The marks are disappearing at an incredible rate.

"Oh, just drive," TrueBias says.

"Will do."

As we pull away, TrueBias shuffles through his coat pocket and pulls out a gigantic mirror and peers at his reflection. He smiles to himself, then frowns and twists his face, distorting it in every direction until the last remnants of the damage, caused by the mesh, have miraculously disappeared.

"Oh! My good man! How excruciatingly primitive of me," he says, replacing his mirror in his pocket, satisfied he's still perfect. "We should have introduced ourselves. I'm TrueBias, capital T capital B. My friends call me True, and this is my whimsical companion, Eliza, Eliza Berry. We're both very pleased to make your acquaintance, and your name, Sir?"

"Oh, we know who you are, Squire; that'll be why no one picked you up." The cab driver peers over his shoulder. "Um, my name is Reginald Blackstock, Squire."

My mouth drops open.

"Shut your mouth, Eliza, you'll catch flies."

TrueBias is right. A swarm of flies are feasting off the rotting flesh peeling off Reginald's scalp. As I snap my mouth shut, my stomach jerks.

"Okay, if we call you Reg?" TrueBias asks.

"Ideal Squire, ideal."

"Grrreat! Well hello Reg. So very pleased to make your acquaintance. Understand why you didn't stop, not a proble–"

"W-why didn't he?"

If TrueBias knew the cab drivers wouldn't stop, why did he bother wasting ten minutes trying?

"Well, fought you'd quiz me about, the uh, the..."

As Reg answers, my stomach flips, air blocks my windpipe, and the retching coughing motion dries my mouth. Gasping, gripping at my neck, the acids from my stomach burn my throat. There's a maggot wiggling over Reg's eyeball and being squished every time he blinks. I hunch over as my stomach spasms.

"I'm going to puke. N-need to get out."

I frantically pull at the handle of the cab door, but it's locked. TrueBias removes my glasses and hands them to me.

"Sort yourself out; you're acting like a child." he says, his face sombre, his mouth ajar, his lip curled and snarling at me. I clear my throat. "There are bigger things than you to deal with, so handle it, and don't be so, so human!"

"S-sorry you're right."

My face is clammy and numb. Daisy said 'don't let fear block your way, be brave.'

"No." He smiles. "I'm sorry. This is a lot for you. Do you

want to go home?"

"Go anywhere you desire, Miss, you just say."

Reg glances over his shoulder at me, giving out a sharp squeal; he swerves the cab before he rights it again and fixes his eyes back on the road.

I'm sure he said *Jumpin' red jellybeans* without moving his lips. Did I read his mind like the cyclist? They can't all be ventriloquist. Can they? Or is this all just my imagination? Well, they can both talk; I'm neither an idiot, nor red.

"Don't mind me sayin' Miss, you're a little flushed."

According to the sign, Reg is driving us towards 'The Old City Centre.' As we wait at the traffic lights, a cat is trotting beside us on the pavement; he is heading in the same direction as us. It is identical to the one that I let out of Mrs Shufflebottom's flat. Skipping merrily beside him is a well-dressed Menax wearing a top hat. With each stride, the Menax kicks out his leg, his hat wobbles, he tosses his head back, and roars with laugher. I point them out to TrueBias, but he's flirting with Reg.

"Soo sorry, Reg. My friend can be a little emotional. We were planning on seeing the sights, so surprise us."

"Oh okay, Squire, we, um cabbies, figured you're after information on the Corpus, the one who got frew the wormhole."

"A Viscorpus through the wormhole. No way! What's a Viscorpus doing on planet Earth? How did that happen, my fine chap?"

"Parrently there was this well-dodgy Dolce who let him in. Opened the wormhole no less, and said, in you come, you is well welcome on planet Earth!"

"You're teasing me, Reg. You sure you aren't pulling my leg?" TrueBias says.

"Yep, no word of a lie, Squire, and guess what..."

TrueBias winks at me as he entices Reg into telling him everything.

"No, don't tell me any more Reg, I can barely digest it."

"This is the god's honest truth, Squire." Reg whispers, as

though someone other than us can hear him. "Got this from my brother-in-law's parents. Now, let me get this right: they're friends with the sister of the Urbe who's helpin' him."

"Complicated, but are you saying an Urbe will help the Viscorpus!" TrueBias says.

"The lady thrashing that man with her handbag. They were Urbes, weren't they?"

As I finish my sentence, TrueBias glares at me and thumps my leg, deadening it.

"Said too much already, Squire. Don't mean to bombard you with my natter."

TrueBias eyes focus on mine, daring me to utter a word. He mouths, "Shut up!"

"No, Reg, it's fascinating. Please go on," TrueBias says.

Maybe I'm crazy, but to me, this is all a massive waste of time. It makes sense to go directly to the museum where the actual Luxlumen stone is. Or even steal the stone for ourselves. Then we can negotiate with the Viscorpus. I'm pretty sure that's what Cecelia would do.

TrueBias seems to think that following the track of the Viscorpus like a dog follows a scent is the most logical way of finding him. I don't understand why his brain can't skip to the end. Maybe, when TrueBias is thinking straight, I'll suggest that we go straight to the museum, but for now I don't want another dead leg.

"Now don't know whether this is true," Reg says, "so don't go quotin' me, but I've heard Lionel Baitley on Swindlers Road. Not sure which house though; well, he's sortin' out all the um paperwork, if you know what I mean?" Reg smiles at TrueBias and winks. TrueBias coughs; I'm not convinced he is finding the maggot appealing either. "All I can tell you, Squire."

"Don't believe it, my charming fellow, but a marvellous story to pass the time. Can you drop us off at the next corner please? It's been lovely to meet you."

Reg lets us out of the cab. TrueBias pays the fare. Over on the opposite corner of the road is a street sign which says,

Swindlers Road.

"Sorry, I didn't mean to mess up. I'm not much use to you, am I?" We stand at the top end of Swindlers Road. "Have you thought about taking the stone for ourselves, and then the Viscorpus can't get his hands on it, can he?"

TrueBias clutches my shoulders and stares intently into my eyes.

"Are you suggesting we commit a crime?"

This is not the response I'm expecting.

"No, n-not really. I'm just saying that maybe we could protect the stone like any security guards would?"

TrueBias' gaze penetrates right through me; he bends his head sideward as though what I've said is either a fantastic idea, or the most outrageous suggestion to commit the most horrendous crime he's ever heard.

"Security guards protect the Luxlumen. It's in one of the most secure places it can be, and the museum is alarmed with the latest technology." He sucks air through his teeth. "We will not be touching the stone unless it's compromised."

"I really wasn't suggesting we did anything wrong."

"Stealing, Eliza, is always wrong."

TrueBias clearly has his own way of saving the galaxy. Maybe he's done it before; maybe he's done it hundreds of times before. After all, I didn't even know what was going on outside my own front door an hour ago. I guess I need to respect what he says, and do whatever it takes to help him, because if I don't, I may never see my dad again. If the stone is as secure as he says it is, and it's impossible to get to it, then it makes sense to find the Viscorpus and zap him to a holding cell in Conexus. Then my dad can come home. It's really, if you think about it, a brilliant plan. I guess!

"I was just trying to help. Didn't mean to upset you." We stroll down Swindlers Road. "Which building do we need?"

"I've no idea," TrueBias says. "We just need to look for the extraordinary."

"Are you from America?"

I imagine he's from a future Earth, maybe a time

traveller. I'm hoping he'll tell me something, which might help me understand him more.

"I'm from a far-off planet." He lowers his head, and with a deflated sigh, adds. "An unmapped black-hole destroyed all life on my spacecraft. There's no way home for me–"

"But you have an American accent; well, it's like a mixed-up American and a posh Englishman!"

"My accent?" he chatters. "Taught myself English through a computer programme but perfected it from the TV. My Insync Harmoniser can translate all known languages, but it's always more polite to perfect accents, you know, rather than relying on technology."

Swindlers Road isn't giving much away. There's an enormous variety of original buildings, combining a mixture of ancient shops and homes.

"This is the original part of the city before it was indefinitely extended," TrueBias says.

It's creepy here. The road relies on the old-fashioned streetlights, making it difficult to see any details on the doors.

"Can Daisy read everyone's mind?"

"No, not necessarily. It's like everything else practice makes perfect. Poppy, your mum, was outstanding; but it depends on the frequency of both minds. As a hybrid, you may only have limited abilities, or indeed intermittent abilities. Some Dolces need absolute silence, others need a heightened state of excitement, but it's not an exact science. Of course, none of them can read computers, androids or artificial intelligence."

I wish he wouldn't call me a 'hybrid'.

"Anything, Eliza?"

"Well, this one's odd."

The house has a tatty emerald-green front door. The sign above reads, *Pebble Book Store, 212a Swindlers Road.* Through the shop window there are towers of ancient dusty books, all sitting precariously on wooden rickety shelves.

"There's nothing out of the ordinary. What are you thinking?" TrueBias says.

"It's not right; these other buildings I've sensed nothing, but as we got to this one, well, I feel there's so much stress around it. Plus, let's be honest, how many people read printed books anymore?"

"Excellent reasoning. It's all we have, so by default, it's worth investigating."

We enter the garden, through the squeaky gate and up the stone steps. A cat, identical to the one earlier, is straggling the garden wall staring at us. TrueBias grabs the lion's head knocker and raps on the door.

— CHAPTER ELEVEN —

Lionel Baitley

"Who is it?"

A squawky voice from far inside the house echoes through the door. TrueBias nudges me and places a finger on his lips. This isn't the best time to ask questions. I nod, whilst rolling my eyes; he treats me like a child. He knocks again, and again the voice, a little closer, calls out.

"Who is it? Answer me, who's knocking at this ridiculous hour?"

TrueBias glances at me again, as though he needs to remind me, so soon, to stay silent. I pull out my phone. Is it a ridiculous hour? It's 10.13 pm, so maybe. The footsteps get closer. He's curious about who's knocking, so late at night, is tormenting the person behind the door of 212a Swindlers Road.

TrueBias whispers, "Urbes, an inquisitive species, always trying to profiteer, shall we say."

The footsteps come closer still.

"Do some Urbes have three legs?"

TrueBias slams his finger to his lips and glares at me. It's not a daft question; there's a clear plod, shuffle, clunk; plod, shuffle, clunk.

The voice at the door demands, "Who's there?"

TrueBias twists his head as though he's listening. The

only sound is the mumbling of the man behind the door and my nostril, whistling each time I breathe in. The anticipation of what's going to happen next is definitely mounting. As my heart makes an uncomfortable, skipping thump, TrueBias knocks on the door again.

"Maddison, we agreed midnight. Come back then."

Shaking my head, I tug at TrueBias' arm. "Say something."

The bolts clunk and the locks turn. The sound cascades from the top of the door to the bottom. The man is huffing and puffing, as though unlocking the door is a genuine effort. There's a final mumble of, "This better be important!" But before the door can fully open, a security chain snaps into place. A pot-bellied man with bushy eyebrows and a button nose peers through the tiniest gap; he slams the door in our faces. The vibration causes a little teal, chipped flowerpot, to the side of the door, to rock precariously before it surrenders trying to rebalance itself and topples over, rolling in a semi-circular motion at my feet.

Distracted by the pot, I didn't see TrueBias disappear. The cat meows and swishes its tail impatiently.

"T-TrueBias?"

There's commotion inside the house, and the door opens. TrueBias smiles like he has just shown me a card trick.

"Come in!"

"Stop doing that!" My foot stamps like a spoilt child as I bark at TrueBias. "Why didn't we agree, in the first place, you were going to disappear through the door instead of just abandoning me on the doorstep?"

Although I'm trying not to overreact, because he didn't actually abandon me, all the same, an irritation, a type of fluttering is swirling in the pit of my stomach. I need to be careful of TrueBias; I can't rely on him to take care of me. Next time, he may leave me somewhere where I might be in real danger. I know I should try to be confident like Cecelia would be, but it's not so easy, especially when you're surrounded by aliens.

"Sorry Eliza."

"It's not nice being stranded, even for the shortest of time, that's all I'm saying."

"Completely understand; how very injudicious of me," he says, "um, inconsiderate, that is." TrueBias lowers his head apologetically whilst holding on to the shoulder of the man. "Please accept my apologies; I will endeavour never to do it again, without being wholly and in absolute agreement with you."

"This is all very touching, but how dare you come into my home uninvited." The old man says, wriggling, desperately trying to escape.

TrueBias drags him towards the seating area of the shop. His tattered tartan slippers leave a polished line through the grubby floor.

Inside the house, the space is divided into sections. To the left is the bookstore, and directly in front of me, along the corridor, from behind an open door, the most delicious aroma of roast beef wafts towards me and my stomach grumbles.

"You must appreciate," TrueBias says, "one can't simply invade people's homes on a whim. How impolite, can you imagine it, popping in and out of innocent folks' homes based on a hunch? Once this delightful chap showed his face, though, we had a definitive right to enter, well, considering the intelligence we've collected."

"What from Reg?" I shut the door behind me.

"It's all we have. Oh, and to make doubly sure, I scanned the building, and this lovely gentleman here is definitely an Urbe."

The Urbe is walloping TrueBias across his arm with his cane, trying to escape his shoulder grip.

"Hey." I leap towards the Urbe. "Stop doing that!"

The Urbe squints and lowers his cane; he's thinking, because his lips aren't moving: *What if Anton or Maddison come back early? What do they know about me?*

TrueBias releases him, and the Urbe staggers towards

the oak-panelled cash desk, trying to steady himself, whilst frantically rearranging his clothes.

"Thank you, Eliza." TrueBias taps his foot. "I would have handled it, but thanks."

The Urbe picks up a phone from behind the cash desk and, with a peculiar rolling gait, shuffles back towards us, whilst cursing under his breath.

"How dare you burst into my home uninvited, treating me like a common criminal. The shop is closed, and you're not welcome here." He waves the phone in the air. "If you don't leave immediately, I'll call the police."

"Oh, my fine chap, you won't."

The Urbe stamps his stick on the wooden floor, causing mini dust clouds to rise whilst he swings his other arm above his head as though he's trying to bat off a swarm of bees.

"Get out. *Get out!*"

TrueBias makes himself comfortable in an old leather-studded armchair.

"My fine chap, we need to chat." He gestures to the seat opposite. "Please."

"Chat? *Chat?* Come back in the morning if you want to chat. I'm a busy man."

"What's keeping you so busy at this time of night, my fine chap?"

"It's none of your business," the Urbe snaps, but whilst snarling, he reluctantly sits opposite TrueBias.

As TrueBias tries to befriend the Urbe, I wander around the bookstore. There are columns and rows of dusty battered books, a tremendous choice, stacked from the floor to the ceiling. The wooden shelves scream under their weight; but what's peculiar is the books are all muddled. Crime books mixed with fantasy, children's books mixed with thrillers and non-fiction books pepper the shelves. How can anyone find anything? These shelves definitely need reorganising.

"Why are your books mixed up?"

"W-what do you mean, girl? They're in perfect order! Don't you dare touch anything. Do you hear me?"

The Urbe is only concerned about one book, a specific book about space, but which one? Whilst TrueBias is keeping him busy, I select several science fiction and a few books on astrology. I leave fingerprint patterns in the dust on every cover.

"Gross, you need to clean these."

The Urbe leaps out of his chair. TrueBias grabs his arm.

"Sit, Lionel." TrueBias forces the Urbe to sit back down. "I've heard plenty about you, from an excellent source; it is Lionel, isn't it?"

I pause and wait for a response. We may be invading an innocent person's home. Lionel squirms in his seat, knocking his cane onto the filthy floor. He stoops over to pick it up. His shoulder looks painfully disfigured. TrueBias is right; Urbes are stretchy, like play dough.

"Um, yes, what of it, w-what have you, um, heard?" Lionel thrusts his chin towards TrueBias. "You've been listening to the Garrae, haven't you? Nasty creatures always meddling, a-and they hate Urbes, you know that, don't you?" Lionel leans further forward and licks his lips as though he is going to say something important. "All I'm trying to do is make an honest living; it's difficult enough without visitors like you putting off my regular clientele."

TrueBias has slipped into a trance, causing Lionel to switch his attention towards me.

"Young lady, please leave my books alone."

"I'm surprised you still get people wanting books." As I remove more books from the shelves, Lionel shuffles to the edge of his seat. "How many shoppers do you get at this time of night?"

"Excellent question," TrueBias says as he snaps out of his gaze. "Who are you expecting? Who is Maddison?"

"You need medicine," Lionel gets up and heads towards the cash desk, collecting papers together and banging them on the counter. "I'm a bookseller, not a chemist! You have the wrong building. Please leave!"

"Oh okay! Have it your way, but before we leave."

TrueBias scratches his head as he strides towards Lionel. "Now, how can we put this... Do you produce forgeries, that is, create illegal papers for travel through the wormhole?"

"Preposterous idea!" Lionel's neck extends, so his head is like a lollipop towering over TrueBias. "How dare you. You will get me vaporised for spreading such rumours!"

As he recoils his neck, his face distorts in such a way it's ridiculous. One eye is in line with his nostril. An ear perches on the top of his head, and his neck, which hasn't gone back far enough, is causing his head to flop from one shoulder to the other. Although I try to suppress an escaping giggle, I can't, and instead release a sound more like a growling bear.

TrueBias glances over. "Are you alright? Found anything amusing to read?"

"Yeah, the head thing is funny, that's all. I'm searching for something; I'll um let you know, if I find it."

"Hey, you're messing up my displays." Lionel shuffles towards me, waving his stick. "You're leaving slimy skin cells all over my precious books."

TrueBias grabs Lionel's arm. "Are you aware, Lionel, that a Viscorpus has got through the wormhole and is seeking a host to help him travel back to Elekron with the Luxlumen? If he succeeds, he will destroy this galaxy and most living things in it."

"Really? Why should that rile me? The Viscorpus and the Urbes have a great relationship. The Viscorpus won't destroy our race."

TrueBias drags Lionel across the room and forces him back into the chair.

"Have you made a deal with the Viscorpus to save your people and planet?" TrueBias says.

"Nooo!" Lionel wriggles awkwardly in the chair. "Please, will you both leave me alone?" He springs to his feet and plods noisily towards the front door and opens it. "Now!"

"Are you mad, man? The Viscorpus will destroy all life in the galaxy. He will say and do anything to get the Luxlumen."

Although TrueBias is pleading, Lionel simply rolls his eyes.

"He's lying; he's hiding something, something behind these books."

TrueBias shuts the front door as Lionel heads, as fast as his short legs will carry him, towards me. I select another book and blow at the cover. A blanket of dirt and grime showers me. Dust stings my eyes as I select further.

"There's something here; I'm sure of it."

"How dare you, girl. Get out. GET OUT!" Lionel pulls at my arm, attempting to stop me from selecting any further books. "GEEEET OUUT!"

I snatch away from Lionel and skip towards the one book he keeps glancing at. It's the second to last book in the third row. It's lying on its spine: *The Hitchhiker's Guide to the Galaxy*. On the back it says, 'Don't Leave Earth Without It' and on the front, 'Don't Panic.' Is this a message? As I remove it from the bookshelf, a series of mechanisms clunk into action.

Lionel steps back before dashing towards the now closed front door. TrueBias beats him to it. The far bookshelf rotates 90 degrees, creating an opening to a secret room. TrueBias marches Lionel back towards the mysterious opening; his shoulder further distorts as he resists TrueBias dragging him across the floor.

"Wow, what's this stuff?" The flashing lights, switches and dials are mesmerising. "Is this the deck of a spaceship?"

"Logical assumption, but no, there is, however, a lot of high-tech equipment here." He drops Lionel to the floor and enters the room, brushing his hands over the dials and switches. "Scanners, printers, microchip equipment and electronic blockers; you have an impressive catalogue of gadgets and equipment to cater to any intergalactic species Lionel."

TrueBias circles round and picks him up from the floor, forcing him into the battered office-style swivel chair in front of the equipment. He swings it around and stares at him.

"Eliza, Lionel has himself a profitable, yet highly illegal business. This equipment creates travel papers, overwrites old papers and removes embedded papers for aliens to travel to and from Earth illegally."

Lionel hides his head down through his neck. He must now be able to see inside his own body. TrueBias rummages through his pocket and pulls out his Insync Harmoniser, pointing it at Lionel. His head pops out.

"Oh no, please," Lionel cries as TrueBias scans him.

I know what that feels like.

"Your own papers have expired Lionel, eighteen months ago. Have you applied for current ones? You're aware you can't stay on this planet without valid papers?" Lionel's eyes bulge like two ping-pong balls. "Your false papers don't fool me."

"I'll do it today," he says.

"Eliza is a stickler for fairness and openness, so explain to me why we shouldn't vaporise you for counterfeit charges against the galaxy?"

Lionel coughs, clearing his throat. "You're right." Since he has all this equipment hidden in his house, he'd find it difficult to plead he's innocent. "I've been creating papers for travel, nothing newsworthy; it's earning a little extra money, that's all. Like she says, nobody really buys books these days, and if there's no profit, I won't be able to stay on Earth. It's just enough to get me by, you know, a bit of pocket money."

I waggle *The Hitchhiker's Guide to the Galaxy* in front of him. "What aren't you telling us?"

"Okay," Lionel says, ducking his head like I'm about to whack him with the book. "Someone called Maddison visited me an hour ago. She's a Simulos, she has made a deal with the Viscorpus to help him back through the wormhole with the Luxlumen. If she does, the Viscorpus will save the Simulos, and, because I'm helping, the Urbe species, and both our home planets. We have no choice; he'll vaporise us if we don't agree to do it."

"So, you're creating papers for Maddison?" Lionel nods. "Is there anything else?" TrueBias asks.

Lionel folds his head downwards, so his nose is resting

on his chest bone. "No, I promise; there's nothing."

"You're not telling us everything, are you?" I fiddle with the dials on a console. "What about Anton?"

TrueBias smiles at me and points the Insync Harmoniser at Lionel's head.

"Lionel, this is your last chance to tell the truth, or I'll transform you, I promise, into a trillion pieces."

Lionel's bottom lip quivers. "Well, maybe one other tiny weeny thing." He raises his eyebrows whilst turning down the corners of his mouth. "An Urbe called Anton also visited, soon after Maddison. He's part of it too. He made the same deal with Viscorpus, guaranteeing the safety of both planets."

"Why two hosts?" TrueBias asks.

"Yes Lionel, what's the plan?"

"Anton is a decoy; forget him, you need to focus on Maddison," Lionel replies.

TrueBias grabs my arm, and he pulls me towards the entrance of the secret room away from Lionel. "Is he telling the truth?" he says.

"I've no idea." The treads of my trainers make designs on the dirty floor. "I'm hardly a lie-detector."

"Well, focus!"

"Okay..."

Lionel's mind is panicking. I can't read his thoughts at all.

"I've still no idea, but I guess it makes no sense to have Anton as a decoy; you only need a decoy if you know someone is on to you."

"Brilliant deduction, Eliza."

"I've just over an hour left to prepare the documents. They'll be back at midnight." Lionel is standing right next to us. "There's not much time."

TrueBias leads me further away from him, but he keeps shuffling towards us, desperate to overhear our conversation.

"What do you think we should do?" TrueBias raises his eyebrows. "If I send Lionel back to Conexus, then he won't be able to forge the papers."

"No, but the Viscorpus will find someone new to create the papers, and we'll be back to where we started, talking to gossiping cab drivers."

"Yeah, you're right." TrueBias says.

"Um, I guess our only choice is to wait for Anton and Maddison to turn up, and then figure it out."

TrueBias nods, "Exactly what I was thinking, Eliza. Well done!"

TrueBias tells Lionel to prepare the papers as planned and not to mention a word of our visit to either Maddison or Anton or we will be back. As we leave 212a Swindlers Road, the cat is heading back up towards the junction. It stops and stares at us as we cross the street to the all-night café. It then disappears into the darkness of the night.

– CHAPTER TWELVE –

The Curiosity Café

The floorboards of the café creak as we enter. A scrawny man, just inside the door, is hunched over his coffee mug. He doesn't look up. The back-lit electronic display boards have no animation, and show a sit-down menu and a takeaway one. This place is very basic; there's no virtual computerised assistant, nor a self-service option, only a live human server.

We must be invisible because despite the squeaking floorboards, neither the server nor the wafer-thin man pay us any attention as we make our way to the counter.

"Um, this may be a dumb question."

"Not another one!" TrueBias grins and nudges my arm.

The server might be deaf or is simply ignoring us.

"Why didn't the Viscorpus come through the wormhole alone? If he's cloaked, nobody can see him."

He smiles. "Cloaking only hides you, you don't disappear. The wormhole uses several probes as you enter; it may have identified the Viscorpus, but as the communication systems had failed, no alarm was raised. The truth is unclear, but to have any chance, the Viscorpus had to come through with someone, and the Menax was a perfect host because he was being smuggled in by Rose, a Dolce." He winks as he tries to get the server's attention. "Excuse me, um, Madam."

"Be right with you." She is stacking mugs on a shelf by

the coffee-making machine. Clearly, she's not deaf, just rude. As she spins round, her plastic smile slides off her face. "Oh, it's you. We're only doing takeaways."

"We'd like to eat in, if it's okay with you, Madam."

TrueBias is being as charming as he can. He grins at the server.

"Sorry, we're full."

Yeah, it's true the café is tiny, with only four tables; the spindly man has taken one of them, but that leave three free. This lady must recognise TrueBias. She doesn't seem to like him at all. A voice from the kitchen calls, "There's room."

We select a circular, metal-legged table with a glass top by the window and position the mis-matched wooden chairs so we have an excellent view of the entrance to 212a Swindlers Road.

"What time is it?" TrueBias asks.

"Oh, uh." I pull out my phone. "Ten fifty-seven. We've an hour."

TrueBias sighs. "Let's hope Lionel is being honest. Well, you can't trust Urbes; they're like the Viscorpus. They warp the truth somewhat." He picks up a sugar sachet from the plastic container on the table and flicks it. "We need to be vigilant; we can easily miss them."

"What do you want?" the server asks.

"Not sure!" The display boards behind the counter lists loads of delicious sounding foods. Some I've never heard of before, but it's been ages since I've been in a café. I squeeze TrueBias' knee under the table. "What do you want to eat?"

"No, I mean, why are you here?" she says.

"Umm, for food, I'm starving!" With TrueBias here, I know exactly what she means, but I'm acting dumb. "I'll just see if my friend wants anything."

She swivels on one foot and flounces back to the counter. The man, sat by the door, raises his head and glances at TrueBias. He drops tokens on the table and scrapes his chair as he stands. I'm sure he's thinking, *There's going to be trouble*. He nods towards me and stumbles out of the café.

"Are we attracting trouble?" TrueBias has gone into a trance and is staring out of the window.

I grab his arm. "Hey, do you want to get something?"

"Yes, sorry, doing routine maintenance. What do you need?"

"I'm starving, but, um, don't have any money."

"This isn't a waiting room," the server snaps, "order something or get out."

"Have whatever. I'll pay."

It's great being on this adventure with TrueBias; he is treating me as though I am his equal. I've never felt so important and useful to anyone before. I reckon if Cecelia knows what I'm up to, she'd be desperate to hang out with me now. If it wasn't for her, I probably wouldn't have been brave enough to search for my dad in the first place. I wave and smile at the server; I know what I'm going to order. She arrives at the table with her digital order pad and stylus poised.

"Okay, I'll have the English breakfast, with all the trimmings, a side order of fries, and a chicken burger. Can I also have a chocolate sundae and lemonade with a strawberry-flavour shot and–"

"And that's plenty, thank you," TrueBias dismisses the server as I'm only halfway through my order.

"You said 'anything.'"

"Yes, Eliza, within reason not the entire menu!"

"Do you not want something?"

"No."

The server, now in the kitchen, is arguing with the cook. It's difficult to understand what the problem is, but I can guess. She kicks the door open and the cook's voice calls behind her, "Whatever."

Placing the strawberry flavoured lemonade on the table, she shows TrueBias her wrist. "We have papers."

TrueBias flicks her wrist away from his face, "Oh Madam, I'm not here for you."

"You're bad for business." She nods towards a couple who have just peered through the window and are now scurrying off across the road.

"Simple Madam, encourage more desirable clientele!" TrueBias' mood towards her has changed.

The digital phone on the far wall rings; the server, realising she isn't getting anywhere with TrueBias, goes to answer it.

"The Curiosity Café, Penelope speaking." Unless you have amazing hearing, it's impossible to know what the other person is saying; plus, they have turned the picture off, so you can't even see who's calling, but it's obvious what the problem is.

"Yes, he's here… dunno… um, probably because he hasn't told me… with a female… yes… okay, bye."

As she replaces the receiver, she glares at us. Her frowning eyebrows join in the middle of her forehead. "See, told you," she squawks, nodding back to the phone as she plods towards us. "You're not good for business."

TrueBias ignores her. She grabs the tokens the man left on his table and rings in the sale.

"The Curiosity Café is an odd name for a café, isn't it?"

TrueBias is staring out of the window.

"Hey, are you listening to me?"

A bell rings in the kitchen, and the cook calls, "Service."

Penelope returns with an enormous amount of food.

"I'll bring your sundae when you've got through this lot." Although Penelope smiles at me, I'm sure she is thinking, *She better not throw up!*

Well, I've ordered plenty of food for sure, but I'll show her.

"When you said the 'head thing was funny,' what did you mean?" TrueBias asks.

"Oh, Lionel, well, it was funny when he overstretched his neck, and it didn't go back right."

"But you weren't wearing your spectacles?"

"No, they broke when I tripped over the tramline. The

glass fell out and shattered over the road, but I-I don't need them."

"No, really? Oh well, how marvellous! You believe in what you see. Excellent, really, that is excellent!"

I muffle my words as I stuff my face. "Can't see them all; Penelope says she has papers, but she's human." Egg drips over my chin. "So, it's only some aliens and not others."

"You gorge like a Dolce, always starving, ah?" He stares at me and points at his own chin. "No, Penelope is not from this planet; she's probably a Simulos like Maddison, the alien we're waiting for."

"Cooool, a shapeshifter? Like we talked about earlier?"

Food drops from my mouth onto the table, and as I pop it back in, Penelope squeals, "Oh disgusting."

She obviously has never been so hungry that her stomach has tried to eat itself. TrueBias either didn't notice, or equally didn't care.

"Yes, the Simulos, a fascinating species. They can mimic the image of any living being, incredible really. Penelope was in human form when we arrived, probably because the man by the door is human."

"That man went because of us."

"Oh, I didn't know he'd left. Well, I'm sure it has nothing to do with us. Penelope, being so rude towards her customers, perhaps made him feel uncomfortable."

TrueBias is probably right, and I'm making this stuff up. The man had finished his drink and was leaving. Penelope and the cyclist, well probably everyone would come to the same conclusion, wouldn't they? I've ordered half the menu and caused a cyclist to have a terrible accident. So yeah, greedy and an idiot then! It doesn't explain how I knew about Anton though, does it? I'm sure that since I've been able to see aliens, I've been more able to read their minds. Munching my way through my fries, I offer TrueBias some of my burger.

"I don't eat."

"Everyone needs to eat. Go on, have some! It's lush!"

"Eliza, you realise I'm a… I'm an android."

"Yeah, right." To Penelope's disgust, I splatter food all over the table as I try to suppress a squeal. "Very funny."

"No, I'm not kidding. I'm an android far superior to anything in this galaxy, of course."

My stomach flips as my heart sinks. An enormous wave of emptiness instantly washes over me. It didn't enter my head TrueBias was anything but a human form of an alien.

"B-but you said you survived your spacecraft coming through the black-hole."

"No, I said, we lost *all life*. I'm not life. As an android, I have no requirement for oxygen or food and could sustain the huge heat spikes the ship went through. All life perished."

I know what you're thinking, and no, you're right, I've spent little time with TrueBias, but I thought because we were on this adventure together that we might end up being great friends. After all, Cecelia has tons of them; all I want is one, but how can anyone be besties with a computer? Everything he knows, a human or alien, has programmed into his brain or his circuit boards. He hasn't got a family, nor can he think for himself.

No wonder he doesn't understand what it's like to be thirteen-years-old. He can't understand what it is to be human. He doesn't have compassion or imagination, or know how to love someone, and he isn't programmed to care about my dad. The galaxy will be the most important thing to him; he's programmed to protect it. This is terrible; it's terrible because I now know I'm my dad's only hope.

"You're a robot?" My burger is less yummy, gluey and quite bulky to swallow. "I th-thought you were alive."

TrueBias smiles at me and holds my hand resting on the table.

"Don't get all emotional. I'm artificial intelligence in human form, but a sophisticated one from a galaxy much more advanced than this one. My emotional circuits allow me to think and feel and hold billions of files on everything."

I slurp my lemonade.

"Yes, but a human or other species programmed

everything into your head; you can't think for yourself?"

"Same as everything in your head, but you're not limited to it. We can both learn for ourselves. Two hours ago, you didn't know that millions of aliens lived on planet Earth; now you're seeing them for yourself, and I thought you'd be completely useless on such a delicate mission, but without you, the secret room in Lionel's book store might still be a secret! I've all your abilities, and can learn in the same way as you can. Consider me another alien being."

"And I knew about Anton."

TrueBias squeezes my hand. He's right. Until a few hours ago, Daisy was lazy and ate too much and aliens didn't exist. Now my dad is in another world, and this galaxy is facing a dismal end, and I'm on a mission to save it. Well, I'm on a mission to save my dad; saving the galaxy is TrueBias' job.

As Penelope brings over my chocolate sundae, I suck the last dregs of the lemonade through the straw. No one has come into the café; well, one couple did, but they left. Others have peered through the window but scurried off. News has spread that TrueBias is in town.

Although I'm stuffed, the sundae is delicious, spooning it in as fast as I can, only causes my stomach to revolt as I belch the lemonade back up, "Buurrpp!" I spray the table with chocolate sauce before getting my hand over my mouth.

"So, when you said earlier you were doing routine maintenance, when you were just staring, you were actually mending yourself?"

"Yeah, the same as you. Your body heals cuts or broken bones, doesn't it?"

"Well, yes."

What TrueBias is saying makes sense, sort of.

"What's the time?"

With a napkin, I wipe off the chocolate sauce splatters sprayed across the screen of my phone.

"It's eleven forty-six; getting late."

Penelope comes over. "You did well." She smiles as she

clears the plates.

"Bill, please." TrueBias requests without looking at her.

"Hey?" Knocking TrueBias' shoulder, I point over to Lionel's house. A man scurries up his steps. With his back to the door, his head jerks in every direction, as though he is being chased and is trying to escape. The door opens, he dives inside.

Penelope doesn't appear to be in a hurry. Is she colluding with Lionel and trying to delay us? Was it Lionel on the phone?

"Bill!" TrueBias demands. Penelope rushes over. He stands, slams his hand against the machine whilst pulling my arm upwards. As he does so, I grab the spare napkins left on the table.

"We've got to go now!"

He yanks me off my seat and out through the door.

— CHAPTER THIRTEEN —

Impostor!

Once outside the café, we cross Swindlers Road and creep into Lionel's front garden. The gate squeals, robbing us of our intention to be sneaky. The temperature has dropped, and although it's late summer, the nights can be as chilly as the winter. I zip my jacket and blow into my cupped hands.

The shop window blinds are partially closed and Anton, well, I assume its Anton, is arguing with Lionel. It's like a pair of wrestlers squaring up for a fight. We should have made Lionel open the window.

"Do you have super android hearing?"

"Shush."

The colour drains from Anton's cheeks as Lionel, who gets particularly animated, raises and lowers his arms, stomping his cane on the floor, which causes bellowing clouds of dust. Anton runs his hands through his hair before placing them on the back of his neck. He then raises them in the air as Lionel shoves him towards the opening to the secret room.

"Get down," TrueBias says, as the determined click clicking of footsteps gets closer.

Placing his hand on the top of my head, he holds a finger over his lips. Pushing hard, he forces me to my knees; both of us crouch behind a flowering hydrangea bush. The flower petals tickle my nose as a lady clip-clops, like a two-legged pony, through the squeaky gate. Snorting, I shove the corner of a napkin up one nostril to quash a sneeze.

This must be Maddison, a Simulos, according to Lionel; she's pretending to be human. I've seen her somewhere before, but it's difficult to make out any features. Once at the top of the stone steps, she knocks using the lion-head knocker, and whilst waiting for an answer, she stands the pot, which toppled over earlier.

"Choo." I scuffle the sneeze, but the grunt is enough to attract Maddison's attention.

TrueBias, trying to silence me, elbows me in the ribs, plunging me backwards further into the bush. It rustles and a branch cracks as I topple onto it. Lionel undoes the series of bolts and locks on his front door.

"Come in, my dear; come in before you're seen." Lionel hurries Maddison inside.

"Someone is out there," she says, peering backwards towards us. "They're hiding in the bushes."

I'm sure I recognise her voice, but where from? TrueBias clamps my hand so tightly, the blood pumps back through my arm, and as I wriggle free, Lionel peers out around the doorway.

"No, no one's there," he says, without actually checking. He knows we're watching, but so far, he hasn't let on to Maddison. He slams the front door behind him.

Through the shop window, we can see that Lionel is saying something, but again, it's impossible to work out anything specific. He swings his arms and points to the front door, then at the books, and then at Anton as he emerges from behind the rotating bookshelf. The conversation escalates into an argument, with Lionel and Anton distorting their forms in a sort of tribal dance. Maddison has her back to us. Her head nods, and she raises her arms defensively before Lionel places his hand on her elbow and ushers her into the secret room.

"I'm sure I've seen Maddison before."

TrueBias is sulking, if androids can sulk.

"What's the matter with you? They didn't catch us."

"More luck than design, Eliza. You could've jeopardised the entire mission."

"Huh! Well, sometimes us humans do odd stuff. We can't help it."

"Maybe you shou–"

"Shush!"

I yank TrueBias' arm. We place our backs to the wall and squat below the window. Anton must have heard us arguing; he's cupping his hands around face and looking out through the gap in the blinds. I hold my breath as a leaf brushes my nose.

"Humph!" I stop the sneeze from making any real sound.

TrueBias again elbows me, but this time in my side.

"Ouch! That hurt; stop doing that."

Fortunately, Anton is now walking towards Maddison and Lionel, who've reappeared from behind the bookshelf.

My jaw drops. I'm struggling to say anything.

"M-Maddison is C-Cecelia Latimer!"

"What?" TrueBias says.

"Cecelia blinking Latimer. She's the girl from my school; the one I wished would *drop dead!* You know I told you earlier." I put up with her because I thought it was *me* who was different and odd, and who didn't fit in. All this time, she was the true alien, and she's only so perfect because she a Simulos. She can shapeshift into a supermodel if she wants to. "What a fraud!"

"They're coming." TrueBias points at the front door. We both crouch behind the bush.

As they open the door Lionel says, "Don't mess up, remember whoever gets through, goes through."

Lionel shuts the door, and Anton and Cecelia head down the stone steps. Cecelia points towards us.

"The rustle came from over there," she says.

"Yeah, I thought I heard something too," he says.

Anton stumbles towards us, tripping over an ornamental rock just as a black cat scurries from behind us and straight through Anton's legs.

"Mystery solved," he says.

"Well, I knew I heard something."

As they head down the path, TrueBias points the Insync Harmoniser at them.

"Okay-jokey, I've scanned them, definitely an Urbe and Simulos."

"We need to follow them." I'm desperate to get out from behind the bush. As soon as Anton and Cecelia go out through the squeaky gate, they split up. Cecelia crosses the road towards *The Curiosity Café*. Anton heads back towards the junction, where Reginald dropped us off. "TrueBias?" I shake him out of his trance. "Which one are we going after?"

I'm crossing my fingers, and under my breath, praying, please don't say Cecelia, please don't say Cecelia. I'm not sure I can face her right now.

"I don't know," TrueBias says, as he battles with the hydrangea. "Did you hear Lionel say, 'Whoever gets through goes through?'"

"Yeah! When Lionel told us Anton was a decoy, I reckon that was, in fact, a decoy!"

"Oh, right!" TrueBias frowns and glances downwards. "Extrapolate?"

"Anton isn't a decoy. Lionel is trying to trick us because he said, 'Whoever gets through goes through.' He's desperate for us to stop Cecelia, so Anton can get through the wormhole and save the Urbe species, the same species as Lionel!"

"Oh, super deduction: a double bluff." He grins. "It's obvious now you say it."

"Well! Cecelia fooled me. What a traitor, pretending to be human." I brush the remaining petals and twigs off my jeans. "If I ever see her again, I'll make it clear to her there's more to being human than being pretty."

Despite how Cecelia has treated me, I still think she's

pretty incredible. It must be fantastic being a Simulos. Maybe, like Lionel says, she has no option but to help the Viscorpus, but that doesn't explain her behaviour towards me before the Viscorpus even came through the wormhole though, does it? I reckon they have been planning this for ages. Equally, I could be totally wrong, but what I do know is that despite being an incredible alien, she's also a spiteful, manipulative bully.

"You're right, Eliza. It's the imperfections of humans which make them human."

"Well! Cecelia could do with a heart for a start."

"She's actually got two hearts; it's me who's heartless!"

It's nice TrueBias is trying to cheer me up.

"Oh, I don't know; you'll make a great tin man!"

"I'm not made of tin!" TrueBias says, his voice harsh. His forehead wrinkles as he wrestles with a twig trapped in the lining of his coat; he snaps it in half and chucks it to the ground. "Tin! How very rudimentary." He didn't get my joke; he probably has never seen *The Wizard of Oz*.

I fasten the gate, and we head in the same direction as Anton. TrueBias is dawdling behind me, messing about with the Harmoniser.

"Come on!" I pull at his arm. "We'll lose him."

"Wait a minute," he says.

His Harmoniser unravels a virtual holographic screen, which is highlighting a flashing dot.

"Wow, amazing! Is that Anton?" My finger traces the flashing dot which is travelling across the screen.

"I've scanned the immediate area for Urbes. He's the only Urbe apart from Lionel; he's by the junction." TrueBias bursts into a sprint, twists backwards and waves at me. "Eliza, come on!" As we dash up the hill, the flashing dot whizzes off the screen. "Oh no, he's gone; we've lost him!" TrueBias' face is like a deflated balloon.

"Are you malfunctioning? The dot flew off the screen, so unless Anton is turbo-charged, he has probably got into a vehicle. Come on, let's go; we need to catch a cab."

"Yes, sterling idea!"

We get to the top of Swindlers Road. "Wait here, allow me!" I'm able to hail a cab in less than thirty seconds and as I get in, TrueBias, as he does, joins me instantly.

"Oh! Didn't know you were joinin' us Guv. Where you off this time of night?"

"Well, my fine fellow, they have dragged me into this awful mess involving the Luxlumen thingy."

"Oh yeah, know what you mean, Guv, madness. Only humans would put the most valuable stone in the universe on a shelf in a museum! Crazy! Um, no offence meant, Miss."

The Garrae smiles at me. Unfortunately, I will never again be shielded from a decomposing body driving a cab. His few burnt-orange rotten teeth wobble as he talks, and a putrid eggy pong wafts around each time he opens his mouth. His scalp is peeling, like an orange skin, as a worm burrows through to his skull.

"I'm not offended, I agree with you; seems mad to me too!" Well, I'm not pure human after all. "They're all crazy!" He twists and again nods approvingly.

My stomach churns.

"Where to Miss? The clock's tickin'." He points to the cab meter, which clicks over another £1. It's £10 already, and we haven't moved yet.

TrueBias is playing with his Harmoniser and isn't interested in talking to the Garrae. I scoot forward in the seat and focus on the Garrae's mind. "Can you make any suggestions?"

"Well Miss, if you're lookin' for the Luxlumen, if I were you, I'd follow the Urbe who's got into my buddy Smithy's cab only five minutes ago; he was just sayin' over the radio 'bout getting the stone; 'parently he's got somethin' to do with it."

"Has he now my fine fellow, and where was he dropped off?" TrueBias says.

"Oh, don't know, Guv, but I'll tell you what, I'll find out in a jiffy, considerin' it's you an all." The cab driver presses a button on his dashboard; a picture appears in front of him of an equally decomposed Garrae. "Ello Smithy, it's me, George."

"Yeah, mate, I can see. What can I do you for?"

"A quickie, mate. Where did you drop that there Urbe off?"

"He's a bad-un he is. Best keep away, up to no good, goin' on bout the end of the world and makin' deals with the Corpus. Bit mad I reckon. Wouldn't trust a Corpus would you, mate?"

"No fear, mate, not my cup of tea. Fanks for the heads-up tho'. Where am I avoidin', so don't run into him?"

"Don't go anywhere near Crystals Emporium. Dropped him outside far entrance on Connaught Road."

"Cheers mate, I'll bear it in mind." George, our cab driver, presses another button, which cancels the connection.

"Crystals Emporium it is." As I instruct George, a feeling of excitement washes over me. "The Connaught Road entrance, please."

George peers at me in his rear-view mirror. "On my way, Miss." The meter is reading £18, and we have only just set off. TrueBias gazes out of the window, surveying the world as we shoot by.

"What's the Viscorpus like?" TrueBias' leg is trembling; he peers at me as I place my hand to steady it. "They must be more than liars?"

"There's not a tremendous amount known about them. Mature quickly, careful with resources, um, they respect heritage and value families, which is all great, but they're also a ruthless race and are known to be compulsive liars. It's said they historically stripped planets of their valuable resources and were known as the universal bullies. There's no more information in my database." TrueBias' expression is blank, his eyelids quiver. He's definitely repairing himself. "I've never come across an affable one," he says, "but I've only met one."

"No, don't get involved with that lot," George adds. "'Ere we go."

George stops outside a huge shopping mall, which sells everything. Well, according to the slogan on their sign:

Crystals Emporium, Everything You Need Everything You Want. TrueBias settles the £34 bill with George, and as we watch him drive off, we climb the granite steps to the main entrance. The metal detectors scan us as we get into the foyer, and then we're manually scanned by a Reus security guard.

I tug TrueBias' sleeve. "I thought they had you then!"

"What do you mean?"

"Well." I cover my face with my hand and lean towards TrueBias. "The Insync Harmoniser: surely they were scanning for weapons."

"Yes, but only for weapons of this world."

The shopping mall is buzzing. Customers are wandering around chatting, arguing, laughing, shouting, moaning and complaining, both in their heads and out loud. It's deafening. I can't imagine what a pure Dolce must listen to all the time, poor Daisy!

"Right Misster, let uss know if you need anything," a guard says as he nods at TrueBias.

A Reus attracts my gaze, and although I focus on what he's thinking, I get nothing; yet I can hear the thoughts of a human, who is deciding what she wants for lunch tomorrow. Another ball-like alien is excited about a party she's going to when she finishes work and tons more shoppers' thoughts are racing through my head.

"Yess Missss?" He lowers his head and stares directly at me.

Surely the Reus won't kick off in here, will he? "Oh! Sorry, I'm um, I'm just having a look around."

The Reus steps back and I check out my surroundings, so as not to appear to be a liar. The huge supermarket is very busy. A Menax with a rather towering top hat is selecting an odd coloured apple. He glances at me and nods.

"Is that the Menax from the road?" I tap TrueBias' arm. "TrueBias."

TrueBias is spinning, pirouetting on one foot. He flings his head backwards and peers up through the many floors in the mall; he's hunting Anton. There are so many shops and cafés; it seems an impossible task. The Harmoniser has twelve flashing dots, so there's twelve Urbes in the mall, but which one is Anton?

I smile at the Reus. "Has an Urbe come in, in the last ten minutes?"

"Yess Misss, sshifty character! He went to Holo." The Reus nods towards the flat-based escalator. "Call, if you need uss."

We've got just over three hours before the wormhole reboots; we've not got much time. The mall is enormous. I've never been here before. Kids from my school come every week shopping with their mothers or fathers, so I've heard all about it, and they weren't exaggerating. We haven't had 'Show and Tell' since year four, but everyone brings in their latest gadgets and wears their most fashionable clothes. So, it's 'Show and Tell' every day at school. The teachers encourage it, well the virtual assistants do.

Striding up the escalator, TrueBias continuously examines the Harmoniser, checking for the changing locations of the Urbes. As we arrive at the top, we're bombarded by virtual images. Holographic shop staff ask whether they can help. Advertising banners float in front of our faces and virtual assistants, doing product demonstrations, hover continuously, always a couple of steps in front of us. TrueBias swipes them away with his arms, with such force, it's odd to have no electronic displays selling something, but it doesn't take them long for them to come back. Each new aisle has a fresh set of advertising campaigns. The Harmoniser shows a stationary dot on this floor.

"Over there!" I point to a sign which reads, *Welcome to the HoloSuite–Dreams Come True Only at Crystals Emporium.*

"He's gone into a HoloSuite." TrueBias stops so abruptly I barge straight into him. "They've tricked us." He slips his Harmoniser back in his pocket.

"What's a HoloSuite?"

"Oh, umm, it's a place where you can programme any virtual environment," he says.

"What like being in the countryside?"

"We can programme any creation you wish, young lady. We have a vast choice of standard programmes. Would you like to peruse our catalogue with a list of options and extras?" A virtual assistant is pestering us.

"Can you get hurt? Can you drown, get shot or even be killed? What I'm asking is, i-is it dangerous?"

"Most definitely not, young lady; we have a 100% safety rating."

"Um, yeah, things can go wrong," TrueBias says.

"It's weird Anton has gone into one. There must be a reas–"

"Well, they've tricked us," TrueBias says. "You over thought it. Lionel is right; Anton is a decoy. If he's messing about in a HoloSuite, he's not bothered about the Luxlumen, or the Viscorpus. Let's find Cecelia."

"Why is it my fault? We agreed, remember: 'Whoever gets through goes through?'" Wow, how quick is he to blame me when things go wrong! "I thought we were a team?"

TrueBias heads back towards the escalator, mumbling. The virtual sales assistants are making it easier for him to do it stroppily; he frantically takes his frustration out on them by batting them away each time they ping up.

"Come on, Eliza!"

"No, wait! If he's a decoy, why would he hide in a HoloSuite rather than stay out in the open?"

TrueBias faces me. His teeth dazzle under the spotlights. "Impressive deduction. Excellent! The only way we can find out what he is up to is to have a look."

I guess that's the best version of an apology I'm going to get. As we head back towards the HoloSuite, another virtual assistant hovers in front of us.

"Can I help you, Sir? Do you need to escape from reality? We can do it all at Crystals Emporium." The assistant grins. "Unfortunately, our HoloSuites are currently occupied. We can offer you refreshments whilst you wait. Or maybe Sir would prefer to book an alternative time slot?"

"I'm after an Urbe called Anton. Which suite is he in?"

"I'm sorry, Sir. Information we hold is confidential. Would you like to read our Confidentiality Policy? It's in a downloadable format, which we can ping to a device of your choice, or we can present it to you on a virtual screen."

TrueBias rummages through his pocket and pulls out his Insync Harmoniser. He scans the virtual shop assistant.

The perky assistant's expression transforms from an up-turned mouth to a rather depressed one.

"Mr Anton and Mr Appollo are in Suite 4, but whilst the programme is in operation, I cannot open the door from the outside. It's a safety measure, which they will not allow me to override."

"Mr Appollo!" My face tingles, and as I try to swallow, a lump of air blocks my throat.

"Are you okay? Do you know who Mr Appollo is?" TrueBias asks.

I gulp. "No, not really; it's just Cecelia said something about him."

Why was Cecelia picking on me? Why was she singling me out? It can't just be random. What link has she made between me and Appollo? Who is Appollo? Questions explode in my head, but as usual, I have no answers.

TrueBias uses his Harmoniser to create an area in the door of Suite 4; it transforms from being solid wood-effect, to a shimmering, water-like liquid. He steps straight through, and as he does so, the door goes back to being solid. It's pretty incredible. The virtual assistant is hovering over me, humming annoyingly. TrueBias opens the door from the inside.

"Come on!" he invites me in.

I pause for a moment as a sense of peace washes over me. The HoloSuite is so serene compared with the chattering mania of the shopping mall.

"Quick!" TrueBias insists.

— CHAPTER FOURTEEN —
The HoloSuite

Now if I wanted to escape reality, and let's be honest, that's most days, my first choice wouldn't be an old-fashioned bar, but it appears this is exactly what Anton has chosen. We find a free booth near the door. The music is by Brick Sity, their latest release, 'Tech Is Killing Us.' It's a great song, but it doesn't fit here. There's no real technology, it's gloomy and depressing. Why would anyone choose to come to such a place?

"Can I help you, Sir? She's a little young to be in here, isn't she?"

A rather round server waddles towards our table; she's showing an awful lot of skin.

"Yes, I'm looking for Anton. Have you seen him?"

"Oh Mr Anton, what a love! He's at the bar with Mr Appollo." She points over to two gentlemen and then leans over the table and whispers: "Between me and you, Mr Appollo isn't so nice."

TrueBias glances over at the bar. "Of course, a cloaking device cannot be effective in a HoloSuite. The entire suite is a cloaking device. What an ingenious way to meet the Viscorpus in secret."

"Sooo, you reckon Appollo is the Viscorpus?"

The bartender is refilling Appollo's glass with a lime-coloured bubbly liquid. The light coming from behind the bar is causing a shadow, so it's difficult to make much out, plus two other men are standing in my line of vision.

"Yes, Mr Appollo *is* the Viscorpus," TrueBias says, nodding his head.

I lean over TrueBias to get a better view. Appollo is human shaped. He has round sunken eyes, an enormous nose and dish shaped ears. What has Appollo got to do with me? Why was Cecelia saying he would laugh at me? Why would he even know or care I existed at all?

"Can I help you, Sir? She's a little young to be in here, isn't she?" The same server distracts us, glitching robotically, standing at the table. "Can I help you, Sir? She's a little young to be in here, isn't she?" She's attracting attention.

"A glass of lemonade, please," TrueBias says.

"Sir." She nods approvingly and waddles away.

The program has crammed the entire bar full of human forms. There's lots of laughter and chattering, but nothing is real. Men sloppily drink from stumpy glasses, whilst there's only a splattering of wild, leather-dressed, tattooed women.

"I'll confront him." TrueBias stands and makes his way to the bar.

As he twists his way past the table and chairs, I dive forward and grab his hand. Is he kidding me?

"That sounds like a dumb idea to me. He doesn't look friendly."

The men, who were blocking my view, have made their way to the bar, so it's now easy to see why the Viscorpus terrifies everyone. Appollo has burgundy-coloured skin with a network of bulging veins, which pulse through his neck. He has no hair, but tattoos, like a road map, covering his head, with only his eyes and lips untouched. He's dressed entirely in leather. TrueBias pulls away from my grip and drags out a three-legged wooden bar stool. He positions himself next to Appollo. I sneak closer and sink into a fake-leather padded tub chair.

"Excuse me." TrueBias taps Appollo's shoulder.

TrueBias is remarkably polite to someone who's planning to destroy the galaxy. Appollo swivels on his stool. His piercing yellow eyes are weird but mesmerising.

"Android, you're wasting my time."

Appollo's voice is threatening; the veins in his head pump as he snarls at TrueBias. An eerie silence smothers the room. Even the holograms seem petrified of Appollo. If TrueBias had a brain, he would agree with him, and retreat to our table, to rethink his plan.

"May I make a suggestion?" TrueBias says.

"Elekron without the Luxlumen is dying," Appollo says. "My people are dying."

"Of course, I understand why you're here. Honestly, I do, but it's my responsibility to protect this galaxy, and punishing trillions for what a few did, 200 years ago, is not the answer."

"It's in the *Chronicles of Elekron*. Do not challenge me on this android. Be warned!"

As he makes his final offer, he stands, kicking his barstool backwards. Appollo towers above TrueBias.

TrueBias, in his wisdom, ignores Appollo's advice and challenges him.

"My good man, let's discuss it properly. Let's talk to the Federation," he says.

"No, it's too late. We did nothing and we've suffered. It's time for them to suffer."

Appollo swipes TrueBias across the face, causing him to slide partly across the counter before tumbling headfirst onto the floor.

My heart instantly jumps into my throat. "Hey stop it!" I bolt upright, glaring at Appollo.

"Go away, little girl," Anton says, shoving me back into my seat. The chair scoots backwards and collides into the table behind me, causing the drinks to topple over. The legs on my chair collapse as vibrant-coloured liquids shoot into the air and spill across the floor. The two ladies, who were sitting at the table, glare at me as I now lie flat on my back, rocking like a beached whale in my tub chair, desperately rolling as I try to get up.

TrueBias is back on his feet. He dives at Appollo, burying his head into his stomach, propelling him across a table that's occupied by three very drunken men. As the drinks on their table spill over onto their laps, the men leap to their feet and clobber each other.

"Fight, fight..." A few other men chant behind me as one of them smacks another over the head with a stool, breaking it into its original parts.

"Your lemonade."

The server, about to place my lemonade on the table next to the two ladies, lifts it again as a rather lanky man comes shooting across the room.

Rolling, creating momentum, I scramble out of the chair and clamber onto my hands and knees. The server gives me the lemonade, but the older lady of the two snatches it out of my hand and chucks its contents in the face of her friend. Her friend grabs the hair of the older lady and pulls it violently. As they yank at each other's hair, they dance around the bar screaming and shrieking like a pair of scrapping alley cats.

People ignore me, yet are happily arguing amongst themselves and across different groups. TrueBias rolls over a table, and Appollo grabs his arms and swings him across the room, slamming him into the far wall. He slides to the ground. Appollo picks up a table and lifts it over TrueBias' head. With all my focus on Appollo's mind, I stand.

"Stop it!"

Appollo stares at me. He drops the table to one side. I sense he is more scared of me than he is of TrueBias. We're distracted by an announcement:

"Please exit the suite. Your bar brawl programme will end in thirty seconds. Remember, dreams come true only at Crystals Emporium."

Appollo taps Anton's arm. He's planning to escape. He's thinking: *Can't get caught.* He stares at me and as I hop back, he says, "We fight in the name of our fathers; we live by the honour of our grandfathers."

TrueBias is searching for his Insync Harmoniser, and as soon as Anton and Appollo exit the suite, the programme ends. The once grubby bar of brawling customers disappears. There's no trace it was ever here.

"Wow, intense; if he d-dropped the table on you, he might have killed you. Can you b-be killed?"

"Well, technically no, because I'm not alive, and, umm, the furniture is just props, but he's knocked my inner circuits out of place, which is tremendously inconvenient. You okay?"

"Yeah, I'm okay."

If I am being honest, I'm not okay at all. My whole body is tingling and my head is trying to convince me to flee as far away from this madness as I can, but I must be brave for my dad. I've never seen a fight before, never mind been in one. What did Appollo mean? Does he know my dad and, more importantly, where is he?

"You don't seem okay. You sure?" TrueBias says.

TrueBias' arm is twisted at a stomach-churning angle. I gulp back a lump of chocolate tasting acidic puke as his elbow twists out towards me. Holding out my hand, I offer to pull him up.

TrueBias tries to stand without my help, but in his frustration and stubbornness his feet keep slipping on the polished surface underneath him. He bangs the floor with his functioning arm as though it's the floor's fault.

"I expected him to be more cooperative," he says, as his eyeballs tremble. He's blinking, but only one eye at a time.

"Are you winking at me?" Smiling apologetically, I again offer my hand and help him to his feet. "We need to forget about decoys. What a mess!" TrueBias is in a trance, probably doing some internal repairs. "I guess our only option now is to go to the museum."

We stagger out of the HoloSuite. TrueBias is relying too heavily on my ability to support him; my knees buckle under his weight.

"Thank you for your custom. Please call again."

The chirpy virtual assistant is waving to us, showing an unnatural volume of perfect teeth. We stumble straight through him. I hold on tightly to TrueBias as we ride the escalator; he's slung his broken arm over me. His head slumps over my shoulder like an inactive string puppet. His arm clunks and cracks back into position as a Reus approaches us.

"We have isssuess Misss. Crysstalss Emporium hass been sshut down. Thiss iss following government protocol until the authoritiess can get here."

"What's happened?" TrueBias says, his voice slurred.

It sounds crazy, but it looks like a truck has driven through the body scanners at the mall entrance; they're all twisted and bent out of shape. A Reus is perched on top, crouching as though he is laying an egg, but he's actually acting as a look-out.

"Nothing to see here. Nothing to see here," a lanky lady with a gravelly sharpness to her voice interrupts, glaring at the Reus. She seems human, but her overly exaggerated pointy features make her less-human. "We can assure you there's no issue. Please continue with your shopping. We're here for you at Crystals Emporium."

TrueBias raises his head and scans the devastation. "Thank you, but we need to leave."

"That's not possible at the moment, Sir, as the automatic security doors and shutters are locked. None of us can leave," she says.

"Saw it all," George says, standing behind us.

"Hello George, lovely to see you!" TrueBias miraculously makes an incredible recovery as he shakes George's hand.

"Ello Guv, thought you'd need a cab."

"How decent of you."

"No problem, Guv, but I'm no use now; can't get out meself," he chuckles. "That Urbe caused chaos when he left." George wobbles his head, causing a worm to belly-flop onto his shoulder. "Didn't see the Corpus, not at first, until they went through the scanner and he uncloaked himself. Saw them both, then. The Corpus was shootin' everywhere, made a right friggin' mess of the scanners." George is animated, re-enacting everything. "Reus went crazy, security lights flashin', and the shutters sealed, but the Urbe and Corpus got out before complete lockdown. They reckon it will be an hour before they'll let us go."

"So, they triggered security to lock us in? Ingenious plan," TrueBias says.

"Did they lure us into a trap?" Holding my neck, I draw in a huge breath of air. "Was Lionel being truthful about Anton being a decoy, after all?"

"Don't worry, I'm not trapped. I'll leave you with George."

"What? No way–"

"It's easier."

"For who?"

"Look; we haven't got time to argue," TrueBias says.

"Right, so you're prepared to dump me whenever it suits you?" A surge of anger builds inside of me. This is now more than a mission to save my dad. "How could you?"

"Someone needs to get to the museum," he says.

"Well, look at the state of you! I'll come."

"It's getting too dangerous. I couldn't protect you in the HoloSuite. You're much safer here with George."

"Fine! So, it has nothing to do with whether you can get me out. Well, congratulations, you've just found a perfect excuse to dump me." My face is getting hotter as the blood rushes to my head. "Newsflash–You're not responsible for me."

"Eliza, you can see what Appollo is capable of."

"Whatever. You probably treated your friends in your spacecraft like this. Abandoned them; left them for dead."

I guess TrueBias' emotional chip is functioning. He glances at me before surveying the floor. I'm sure there's a tear in his eye. But that's impossible.

"Leave me alone."

My guilt-ridden heart flutters. How could I be so cruel?

It's the sort of nasty thoughtless thing Cecelia would say.

"I'm sorr–" but before I finish my sentence, he's gone.

He'll be better off without lookin' after her, George is thinking.

"Aaaaah." Raising my hands to the back of my neck, I twist my head in every direction. "God, I can be a right nasty–aaaahhhh." Tears bubble in my eyes for the hundredth time tonight.

"You alright, Miss? You're a bit flushed," George points to his own face.

"Yeah, sorry, just wish I'd engage my brain before my big mouth sometimes."

"Oh, he'll be fine. Don't you go frettin'. Fancy a snack? My treat."

"No, but thank you. You are really lovely."

George blushes. "Fanks! Never been called that before."

We wander through the grocery section of the mall; the customers are still shopping as if nothing has happened. The same constant mental dumb brain chatter rings through my ears. A teenage human boy has just finished helping a swanky lady pick some grapes off an animated vine who's reluctant to let them go. He shifts to restocking purple-coloured apples, the same apples the Menax selected. He is singing a song in his head.

"Is that Brick Sity?"

"Sorry Miss; didn't mean to sing out loud."

He wasn't.

"Can you tell me if there's a way out, please?"

The teenager twists his head. He is thinking: *Is she stupid?* But says "Sorry, Miss, there's no way out in lockdown. You must wait until they issue the all-clear."

"There we go, Miss. Stuck for the foreseeable." George cheerily reinforces what we've been told, but this human is not telling me everything.

"Thank you, George. Let me handle this."

George thinks I'm being stroppy and raises an eyebrow, probably because he only has one. He then holds up both hands as though he is surrendering and steps back.

"Hi, me again!" The shelf stacker is now restocking green coloured oranges, or maybe limes. "That's not true, is it?"

"What Miss?" he says whilst thinking: *Leave me alone.*

"That there's no way out?"

"No, but that's what I'm supposed to say."

"Okay, tell me what you're *not* supposed to say."

"The bakery emergency exit is always unlocked." He's picturing, in his head, the unlocked emergency exit.

"Thank you!"

"You're welcome, Miss."

He unwraps a tray of bananas; I'm oddly relieved they're yellow.

"Oh, one other thing."

"Yes, Miss," he sighs.

"What colour would you say my skin is?"

"Um, I'm not sure what you want me to say, Miss."

He's puzzled. He thinks it's a trick question. I guess it is.

"My skin, is it purple, pink, green?"

"No, it's, it's um, a brownish colour, Miss."

He is so reluctant to tell me. Well, I guess it's an odd question. It's all making sense now. Cecelia only called me *Cherry Berry* because she was the only one who could see my true colour; that's why her friends looked confused. I saw my face in George's windscreen mirror; the same face I saw with the spectacles on in my bathroom. My skin is a perfect shade of... me. Humans don't see my true alien colour, any more than they can see a Reus, or the insects climbing all over George. The boy continues to restock the fruit. I'm sure the animated grape vine is chuckling.

"Wow, you make it seem easy. No thumb twists or teeth pullin'. He told you what you needed to know!" George chuckles, while one of his eyeballs pops out of its socket. "Oops, sorry." He slaps it back in with a pop.

"That's because I'm a Dolce George."

George grabs his throat and chokes as he stumbles

backwards onto the floor. Anyone would think I've shot him the way he's carrying on. My face burns.

"You okay George. I didn't mean to scare you."

His jaw vibrates as he tries to answer, making his bottom lip quiver and several insects abandon him, scurrying in all directions across the floor.

"O-oh fine, Miss. Y-yes I'm fine. You're a bit, well, red for a Dolce, that's all."

"Well, I'd rather be red than a dull, scaly grey!"

"N-no offense intended Miss. It might be my eyesight or the smog you know. I don't know 'bout these fings; you don't look like a Dolce. Not that I've seen many, in real life, mind."

I offer to help him up, though I soon regret it. He grabs my hand as the worms underneath his skin wriggle.

"Come on George, let's go."

We escape through the bakery emergency exit. As I fling open the door into the alleyway, it bangs into an industrial waste bin tucked behind it. The black cat, who's snoozing on the lid, is rudely awoken and is not amused. It stretches and swishes its tail as I clamber into the back of George's cab. Within seconds, we're heading towards the museum.

"I've no money, George. Sorry."

"No problem, Miss." He switches off the meter.

– CHAPTER FIFTEEN –

The Museum

George drives towards the museum. He's saying something about his nephew, Yardly, who only travelled back through the wormhole a while ago, and something else about the Viscorpus being on planet Earth.

My mind isn't focusing on him, but I smile and nod, hopefully in the right places. I'm disappointed, not only because I was cruel to TrueBias, but because he was so quick to abandon me at Crystals Emporium. Saying it wasn't safe was an excuse. Hunting aliens will never be safe; we're hunting a universal criminal. What did he expect? It was clear from the offset he hated me being around; he said as much.

We should have followed my original plan, which was to steal the Luxlumen for ourselves; at least then we'd know it was safe. Now, if TrueBias is wrong and Appollo has got into the museum, then we're all in real trouble. I've no option. I need to get into the museum and snatch the stone for myself, so I can at least trade it with the Federation, or Appollo or whoever I need to, to save my dad.

"Nearly there, Miss. Just round this corner."

The city is bustling. This is the first time I've visited the museum. Dad says his job as a janitor is only a cover story; he's really a secret agent, and that the museum is his headquarters.

"'Ere we go Miss."

George parks the cab in the middle of a brightly lit street.

"George, I know it's, um, dark, but uh, where's the museum? You sure you're in the right place?" George chuckles as hordes of woodlice climb out of his mouth and march over his chin. How can he not sense hundreds of legs parading over his face? Can't he feel them?

"The museum, Miss, is in front of you."

I get out of the car as George lowers his head and nods through the windscreen. Mirrors disguise a humongous structure in front of me. It's no wonder I couldn't see it. The building is reflecting the road we've driven on, the trees and bushes in the children's park beside us, and other traffic driving by. The museum is practically invisible. I can't even figure out where the door is.

"How am I supposed to get in?" I'm hoping George will volunteer some advice on what to do next. He doesn't take the hint. "Any suggestions, George? It's a mirrored fortress!"

"Yep, it's locked, Miss." George states the obvious as he gets out of the cab; he wipes the last few insects off his chin with the back of his hand. "Alarmed too, I bet."

There's a reflection in the museum's wall of the Menax in the top hat with the black cat. What's he doing here? Is he following me?

"George, do you know who that is?"

"Who, Miss?" George asks puzzled; he's staring where I'm pointing.

"Over ther–" Swinging back around the Menax has disappeared. Was I seeing things?

Something shuffles in the bushes behind us. There is a scuffling sound and then: *THUMP!* It might be an animal, but as the swishing sound comes closer, I grab George's shoulder and we crouch out of sight. My heart pounds in my head like a drumbeat. What isn't helping is George's constant negative thoughts.

He's panicking: *Oh no, who's there? They may kill us. I*

want to go...

I poke him in the ribs and jam my fingers to my lips.

He stares at me, his eyes wide, mouthing, "What?"

I've told him off for being silent. All he's doing is thinking, and it's stressing me out.

The bushes right by the car rustle, and from the children's park a Reus appears holding a canvas bag. As he lollops past, he doesn't notice us huddled together on the other side of the cab. He's making his way to the museum. This may be my only chance.

I place my hand on George's shoulder. "Wait here!"

Sprinting towards the Reus, I get within a couple of metres before he senses me. I've startled him, but before he says anything, I place my hands on my knees and pretend to catch my breath. In reality, I just don't want to appear to be a threat. His beady eyes stare right through me. Why isn't he doing anything?

"Hi! Sorry, didn't mean to scare you."

"What do you want?"

"I need to get into the museum?"

"It's open tomorrow. Come back then."

"No, I need to get in now." I use the same tone as with the fruit stacker. "You're really eager to help me, aren't you?"

"I'm trying to get in myself."

"Are you the museum's security?"

"The Reus are security."

The Reus presses the button for the intercom. As he does so, I stand to the side, in his shadow. I'm sure cameras will be everywhere.

A voice buzzes over the intercom, "Ainssil, forget protocol, just type in the code. I'm sstarving."

The Reus types 14362 into a keypad. He glances at me as though I've stolen his PIN number. The electronic locks unbolt, clunk, clunk, clunk, and the sliding doors open. The Reus steps in and as I sneak in beside him, George calls to me. He's a few metres behind the cab in its shadow. I'm not sure what he is holding; he's jumping up and down, with one hand holding what appears to be a massive snake and the other waving frantically. The Reus whips in his tail, allowing the museum doors to lock behind us. Clunk, clunk, clunk. Through the window, George has stopped jumping and has dropped the snake. I hope he's okay. What is he trying to tell me?

According to the notice on the wall, I've just entered a lift, which will automatically take me to reception on the third floor. I crouch beside the Reus, hoping no one is checking the cameras.

"Where's the Luxlumen?"

"The sixth floor in *Precious Stones*."

Something is odd with this Reus. The others seem aggressive and have a lisp. I could neither read their minds nor influence them until now. This Reus' voice is softer and is desperate to get his hands on the Luxlumen. Did I place the thought in his head? Or does he know it's compromised?

"Leave the lift; you're in danger.
The Reus in here is not a stranger.
Take the stairs to level six.
Be very quick, the clock does tick."

"Hey Jack! It's great to hear you."

"Who's talking?" the Reus says.

"Oh. It's just the lift. Don't worry. It's fine."

The lift doors open at reception level and, following Jack's advice, I get out. He's right; staying with the Reus increases my chances of being caught. The Reus stays in the lift and presses the button for the ground floor. It's madness; we've just come from the ground floor. Why would he go back down? The voice over the tannoy said he was starving, so maybe the canteen is down there. It's probably their snack time.

Reception is deserted, lit only with a desk lamp, and a couple of glowing wall lights. My trainers squeak annoyingly on the marbled floor. Tiptoeing like a comic thief, I sneak around, silently searching for the stairs to level six.

Just as I find the exit, footsteps, well more like claws, clip-clop-click, across the marble floor towards me. Diving behind a metre-wide pillar, I hold my breath. A security guard, another Reus, is making his way to the reception desk. He picks up the intercom.

"Ainssil, where are you, where'ss my food? You better not be messssing me around, mate."

He pauses, gently banging his intercom on the surface of the desk, gazing in front of him as he waits for a reply. He taps his computer screen.

"Ainssil, it looks like the fire exit is showing as faulty again."

I gulp heavily. He looks in my direction.

"Ainssil, come in." The intercom hisses. "Ainssil!" He taps something else on his screen. "What the..." He presses a button and calls through his tannoy. "Code red, code red, code red." Red lights flash and the entire building bleeps, steel shutters grind and hum as they drop, sealing the external windows and the doors to the lift. The building transforms into an even bigger fortress. "Ainssil we've a Ssimuloss in the sstairwell on level four and a human, um, a human hybrid at reception level." He replaces the tannoy and switches on his massive flashlight. My chest heaves as a huge gulp of air gets trapped in my throat. "Come out, now. You're on the monitor. There'ss no esscape."

I'm desperate to bolt, but instead keep silent and hidden, but he's heading towards my exact position. He must have similar tracking software as TrueBias has on his Insync Harmoniser.

Wait a minute; did he say there was Simulos in the stairwell? It all makes sense. So, it was probably Cecelia in the lift with me, pretending to be a Reus. She must have known it was me all along. No wonder she never acted like a Reus, because she's not one. She's off to get the Luxlumen and Jack knew it was her. He told me I was in danger and the Reus was not a stranger. I'm so dumb. I thump my forehead with the palm of my hand. What an idiot. An agonising pain shoots through my head. But why did Cecelia go back to the ground floor? George was probably trying to warn me, the snake. Was it Ainsil's tail? Did Cecelia kill him once she got the pass code? She must have tricked him by pretending to be a Reus. A Reus wouldn't surrender their security codes to just anyone.

The Reus heading towards me is enormous. I sprint towards the door with the emerald illuminated stairs sign above it. He's hot on my heels.

"Hey sstop!" he shouts. I whack the slow-moving, swinging fire door back onto him as I sprint up the stairs.

Now I'm great at climbing stairs at speed; I've done it millions of times at home, but I'm not used to being chased, especially by an alien who can scale the stairwell as easily as a monkey swings through trees.

I'm no match for the Reus. He hops over the handrail, and as I get to level five, he's standing in front of me. Other than our breathing, there's silence. We stare at each other; neither of us turns away nor blinks. My heart is thundering through my chest, and although I'm concentrating, I can neither read his mind nor convince him telepathically to let me pass. He's waiting for my next move.

Dad always says you can never outrun a dog, despite what the movies show, and it's impossible to outrun a Reus, especially if they cheat and climb vertically.

"You're coming with me."

This Reus decides I'm no threat to him and grabs my sore elbow with his claws; he lifts me by the arm and dangles me, like a rag doll, over the stairwell. Is he going to drop me? Is this what Jack meant when he said I was in danger?

"Aaaahhhh, you're hurting me. I'll walk."

He springs over the railings, and clambers one-handed back towards reception. He sways back and forth over the stairwell like a gorilla, gripping and swinging from the handrails to the spindles. If he drops me now, well, to be polite, there'd be a mess.

"Can we use the actual stairs? You're killing my arm."

I'm not trying to be clever, but am terrified of being dropped. Plus, his humongous talons are making fresh puncture holes in my elbow.

"I promise, I'm here to protect the Luxlumen, not to steal anything. The Simulos, Cecelia, well she's here to steal it. If she does, she'll give it to the Viscorpus."

Nothing I'm saying is having any effect. This Reus ignores me as he scrambles down the stairwell with me in his clutches.

"You need to let me go, oh uh, not immediately."

If he does as I ask, I'm sending myself to my death.

As we nearly get back to level three, reception level, the entire building wails into a higher level of panic. A deafening alarm pierces through it. The red flashing lights are no longer visible; much bigger white spotlights switch on and illuminate every shadow in the stairwell. Cecelia must have removed the Luxlumen from its casing.

The Reus drops me; for a split second, like a cartoon character, I'm suspended in mid-air. Then I fall, not far, but enough to churn my stomach inside out, and my dad's face to pop into my head. I catch one of the spindles as I fall, my legs swing in mid-air, and my body spins. I'm dangling from the stairwell as my moist palms slide slowly down the highly polished spindle.

My back slams against the side of the staircase. Only a few sweaty fingers are preventing me from plummeting to my death. I'm losing my grip, but I must hold on. With the weight of my body and the pull of gravity mixed with the clamminess of my hands, I slide a little further. My shoulder and arm are in agony. I don't want to die.

Sucking in a deep breath, I swing myself around to face the stairwell and grab the bottom of the next spindle with my other hand, and try to climb them, but my hands keep sliding. My arms scream, begging me to let go, to surrender, but my optimistic, well desperate brain is telling me I've no choice; I can't let go.

Building momentum in my hips, I grip the spindles whilst swinging my legs, missing the first time, but on the second attempt I wedge one foot awkwardly through two lower spindles and spread the weight of my body across the side of the staircase, which not only relieves the throbbing ache in my arms but also the panic building in my head. Clawing my way up the spindles, I grab hold of the handrail.

My heart pounds. TrueBias is right; this is dangerous. Taking a few deep breaths, I clamber over the banister and drop onto the staircase to safety. As I do so, I whack my hip on the corner of the granite edged stairs; a stabbing sensation shoots through my leg.

The Reus has just climbed over the handrail at level six. Dragging myself to my feet, I hobble back up the staircase, heading again for the Luxlumen; it's clear I can't mind read or influence a Reus.

As I get to level six, chattering and quick feet, tip-tap, tip-tap are coming from below. It's Appollo; he's telling Anton to hurry as they scale the stairs. My hip wails as I open the doors with the sign, *Precious Stones,* above it.

– CHAPTER SIXTEEN –

The Luxlumen

Glass is popping and shattering all over the floor. The broken and bent, wooden and metal casing, once protecting precious stones, are being used by the Reus as trampolines, as they bounce from one display cabinet to another.

Precious rocks are being used as missiles, and magnificent stones are kicked in every direction as the Reus slog it out. A mythical decorative object, displayed on the window ledge, is preventing the steel shutters from closing. Their motors roar in desperation, repeatedly bashing the head of the figurine.

A central display cabinet has a sign saying, *The Luxlumen*, but the stone, which was once nestled in the indented velvet cushion, is missing. The Reus' continue to dance around the room, avoiding each other's razor-sharp claws and flicking tails.

TrueBias is leaning against a pillar; he's a little battered, and must have been battling with Cecelia before the real Reus arrived. He's oblivious to the chaos going on around him. Is he injured? Or more accurately, electronically damaged? He wasn't in great shape when he left Crystals Emporium. He's fumbling through his pockets. Has he got the Luxlumen?

Despite the way he abandoned me, a sense of calm

washes over me; at least we're in the same room together. Trying to stay in the shadows of the pillars, I creep towards him. The broken shards of glass crunch under my feet.

Dodging a flying rock, I slip and stumble over a twisted metal frame. As I do so, I slam my hand into a pivoting piece of broken wooden casing, which causes a small marble stone balanced on the other end to launch, like a slingshot, a mini missile, heading straight towards the brawling Reus. It whacks Cecelia, the Reus with the canvas bag, on the back of the head.

Cecelia swings round and sees TrueBias pull out his Insync Harmoniser. Anticipating his next move, she pounces towards him. Her huge claw swoops down and knocks the Harmoniser across the room, ripping off ribbons of skin, and exposing the electronics in his fingertips.

"Umph." I jam my fist into my mouth, trying desperately to suppress a scream, but TrueBias ignores his injury, and scoots across the floor to retrieve his Harmoniser.

Cecelia doesn't notice that the real Reus has positioned himself above her head, hanging from the ceiling. He plunges and swipes her across the floor; she drops the bag. The Reus leaps towards her, grabbing her by the shoulders and slings her against the wall. *WHACK!* She slides to the ground; she's unconscious. I dive for the canvas bag whilst the Reus taps Cecelia's face. He peers over at TrueBias. Surely, he recognises him. TrueBias is on all fours, searching through the debris for his Insync Harmoniser. Before I can warn him, he's in danger, Anton and Appollo burst in.

Appollo fires his Terminator at the Reus. A red beam shoots across the room. The Reus reactively leaps in the air, hurdling the shot, which pierces a hole in the windowpane. Glass shatters everywhere. Realising he is no match for the weapon, the Reus dives out through the now broken window; his enormous body dislodges any remaining pieces of shattered glass with him. The cool night air blows in, sending a shiver down my spine. Appollo and Anton scurry across the room after the Reus, and I creep towards the door.

"Eliza, the Harmoniser," TrueBias whispers.

The Harmoniser is at my feet, and I skid it across the floor towards him, but before he can grab it, Anton shoots a laser beam at TrueBias, which freezes him, like a statue, on the spot.

"Found this by the exit. The Reus must have dropped it," Anton says to Appollo as he passes the disc-shaped object to him. The beam continues to pulse towards TrueBias.

"Not seen a Carcer in years." Appollo places the object on the ground, which is still imprisoning TrueBias. "A confinement beam should keep him silent for a while. Let's find the stone and get out of here."

I hide in the shadows as they head towards Cecelia.

They shake her.

"Get the stone. We'll leave her," Appollo says.

As Anton searches for the stone, I head towards the door. TrueBias is in a trance. The Insync Harmoniser is too far away. Not that I know how to use it, even if I had it. I've got the Luxlumen, which is what I've come for. My heart is pounding. It should be easy to outrun these two. As I push against the door, a hand clutches my shoulder and pulls me back into the room. It's Appollo.

I focus all my attention on Appollo. "Leave me alone." He isn't listening and although I try to wriggle free, he's so strong that I'm practically floating across the room; nothing I do makes any difference.

"Let go of me."

He continues to drag me, only releasing me when we get towards the far side of the room.

"You've got something which belongs to me, young lady."

Cecelia is still lying on the floor behind me.

"Look okay, I get it. The Federation shouldn't have stolen the Luxlumen from Elekron, but, um, I–I need it to save my dad."

Appollo eyes crinkle at the edges. "Your father will be proud of your courage. There's no higher vocation than fighting in the name of our fathers," he says. "With the stone, you have the power of the universe in your hands."

"Let's get going," Anton says, in an irritated voice, as he steps towards me, trying to snatch the bag from my shoulder. I twist out of his reach. Although I'm acting tough, inside my body is trembling.

"Wait!" Appollo says. He frowns and pulls Anton away. "Let's check the stone is in the bag first, shall we?"

He has a point. Taking the bag off my shoulder, I unzip it. An incredible white round shiny stone winks at me as it catches the light. I lift it out; its mesmerising beauty silences us. It transforms into the palest pink colour, and a series of rhythmic swirls dance around it like candyfloss, creating odd shapes and designs. It's warm in the palm of my hand, and there's a tingly sensation pulsing through my arm.

"You've a gift beyond this world, young lady. The stone doesn't alter like that for anyone. You should come with us."

Appollo is being genuine. He's smiling, holding out his hand, not for the stone, but for mine. I don't know why, but I'm tempted to go with him. But instead, I scramble backwards.

"I'm sorry; I've got to save my father."

"You can save your father without the stone, but Elekron is suffering and needs its sun. My planet is dying. We need our planetary heart. Our people live in darkness, our energy source is depleted, and our species will become extinct without the Luxlumen. We've little time left."

"Well, yeah, of course; I agree that doesn't sound great, but why was it stolen in the first place? Why would the Federation force your people and your planet to suffer?"

"Come on, let's go; we're wasting time." Anton is becoming impatient and lurches towards me. I swerve as Appollo shoves him backwards over some casing.

"Wait! Have patience," he says.

My knees tremble as fear erupts through my body. TrueBias hasn't flinched; he's frozen in a crawling position on the floor. The fact the Reus abandoned the museum, when he saw Appollo, sort of makes it obvious that I'm in real danger. The cool evening breeze blowing through the shattered window isn't helping. I cross my arms and hug myself.

"Hey," Appollo grabs my arm.

I swallow a lump of air.

"Don't be afraid." His voice is mellow and comforting. "The Federation feared us. We were powerful, and they felt threatened; that's all."

"Well, you must have done something wrong."

"Our only crime is to live in paradise. We don't need a sun as others do. The Luxlumen act as our sun, it connects to our planet's core and generates enough energy to make us the most powerful race in the universe. Our planet is over a hundred million Earth years old and the Federation is, and always has been, fearful of us."

Appollo is making sense; he believes what he is saying, but he's thinking: *The Medeis brought it on themselves.*

"What about Medeis?"

Cecelia is moaning and groaning behind me. Let's hope she has a headache.

Appollo twists his head to one side. He looks confused. Did he misunderstand the question?

"They, um," he says, playing with his hands, fanning his fingers before clenching them back into a fist. "The Medeis were a greedy race. We used to trade with them, but they pilfered our minerals and offered nothing in return. All they did was steal from us."

"So, what happened to them?"

"We, um, drained their sun, but they were stealing from many galaxies and planets. It was the right thing to do–"

"I'm not sure killing millions of people is ever the right thing to do."

"It's a noble thing you're trying to do, very courageous. We've so much in common." Appollo's words match his thoughts. He's not trying to trick me. "The most important thing is to earn the respect of our fathers and their fathers before them. I understand and respect your intentions, young lady." He smiles. "If it's better for you, I'll bring your father here. He's safe."

"How do you know my father?"

"Your father has been helping us to get the stone back. Once you held the stone, I knew for sure who you were. Your father believes in us."

"My father wouldn't help you. He doesn't know about the Viscorpus race."

"Are you sure?"

Appollo stares at me, lifting his head as though he is waiting for an answer.

"He left the emergency exit to the museum open when he finished work today," Anton says.

"He wouldn't do that."

Although I'm sure my father wouldn't help, he was in a foul mood today, and before I knew I could read minds, I sensed he was regretting something. What has he done? Did he help them and feel guilty, or not help them and fear the consequences? Did Mrs Shufflebottom knock him through the wormhole as punishment or reward? Is Appollo being truthful? Can I trust myself, my own judgement?

"You can't bring him through, not until they reboot the wormhole."

"I'm from a galaxy far beyond this one; I can bring him through to us right here," Appollo says.

I'm sure he is being honest. TrueBias said there's no knowing the Viscorpus' capabilities. An enormous wave of peace washes over me. If Appollo can bring my father back, I'll ask him, to his face, what he knows and what he's done, or not done. I'm sure he will explain everything.

"Turn around!" Appollo says.

My father is standing behind me. I drop the bag. He smiles and opens his arms. I leap towards him and hug him like I've never hugged him before. Tears pour over my face. This nightmare is finally over. My words trip over in my mouth as my voice shudders.

"T-thank you Appollo." But both Appollo and Anton have gone. "W-where are th-ey?"

"Oh, I'm sure they're only outside; they're probably giving

us some privacy. I'll go fetch them. You help him." My dad's voice is strange, but maybe it's because he has just travelled in a zillion pieces to get here. He points to TrueBias and goes to find Appollo.

"I've missed you, dad. I've so much to tell you." My heart pounds through my chest. "Daisy, well we have to be kinder; we can't have bad thoughts either." I crouch to pick up the Carcer, but it isn't budging; it's stuck to the floor. "Dad, can you help me with this? It's stuck?" As I kick at it, little suction pads pop and release. "It's okay. I needed to be tougher. Dad?"

TrueBias hasn't moved throughout all of this, but where is Cecelia? When did she leave? Dad hasn't come back either. Something is not right; my heart flips. Was it Cecelia pretending to be my dad? I drop the Carcer and dash out of the room. They've tricked me; they've all gone, and they've taken the Luxlumen with them.

"What an idiot; how could I be so dumb?"

This is disastrous. I was so desperate to see my dad that I trusted a complete stranger, and not any stranger, a universal criminal. Why don't I ever fully engage my brain? It's one thing to lose the stone after fighting over it, but to be tricked out of it. How embarrassing. Does TrueBias know what's happened? He is in a trance, so maybe not. After the way he's treated me, I should leave him confined by himself, but I probably need his help to find my real dad. I pick up and twist the top of the Carcer to the off position; the laser disappears.

"What's happened?" he says.

"They got away with the stone, sorry."

"Oh no! Well, there is no need to pout. It's not your fault. We've still got time, haven't we?" TrueBias smiles and crawls over to his Insync Harmoniser and drops it in his pocket.

I pull out my phone, "Yeah, we've thirty-five minutes before the wormhole reboots."

"Well! Let's get going." TrueBias holds out his hand and I pull him up. "Great to see you, Eliza; this team doesn't function without you."

He squeezes my hand and smiles as we head towards the emergency exit on the ground floor.

"Can Simulos transform into any species, like, um, could Cecelia mimic Mrs Shufflebottom?"

"An excellent question. Yes, she can copy anyone she sees. I'm not sure Cecelia knows Rose, though, nor why she would want to mimic her. What are you getting at?"

"Oh, nothing... just wondering."

Cecelia has seen my dad tons of times when he's taken me to school and when she lingers around outside the flats waiting to pounce. It wasn't my dad I hugged; it was definitely Cecelia conning me. How disgusting! I bet they are all *roaring* with laughter, having tricked me so easily. Cecelia was never nice to me, and she was only popular at school because nobody really knew her. It doesn't matter whether she's an alien or human, all she is, is a nasty, manipulative bully. Why would anyone choose to be like her? Why did I want to be like her? My stomach churns. It seems I was so desperate to find a friend that I would have accepted anyone.

We arrive at the emergency exit. They've wedged the security shutters open with a statue of an ancient God; the name plate says *Dolos*.

"Did you come through this door when you arrived?" Not that it really matters how he came in, it's just I want to know whether the emergency exit door was left open or not.

"Yes, changing the molecular structure of mirrors or, more accurately, glass can lead you into a different parallel dimension if you're not careful. It's the reflection thing; it can be problematic."

"Was this door locked?"

"Didn't try it, but that statue wasn't there. Why?"

"Just wondering."

"Um, are you now? Your line of questioning is getting ominous; that means worrying. What are you hiding?"

"I'm not dumb; you don't have to be a walking thesaurus. I understand what you're saying. I'm just curious, no hidden messages, and no secrets, right?"

Okay, I'm an idiot, but if I let on to TrueBias what I've done, he'll be pretty disappointed in me, well, probably angry. Worse still, if my father finds out how naive I've been, confusing Cecelia for him and losing the stone so easily, he'll be more ashamed of me than I could ever be of myself.

The Reus, who dived out of the window, is chatting to George whilst helping his friend, Ainsil. Ainsil's not dead, but the way he is thrashing around and thumping the air with his claws, it's obvious he's furious. The shattered window litters the road with pieces of mirrored glass; it cracks under our feet as we head towards George, who's flapping his arms as if he is landing an aeroplane.

"The cops are on their way. We need to get movin'," George says, opening the doors of his cab and hurrying us along.

It's baffling to me that the regular human police force has no way of catching Appollo, Anton or Cecelia, or any clue about this other world, unless the regular police are, of course, the Reus.

George and TrueBias seem eager to leave before the police get here, so for now, I won't find out the answer. We bundle into the cab and George starts the engine.

"Thanks for releasing the Carcer," TrueBias says.

"Well, I'm sorry that I was so mean to you earlier at Crystals Emporium. I-I really didn't mean to say you abandoned your friends–"

"But that's exactly what you said, Eliza."

George looks at me in the windscreen mirror and smiles sympathetically.

"Appollo said the Federation stole the Luxlumen to punish them for destroying the planet Medeis; a race of thieves."

"Over so many years they've twisted the truth," TrueBias says. "Adults tell their children what they remember, and their children tell their children what they believe to be true. It's like Chinese whispers. Ever heard of Chinese whispers? My understanding is the Viscorpus species threatened planets with destruction if their demands weren't met; they exploited worlds. They were a ruthless, powerful race–"

"Where to, Miss?" George says.

"Lowry Heights Flats."

I've no way of knowing if TrueBias is telling the truth. I can't mind read or influence an android. As we drive away, Ainsil is still marching around, shaking his head and continuing to wave his arms.

"Was tryin' to tell you, Miss," George says, as he drives towards home. TrueBias is sulking beside me. "It was too late. You were in the lift when I found him."

"It's fine, George; it's not your fault."

George smiles at me and I wish he wouldn't. A worm swings out from one nostril before it burrows up the other one. I really like George, and it's not nice watching his rotten body being eaten by parasites.

"George, you've been great, thank you."

— CHAPTER SEVENTEEN —

The Parking-Bay Fight

Police cars zoom past us in the opposite direction, heading towards the museum. I close my eyes and let out a huge puff of air; my legs are trembling, and I've never been so frightened in my life. I shan't tell TrueBias about free-falling down through the stairwell; I don't want to give him another excuse to dump me.

No, George isn't to blame," TrueBias says, whacking his hand on the seat beside me. "You are!"

"W-what's wrong? You're scaring me. Are you okay?"

"You messed up, didn't you?" He glares at me. "I've gone over my recordings and you had the Luxlumen in your hand and didn't tell me. That's the same as lying."

"What, so you recorded everything?"

TrueBias' forehead creases and his eyes narrow; his stare is so intense it makes my chest flutter. I gulp. The urge to bolt is overwhelming, but I can't go anywhere sat in the back of a locked cab.

"Well, if you recorded everything, you may have noticed you weren't much use either." TrueBias rummages through his coat pocket. The thought he may pull out the Harmoniser makes me shudder. My shoulders and neck ache. George glances at me through his rear-view mirror. "You didn't even get near the stone."

"Do you want to destroy this galaxy? Are you proud of yourself? Appollo's made promises to you, hasn't he?" TrueBias is barking at me in the same way he did at Mrs Shufflebottom, and we all know how that ended. "Well, at least we've found out your father is a traitor; did you know all along? Humans, all the same, out for themselves."

"Now, now, Sir–" George says.

"I'm not proud. I never said I was proud!" Wiping a tear from my eye, I press the button to open the window. The cool evening breeze rushes in, refreshing the stale air in the cab. "Neither of us knows what my father did, and I'm fed up with you treating me, when it suits you, like a child. You need to ponder over your own mistakes rather than picking over mine."

"Yep, she's got a point," George says.

"My mistake was to babysit a thirteen-year-old."

"You'll find I've saved your electronic circuit board more than you realise, and my father may appear to be a traitor, but we don't know for sure." Twisting in my seat, with my back to the window, I face TrueBias. My blood is thundering through my veins and my head is throbbing. "He's spent years caring for my mother and Daisy, so maybe you shouldn't judge him so quickly, or at all. If it wasn't for Mrs Shufflebottom, none of us would be in this mess."

TrueBias appears stunned. His lips are pursed, and his eyes are darting suspiciously in different directions. Although I'm defending my dad, I'm not entirely sure how innocent he actually is.

"Oh, how is Rose? She's always travelling with us," George asks.

"Sent for trial in Conexus, she's been charged with crimes against the galaxy," TrueBias says, sweeping back his hair.

"Oh, no!" George says, as he swerves to avoid a pothole in the road. "Sorry."

"I think you need to repair your judgemental chip; it's defective." My vision blurs as I glare intensively at TrueBias.

"I'm so sorry." He pulls out his Insync Harmoniser. "But this–"

"Oh, my goodness," George says.

We've pulled into the parking bay outside the flats. There's a tremendous amount of commotion. The Reus are wrestling amongst themselves, whilst also brawling with the Urbes.

"Wait here," TrueBias says, as he leaps out of the cab.

What just happened? I wipe over my cold, tingly forehead with a napkin from the café. Was TrueBias going to vaporise me? Why else was he pulling out his Insync Harmoniser, saying he's sorry? Has George just saved my life by distracting him?

I've no intentions of waiting anywhere, and certainly not in the back of a cab. Opening the car door, I place my hand on the mesh cage screen, which separates me from George.

"Hey, are you coming with us?"

George is itching to drive away: *We need to go, need to go. She shouldn't be here, madness. We're all going to die!*

"No-o fanks, Miss. Be better if you come with me. Ain't safe 'ere."

As I scoot out of the cab, a stabbing pain shoots through my hip. "Thank you, George, for all your help, and for caring, but this is for my dad."

"Good luck, Miss."

As soon as the door slams, George drives off with such speed, he's around the corner before I'm able to raise my hand to wave goodbye. I've no intentions of getting involved in this, but I need the stone.

It's clear from the number of aliens fighting that word has got out. There must be over fifty Reus and Urbes. The Simulos, who have disguised themselves as Reus, continue to ambush the real Reus, causing them a tremendous amount of confusion and frustration. There are at least twenty Urbes distorting themselves, trying to dodge the enormous claws of the Reus. We've only got about fifteen minutes before the wormhole reboots itself.

TrueBias is at the centre of the chaos. He's ignoring the Reus, Simulos and Urbes, hiding behind a wall, staring at a pillar supporting the overhang of the flats. He waves his arms, indicating I should take cover. Standing out in the open isn't a brilliant idea, but no one is paying much attention to me; they're so busy brawling amongst themselves.

The dazzling streetlights create vast shadows, leaving several excellent places to hide. I sprint to the back edge of the building and crouch behind a wall. TrueBias' head is following something in the distance, a black figure: it's Appollo.

TrueBias aims the Harmoniser toward Appollo; an electric-blue beam further highlighted by the darkness of the shadows clips the corner of the pillar. The concrete burns and fades, and as Appollo returns fire, TrueBias ducks. The beam overshoots the wall, missing him by millimetres, burning into the ground and again disappears.

Every time either of them tries to change their position, they get forced back. Each one is taking it in turns to try to vaporise the other, like a leisurely game of tennis. Presumably he's not using his cloaking device because he's fighting. Or perhaps the Harmoniser exposes him. Either way, TrueBias needs to stop him.

A Reus is sneaking up behind TrueBias, but I'm pretty sure it's a Simulos disguised as a Reus.

"TrueBias behind you. Look out!"

He can't hear me over the chaos. Just as the Simulos is about to pounce on TrueBias, a real Reus leaps from a standing position over two metres away and onto the back of the Simulos. They roll to the ground and bash each other.

Sneaking around the corner, I force my back against the wall as if I'm balancing on a narrow ledge. I creep out into the open, shuffling towards the brawling aliens and heading for the entrance to the block of flats. TrueBias and Appollo continue to play their firing game, but despite my desperate need to go unnoticed, Anton, the apparent decoy Urbe, sees me and bounces over. He splats against the wall as I dodge his lunge, and as he chases me towards the flats, he dives, grabbing my leg, bringing me crashing to the floor: *THUMP!* My elbow screams as it saves my head from bouncing off the tarmac.

Before I'm able to say anything, Anton's hands slip around my throat, trapping any words from coming out of my mouth. His tightening grip forces blood to pump fiercely through my head. My brain is about to explode. All I can think about is him throttling me. I'm suffocating. He lifts me off the ground by my neck; my legs dangle in mid-air. My breathing is now so faint I can hardly hear it. My heart tires into a lazy drum. The noise of the brawling aliens sounds like they've gone underwater as my ears pop, the intense lights of the parking bay dim into a misty haze.

As my eyes shut, probably for the last time, there's movement, a shadow behind Anton. Just before I lose consciousness, he releases his grip around my throat and I drop to the ground. One of the Reus, the one who slashed my cheek with his tail, has come to my rescue. He lifts Anton above his head and splats him against the wall beside me. Anton slides onto the floor like a pancake being slid out of a saucepan. Disfigured, he wraps himself into a cylinder shape and rolls away. I'm guessing he needs to remodel himself.

Hunched over, kneeling on the floor and gasping for air, I try to clear my lungs. Coughing makes my throat scratch like I've swallowed a handful of sand. Holding my neck, I generate enough spit to swallow. Every part of my body is aching: my mind is confused and fuzzy and starved of oxygen. The Reus, who has been guarding me for a few moments, nods his head as I regain consciousness and leaves, leaping back into the mix with the other aliens.

The Reus have disfigured the Urbes; they've flattened, knotted, shredded or distorted them. The Urbes have all but abandoned the fight, and although the Reus seem to be beating each other up, they're actually wrestling the Simulos. It's now easy to tell the difference between them. The Simulos are no genuine match for the athletic Reus. The Reus clearly have agreed on a method of ensuring they don't batter each other. They leap high into the air and climb the pillars, landing on the Simulos, who can only defend themselves from the ground, and have no chance of winning. Many, realising they're losing, scurry away, transforming into human form as they do so.

There are no crowds standing on the walkways of the flats. This brawl is not attracting any attention from the residents. Is it filtered out from human reality as it was for me before I put on the spectacles? Or is it that people are so petrified they stay inside, keeping their noses out and hiding behind their own front doors?

I sit with my back to the wall. TrueBias and Appollo are still battling it out. Lionel, the Urbe from the bookshop, is by the lift entrance. He is trying to force the lift doors open. He's arguing with Jack. Each time he fails to open Jack's doors, he whacks them with his walking cane, stamping his foot and raising his arms in a frustrated manner, before he tries to force them open again. He signals for help and another Urbe dashes into the foyer, and between them, they force the lift open. Lionel wedges his cane in the gap between the doors, preventing Jack from closing them. He shuffles out of the entrance and whistles over to Appollo, waving the canvas bag in an *over here* type of motion.

Inside the lift, the wormhole is pulsing, as it was on the TV. Nothing is coming through and no one is leaving, but it is clear Lionel is trying to help Appollo escape.

The doors to the lift close slightly and reopen. Jack is trying to snap or dislodge the cane, but he is failing. I need to help him.

Using the wall to clamber to my feet, I stagger towards the entrance. My mind is fuzzy, and the brawling aliens still sound hazy. The Reus have defeated the Urbes; many are tending to their injuries by reshaping themselves and those who can walk are leaving.

I step over a deformed unconscious Urbe who's sprawled across the walkway under the overhang; he has fluorescent green blood oozing out of his nose. I hope he isn't dead. Just as I get clear of him, his arm lashes out, grabbing my foot, yanking me to the ground. He then jerks me towards him, jolting my leg like a dog rattles a toy.

My hip screams and despite my attempts to kick him off, his body swallows any contact I make with him. Trying to stamp on the hand holding my leg is equally impossible; I'm spending more time kicking my foot and completely missing his hand altogether. I need to help Jack.

I concentrate on his thoughts. "Release me."

His fingers reluctantly unwrap from around my ankle, and before he has time to reconsider, I pull myself free and sprint off towards the flats.

Embers burn like mini campfires as TrueBias and Appollo continue to laser it out. TrueBias' skin is peeling off his face; miniature flashing lights glow from his head, revealing his circuit boards.

Lionel has seen me sprinting towards him. He shuffles backwards, through the foyer and towards the lift. He hides the bag behind his back.

"Lionel, don't jam the lift. We can capture Appollo."

"No, we can't; even if we can, there'll be others."

"The Viscorpus race might not save your planet."

"No, but if we don't help, they definitely won't!" he says.

"Give me the stone Lionel."

I step through the main entrance into the foyer and across to the lift. I shove Lionel aside and kick the wedged walking cane out of position, allowing Jack to shut his doors, but he's not quick enough. Lionel grabs the cane from the floor and forces himself across the threshold like a human wedge, or in his case an Urbe wedge. Jack cannot fully close the doors and is now shutting them onto Lionel's chest, which is compressing his body in the most peculiar way. The bag with the Luxlumen stone inside is now in the lift.

"Lionel, you don't–"

Lionel isn't paying any attention; he's staring beyond me. Trembling, his eyes widen and his jaw drops as he lifts his arm to point at something.

Appollo is hurtling towards us, his Terminator aimed at me. But maybe Lionel thinks it's aimed at him. As Appollo fires, the automatic foyer doors shut. His fire clips their metal frame, immediately forcing them to reopen. He continues to race, lifting the Terminator again; he's definitely aiming it at me. I'm eager to escape, to hide, but until someone is shooting at you, it's difficult to figure out what to do. My feet are pinned to the floor; all I can do is focus on him.

"Don't shoot me."

He pauses for a split second and disappears. Behind him is TrueBias, his Insync Harmoniser aimed at where Appollo was. Has TrueBias vaporised him, or did Appollo just cloak himself?

TrueBias crumbles to his knees, landing on the ground, his limbs twisted and bent out of shape. He's malfunctioning. As he clicks and twitches, the Insync Harmoniser, in his hand, fires a constant laser beam, channelling the ground and the concrete pillar in a straight line. He does it again, and again, grooving a perfect arc shape into the pavement and pillar. His programming is messed up. I dash over to him and unpeel his finger from the Harmoniser and take it out of his hand; the motion of his arm continues to rotate in the same direction without it.

The Simulos have scattered, transforming into different species as they do so. The Urbes have also dispersed, either hobbling or rolling away, all disfigured, and the Reus are standing their ground, panting; they're exhausted. Now Appollo has gone, there's no need to fight.

"Um, problem." Jack's alarming voice distracts me from TrueBias. Lionel has released himself from the doors and is heading through the wormhole. Has Appollo cloaked himself and gone with him, or did TrueBias vaporise him?

"True, are you okay? What do you need?"

"Eliza quick, don't be slow.
It's imperative that you must go.

The galaxy's troubles you need to face.
You really must now leave this place.
Your struggles await; you'll save the day.
The wormhole is closing, so don't delay.
In you, jump through the hole.
It's time Eliza for you to go."

I've no choice. TrueBias is no use at all. Racing towards the lift, I leap into the wormhole and, as I do so, I'm sure there's a black cat sitting at the bottom of the first flight of stairs.

— CHAPTER EIGHTEEN —

Through the Wormhole

The temperature has dropped. My face is being blasted with icy air; I'm not running but standing, being propelled forward on a moving virtual conveyor belt. Hunched over, I shut my eyes and through chattering teeth, blow into my hands to warm my numb fingers. What's just happened?

Drawing in a deep breath, I lift an eyelid. I'm heading towards a red glowing light in the distance. Have I died and am I on my way to hell? Was this a trick, and I've plummeted through some sort of lift-shaft to my death? My heart jolts as I stretch out in all directions, but there's nothing to grip hold of. I've no choice but to go forward.

"I can't go to hell!"

You haven't died, Eliza; you are a funny thing. Daisy enters my thoughts.

Daisy, where are you? My heart flutters. I'm so relieved to hear her voice.

I'm at home, darling; you're travelling through the wormhole. You've no papers, so you'll go to the 'Something to Declare' platform. Don't worry! Be confident, concentrate and tell them they've seen your papers and to let you through.

Lionel has the Luxlumen.

Lionel is going through 'Nothing to Declare.' I'm trying to alert security, but the communication links are still offline.

Don't panic, you'll be fine.

I'm scared.

Have courage, my darling.

TrueBias: h-he's outside the flats malfunctioning. I'm on my own!

Eliza, be brave; you are strong. An enormous wave of warmth smothers me. *Believe in yourself.*

Daisy, your voice is fading.

You're too fa–

Daisy... Daisy?

Her voice has gone from my head, and although I'm focusing, I can't reconnect to her.

The hairs on the back of my neck tingle to attention. Will they vaporise me when I get to the light? Going back isn't an option. Behind me is, what appears to be, a solid moving shadow-like wall escorting me on my journey. The whole wormhole is moving towards the light, and I'm pretty sure that if I don't volunteer, then the wall will simply shove me out the other end.

I stop just before the entrance to the room and swallow. What am I about to see? What's going to happen to me? Stepping out of the wormhole, I'm instantly bombarded with jets of warm air; beads of sweat burst out across my forehead.

The room is not much bigger than the lift. The ceiling is a glowing blood red and the walls and floors are the shiniest marbled polished stone. Opposite me is a metal circular door with no handle. Is this another lift?

"Jack, can you hear me?"

There's a rumbling. The wall behind me finally catches up and seals off the wormhole, it creates a perfectly mirrored surface.

"Jack, is that you?"

The rumbling is growing, then some hissing. This isn't Jack. From the ceiling, clouds of green gas spiral over me.

"Umm, hello, anyone there?"

I tap the door at first, and then bang as the mist engulfs

me. Eventually, I strike it with such force my fist throbs. The stench is too much. Sliding to the floor, I try to keep my head below the dense green haze. My hands continually bang on the door as I cry out for someone to come.

"*HEEELP!* Please someone!"

The vapour completely packs the room, but there's no escape. Choking, I pull off my jacket and wrap it around my face and hold my breath, but I'm suffocating. My eyes sting, and tears and snot absorb straight into the lining of my coat. I flip over onto my back. The smoke is so dense it's impossible to make out the red-lit ceiling.

Daisy, h-help! I'm being poisoned.

As quickly as it came, the trails of green cloud snake upwards back through the ceiling. I'm alone, lying on my back as the red light bursts through the smog. My mouth is burning. I scoot across the floor on my backside and lean against the mirrored wall opposite the door. I allow my heart to calm into a more peaceful, rhythmic beat and my breathing settles. An acidic belch travels from my stomach into the back of my throat. I spit into a napkin from the café. Standing only makes it worse. My stomach rejects all the stinking, putrid gas I've swallowed. Burping the gases up reminds me of rotten eggs, combined with someone's ancient, musty, cheesy socks. It's disgusting.

Daisy, what's happening? A hissing sound echoes through the room. Oh no, not again!

The doors to the room swish and separate, opening horizontally. Half the circle drops into the floor, and the other half goes into the ceiling, leaving a huge circular hole to an outside world, well, to an outside corridor. A yellow waxy species comes into the room and the doors, with a whirl, snap closed.

I don't recognise this species; she isn't human. She has massive bulging eyes, stumpy arms and legs, and the only little hair she has runs like a Mohican through the centre of her forehead and down her back. She's wearing a pink satin shirt and a pinstriped skirt. Her ears are flapping at the side of her head, her nostrils flare and her lips are huge and pouting.

"Name?" she says, with a voice that reminds me of someone gargling water.

"Um, burp, phew. I need the bathroom."

Her eyes roll upwards as if she's heard that request a zillion times.

"You have entered Conexus, with no legal papers contrary to subsection 9.746 of *The Convention of Intergalactic Law of 1674 as amended*. Name?"

"Don't feel well. The gas stuff has made me sick."

"The purifying spray is harmless to you; it has killed bacteria, parasites and all known viruses, and in fact, it should have the opposite effect of making you unwell. You should feel re-energized." It's obvious this creature is losing her patience with me. "Your name and I'll escort you to a holding cell for trial." She taps her foot.

"Where are the holding cells?"

"You'll soon find out!" Her lips curl into an unpleasant smile.

Taking a deep breath, I focus on this creature's mind.

"I told you my name, and you saw my papers. Don't you remember?"

"Um, I–I've nothing written down."

The creature inspects the underside of her tablet computer, like it has hidden something from her.

"Eliza Berry, I've papers; you checked on the system and you said they were up-to-date."

"O-oh yes, um, I must have come into the room too soon, a-and the gas jumbled my memory."

"I thought you said it's harmless?"

"I-it is for you. Some of us rely on parasites." The fishlike alien grins, displaying several rows of chiselled razor-sharp teeth.

"Oh, okay, can I go?"

"Yes, of course, I'm so sorry, but our communications are malfunctioning, and you can only imagine what problems that has caused. The system has sent you to the wrong place. I'll escort you to Promenade Square, and you can select your onward journey from there."

She tells me her name is Lora, and she has been employed as an immigration officer at Conexus for 106 Earth years. Lora requires no prompting; she continuously chatters away as though she hasn't spoken to anyone for ages. We march through plush carpeted deserted corridors, passing many circular doors, probably leading to other worlds or more likely to featureless offices. We travel along travelators and up escalators, passing signs and notices for everything imaginable, but none say *Holding cells* or similar.

"W-where are the holding cells?"

"Why?"

"Well, umm… It sounds a bit silly, but I'm worried about the criminals on Conexus."

"You're safe." Lora smiles. "The holding cells are a prison shuttle, docked on a remote terminal; it's very secure and highly guarded."

I'm guessing Dad is on that shuttle, and it's possible that any one of these circular doors will lead right to him. The further we walk, the noisier it gets. Aliens are travelling in every direction; they ignore me, continuing with their journeys as though travelling through intergalactic space is the most normal thing in the world or in their case, the most normal thing in the universe.

I'm distracted by a diagram on the corridor wall, and let Lora carry on walking without me. It's a massive drawing, like a map. Lora stops and turns around.

"That's the layout of Conexus," she says.

She taps the map and two flashing lights flicker. She touches the lights and our faces appear.

"See, here we are in the fourth quadrant."

"Wow, that's amazing."

Maybe I can find Dad with this map.

"Can I find anyone using this?"

"No," Lora gargles. "For confidentiality purposes, it will

only display *your* location on the space station."

"It's massive!"

"Conexus is approximately three kilometres square," she says proudly. "We're going to, umm, there, to Promenade Square."

She points to a large pink-shaded area at the far end of the map; it's practically around the next corner.

As we arrive at Promenade Square, a lump blocks my throat, preventing me from thanking Lora for escorting me. She says goodbye, and as I feebly wave to her, my lips form a silent "WOW." My heart flutters as my hands tremble, and my knees, well, they buckle. I shut my eyes and collapse on the nearest chair next to where I'm standing. Promenade Square is a magical place.

"Oi, I'm sitting here."

I'm being shoved, like I've sat on someone. I spring to my feet, but there's no one there. Or is there? An image, an outline, which is all but transparent, is sitting on the seat.

"Soo sorry, I didn't see you."

"That's what they all say."

"Well, it's true. I'm sorry." I shuffle to the other end of the row. In case he has a family. You'd think I'd sat on him on purpose the way he's carrying on.

This place is amazing. The room is enormous; the walls and floors are the whitest polished stone with ribbons of crystal threaded through them. The stairways, escalators and travelators have raised rubber treads but with the shiniest of handrails. There are multiple floors, and from this central position, the glass-walled corridors and translucent lifts create an atmosphere where people seem like they're floating in mid-air, and the ceilings on each floor are lit with the sharpest white light, with dangling pendants like crystal chandeliers running the entire length of each walkway.

I draw in a huge breath of air, but there's no taste, no grit is sitting in the back of my mouth. This must be what fresh air tastes like. I'm surrounded by signs and notices; departure and arrival boards and virtual assistants are hovering everywhere.

The most incredible thing is the gigantic window at the far end. The view is not of a concrete city with illuminated advertising boards on the sides of buildings, nor of a murky sunless sky, but it looks out into a magical darkness. Stars sparkle like glitter; planets pepper the view, and the closest one is the most colourful turquoise, with pink and green ribbons swirling through it. It's mesmerising.

I calm my racing heart; as incredible as all this is, I don't know what I'm doing here. To say this world is alien to me would be an understatement. I have no plan and no idea what to do. What isn't helping is the constant thoughts and chatter of these aliens, who, by all accounts, are not impressed that they have been stranded on Conexus. As I focus on individuals, I think I can figure out what is going on in their heads, but otherwise, it's just endless noise and a general feeling of frustration.

The transparent man is a perfect example.

Everyone treats me like I don't exist. I'm sick of it. He is still complaining.

He's incredible. I'm sure he'd make an excellent bank robber. Sometimes you just have to work with what you've got.

A family comes and sits opposite me. The adults are similar in appearance; one is rounder than the other. They have triangular shaped heads with short, narrow chins and their mouths fill the entire widths of their faces. Their gigantic eyes are pear-shaped, with lumpy bumpy foreheads that fill half the length of their faces; it's like their brains are punching their way out. Their noses and ears are holes like the Reus. The child, well assuming it's a child, is analysing me. She keeps twisting her head, but her parents aren't paying any attention to her. Their thoughts and conversations are focused on their home planet. It's confusing listening to these creatures' minds and voices all at the same time: my brain hurts. This must be how Mrs Shufflebottom felt in the lift.

My hair fascinates the child, and she's itching to play with it. This species is bald, so it's understandable. She's probably obsessed with hair. She innocently skips around the chairs and positions herself behind me. I ignore her little clawed fingers grasping at one of my ringlets. First, she tugs gently and then with a *yank*, she rips a clump of hair right out of my head.

"Ow! That hurt!"

I jump out of my seat and turn to look at the spiteful little thing, rubbing the back of my head as I do so. The child inspects me, staring directly at my face. She smiles, opens her mouth and reveals a set of pointed black teeth. First, she makes a faint chittering sound, and then holds up my lock of hair triumphantly. Her parents, realising what she has done, screech at the top of their voices. Are they cheering the little girl on, or terrified of the consequences? It's impossible for me to tell. The child joins in the screaming. A Reus clambers towards us. If I'm caught, I'll be in real trouble. If I move, they will chase and catch me.

"Shush, it's fine."

I put a finger to my lips and wave my hand as I sit back down, hoping it's a universal calming motion, but it's too late; the Reus' threatening presence instantly shut the family up.

"Paperss pleasse," the Reus asks the family first.

As he scans their papers, he nods at me.

"Paperss pleasse Missss."

"Yes, of course."

What do I do? I can't mind read or influence a Reus. As I lift my wrist, a message comes over the tannoy.

"All Promenade Square Reus to report to security.
A Caecus has tried to rob the Currency Exchange."

The Reus swivels and heads towards a door which says *Guards* above it. The family opposite me stands and glare, as though I've caused them a monumental problem.

What a grotesque creature allowing so much protein to

cover her head, the spindly one thinks. I'm guessing he's referring to my hair.

"Can I offer you any refreshments?" A virtual reality hologram appears in front of me. "Would you like me to list, or show in pictorial format, today's specials?"

"Neither, none, no thanks." As the hologram disappears, another replaces her.

"We have a magnificent offer on perfumes and duty-free items at our shop. Please allow me to escort you there to make your choice."

"No, no, thank you." Being bombarded with constant chatter is affecting my concentration. I need to get the Luxlumen and save my dad.

"We have designer clothes for all human shapes at incredible prices."

"Stop please!"

— CHAPTER NINETEEN —

Yardly

"Just opt out, Miss."

A young Garrae is standing over me. Well, I'm guessing he's a Garrae. I'm sure a leg shot back up his nostril, and if he went through the purification spray, he has probably lost most, if not all, of his other companions, but he isn't as decomposed as Reg or George.

"I don't know how."

"Of course you don't." The Garrae crouches down, sitting half on the seat beside me. "Scroll to the *opt out* section in your papers; 'ere, I'll show you." His sausage-like finger presses an invisible button on his wrist, and a virtual screen hovers in front of our eyes. The Garrae scrolls through several pages until he gets to what he's searching for.

"Ah 'ere it is. See, press that button; the one which says, *Opt out of all marketin' at Conexus space station,* its well, straightforward, once you know how, eh?"

All the virtual salespeople disappear.

"Oh, okay thanks." With no papers, they're going to pester me forever.

"Where're you 'ravellin to, Miss, goin' far? Of course, it's bafflin' me brain seein' a human 'ere."

I place my hands on my lap; it's a struggle to keep them still. My entire body is trembling.

"Hey, Miss, not meanin' to frighten you. I fought you seemed a little lost. Only being friendly... Um, I'm Yardly."

As he holds out his hand, a tiny money spider scrambles out from inside the sleeve of his coat. Another survivor! *Yardly*, now where have I heard that name before?

"Eliza," I shake his hand, shoving the lectures my dad gave me about talking to strangers to the back of my mind. Well, I'm not on my own planet, so the rules can't apply. Can they?

"Of course, it's stupendous to meet you. Are you 'ere on your own?"

Yardly holds on to my hand a little too long. The corners of his mouth turn upwards and his cheeks puff out like a hamster's. This is a little creepy, despite him only being about my age. Maybe I shouldn't talk to strangers after all.

"I'm trying to find my dad."

"Of course you are, but how bothersome you've lost him. Don't go frettin' though. Just go to Customer Service." He points to a kiosk at the far side of the seating area. "They'll sort it out."

"Can you tell me what a Caecus looks like?"

"Of course I can, but why would you be lookin' for a Caecus? Fought you were lookin' for your dad?" Garraes have dreadful dental hygiene; his chirpy voice is no distraction, as the plumpest maggot crawls between his wobbling, stained front teeth. "Of course, your dad ain't a Caecus, is he? Cause if he is, 'e'll be a stinker to find!" His amber eyes sparkle as he reclines back in his chair snorting with laughter.

"Um, no, he's not. He's human." The tension in my shoulders eases as Yardly snorts loudly, and stamps his foot, rejoicing in his own amusement. "They said over the tannoy something about a Caecus."

"Huh, of course they did." Yardly's eyes narrow and his face is sombre. "Caecus, they're 'ard to find." He uses the back of his hand to flick the insect emerging from the end of his nostril back inside. "I reckon the one they're on about is the guy I sat on earlier. He woz sittin' over there a few moments ago." Yardly points to the chair I sat on. The same chair which had the practically invisible person on. "Stinkin' attitude he had. All I did was sit on him by accident, but you'd fink I did it on purpose, the way he went on."

It's no wonder the Caecus is so grumpy; people must squish him all the time.

"So Caecus are invisible?"

"Of course they are. I don't usually go sittin' on folk on purpose." He scratches his head as if he's looking for inspiration. Bits of flaky skin fall onto the floor. "Of course, it's all a little odd, 'cause usually they're not a bothersome race, but that one, well, I wouldn't have believed it meself, unless I saw it with me own two eyes." He points to his eyes, to prove he saw it for himself, or that he has eyes. "Pretty sure it was that one who tried to rob the Currency Exchange. Heaven knows who put that idea into his head. They will vaporise him, no doubt."

"No, that's not fair."

"The law is the law; you can't go around robbin' places 'cause you're invisible." He leans forward as though he's going to tell me a secret. "Of course, what's odd 'bout that one is when they were draggin' him away, he said he woz workin' with what he got! What do you fink that means, ah? Reckon there's a gang of them, but who can see them ah? Who can see them indeed?" As he chuckles, his belly vibrates and his few remaining teeth sway in his mouth.

I caused this; my fingers widen the already existing hole in the knee of my jeans. They will vaporise an innocent man, because I suggested he'd be good at robbing banks, and the next thing he's trying to do is to rob the Currency Exchange. Maybe I should hand myself in to save him? This is so unfair.

"You're lookin' a little flushed, you okay?"

"Where are the holding cells?"

"Don't be ridiculous. You can't go savin' the Caecus, you mad fing. Of course, neither should you. The prison shuttle is burstin' with criminals and there are guards everywhere. You need to keep well away." He smiles and taps his foot on the floor, whispering, whilst nodding knowingly. "Of course, it's in the bowels of the space station. Where else would they put um?"

It's funny, getting information out of a Garrae is so easy; no wonder they're perfect cab drivers! I now know of at least two people in the holding cells who aren't criminals. If I try to get to them, the Reus will probably catch me, and chuck me in with them. That won't help anyone. They don't seem to treat people fairly here. They either vaporise or jail you without letting you prove your innocence. My only option is to find Lionel and get the Luxlumen. They'll have to listen to me then.

"Oh, um, I'm searching for someone else too, an Urbe called Lionel."

"What in the prison shuttle?"

"Nooo, in the space station somewhere."

"Of course he is. So let me get this straight. You've lost your father, who you say is human and therefore can't be the Caecus who robbed the Currency Exchange?"

"No, my dad wouldn't–"

"Yet you have an unfathomable interest in where the Caecus is, whilst lookin' for an Urbe called Lionel?" Yardly reclines back in his chair, rubbing his chin, "You seem to have a very chaotic life."

"Well, no, not really, it's just been the past few hours, that's all."

"Are you hidin' somefink. Some criminality?"

"No, well, umm, not really."

Yardly lurches forward. I catch my breath. "Of course, you have to tell me everyfink now." He's swirling his hands in the air, encouraging me to hurry with the information. "Now, Urbes aren't keen on humans. So, he ain't no friend of yours." Twisting to face me, he squirms so his backside is half on his seat and his eyes are dancing. "Go on; tell me, what's goin' on?"

"It's complicated. It's, um, a secret."

"Hey, Urbes don't like Garrae neither. Not sure they get

on with anyone and, of course, it goes without saying, anyfink you tell me will be confidential." He zips his lips, pretending to lock them and throw away the key.

Lionel said something about Urbes not liking the Garrae when we were at his shop. Yardly is practically hysterical, but considering he's a Garrae, I doubt anything I tell him will remain a secret for long.

"You can trust me," he says, his voice chiming as his bottom shuffles on the chair.

He's attracting the attention of one of the Reus. He reminds me of George when he was trying to show me Ainsil's tail.

"Shush," I say, jamming my fingers to my lips.

"Sorry, me uncle says I can get a little enfusiastic."

He leans back in his chair and, with a huff, peers silently at his fingers. His silky auburn hair, trimmed as if someone has placed a mixing bowl over his head, swings forwards like a curtain around his face.

I grab Yardly's shoulder. "That's it!"

My voice causes him to leap in the air and swing around; his head darts in every direction. Once he realises there's no immediate danger.

"Whaaat?" he says.

"Are you George's nephew?"

There can't be many Garrae on Conexus called Yardly.

"Yeah, wow! You know Uncle George?"

"He's one of my best pals, really a great guy. He dropped me off at the wormhole about an hour ago."

"Awesome. Of course tell me everyfink. How did you meet him?"

"It's a long story, but it's fantastic to meet you. George has been helping me sort this mess out. He's been brilliant."

Yardly holds my hand; his skin is soft and warm. "Just tell me, why are you here? Why are you lookin' for all these people?"

"Huh, I'll tell you, but you have to promise me you won't tell anyone else."

"Of course I won't. I know when to keep quiet and besides, any friend of Uncle George is a friend of mine. You've got me full attention, well 'til I leave for Loquor."

Garraes seem to be a very helpful species. Well, Reg and George were anyway, so this one shouldn't be any different. His thoughts haven't considered reporting me, but he doesn't understand the seriousness of this secret either. At least he knows this place, and what can I do without papers? I've no choice. I lean forward, trying not to attract attention or be overheard.

"Lionel, the Urbe has stolen the Luxlumen from planet Earth, and has travelled to Conexus, probably with a cloaked Viscorpus. We need to find him before he, or someone else, leaves Conexus with the Luxlumen stone for Elekron. My dad got mixed up in this, and I'm guessing he's in the prison shuttle with the Caecus."

Yardly gulps, pauses for a few moments, and scratches his head.

"Of course, your dad will be safe. The Caecus–he's no risk to no one. They're not really an aggressive lot. That one must have been a rotten apple." He rubs his chin, causing a tiddly head-louse to lose its grip, well I'm assuming it's a head-louse, and drops onto his bushy eyebrow. "So let me get this clear. You tellin' me they've stolen the Luxlumen from Earth and it's headin' to Elekron?"

He's not so keen on knowing my secret now.

"Yep, that's why I need to find Lionel to get it back and save my dad. Have you seen any Urbes?"

"Well, weren't expectin' that for sure." His smile has gone, and he taps my leg with his fingers. "I'll help, if I can. That's all I can say."

Yardly gazes out into the distance, probably absorbing what I've just told him. Hundreds of aliens are hanging around, some sitting, others shopping and eating. Some are reading the departure boards, whilst others behave as if they've been waiting for hours and are slumped across seats with piles of discarded bottles and snack packets scattered around them. They must be the travellers waiting to go through the wormhole to Earth.

Several disfigured Urbes walk past, a few Menax, a couple Lora-type species and many other species I've not come across. Tons of virtual assistants dangle in the air, selling their items. The one species I definitely recognise is the Reus, guarding departure gates and entrances to shops.

If I tell the Reus, and let's assume they listen, we can sort this out, but it'll take ages and Lionel and Appollo will have left by then. Lora strides past us; she is gargling into a microphone embedded in her wrist.

"No links aren't up… not protocol… no." She straightens her skirt and flicks an imaginary speck off her leg. "The portal is still malfunctioning… I think only three came through, a human hybrid, a Simulos and an Urbe… well the probes are down… yes okay, we'll ease the backlog."

Maybe I should tell Lora what's going on. "Umm excuse me!"

"Yes, how may I help you?" she gargles.

"We are all in danger."

"The Caecus has already been apprehended, and although I know you are worried about criminals on this station, I can assure you it's the exception, not the rule." She bends over and pats my head. "He's already in the prison shuttle; you are safe."

"No, but you don't underst–"

"Any further concerns about your safety need to be directed towards the Reus."

She gives me a dismissive smile and continues to chat into her wrist.

As Yardly peers up through the five other floors, I shut my eyes. My breathing shudders. "The Luxlumen might already be on its way to Elekron."

"It's okay Miss. Don't you go frettin'."

Yardly strokes my hand, and when I open my eyes, he's smiling at me.

"It's unlikely Lionel will stroll past us whilst we're sitting here, plus you don't even know what he looks like. We need a plan."

"Agreed, of course we need a plan, a good one," Yardly says as he scratches his chin in deep thought.

"Which terminal will take us to Elekron?"

"Not sure there are any routes; 'pparently it's a horrible drab place, not a holiday spot."

"Well, how would you get there? How would anyone get there?"

"They don't. Nobody goes there, and neither is anyone 'llowed to leave, well travel to 'ere, anyway."

"Somebody must go or know how to get there."

"Of course they do. I guess you'd have to go to a planet that trades with them and travel onwards from there," Yardly says.

"Well, which pla–"

"Of course, I don't know which planets before you ask, so I can't help there, but you'd have to travel outside of this galaxy, or commission a private spacecraft or somethin'."

"Brilliant! Thank you." My mini applause pleases Yardly. "How do we–"

"Of course, a travel agent, travel agents know everyfink about this universe," he says.

"Of course!" I hope Yardly doesn't sense my sarcasm, or am I just being unkind?

Around the edges of Promenade Square, travel agents advertise their latest deals, but which one should I pick? I grab Yardly's hand and pull him towards:

The universe is yours... Wander... Explore... Discover.

"This one."

As we approach the desk, a virtual assistant pops up.

"Of course, it would make sense for me to handle this." Yardly prods my arm. "We have to travel to Elekron, which terminal do we need?"

"Hello, my name is Beta; please show me your papers."

Yardly glances over at me, I shrug. He holds out his wrist.

Beta scans it and says, "There's no travel to Elekron."

"Of course, there may be no direct travel, but how do I get there if I need to go for business?"

"They do not allow business transactions with Elekron."

This isn't helping.

"Hi," I say, nudging Yardly out of the way. "I'm trying to find a friend and they're planning to go to Elekron. Can you tell me which terminal they would have to go to?"

"They do not consider the Viscorpus friendly, and there's no travel to Elekron."

"Can I see your supervisor, preferably not a virtual one?"

I'm hoping a *live* alien being may be less robotic, and I might be able to read its mind.

The virtual assistant disappears as quickly as she arrived and is replaced by another being that comes through from a back room.

"Heello, my name is Albeert and I'm the duty supeervisor for *The univeerse is yours... Wandeer... Explore... Discoveer.* What is your deestination?"

Although Albert is not a virtual assistant, he is artificial intelligence, a robot, equally useless! He is singing his words, and it's annoying.

"We need to get to Elekron and although Beta says there's no direct passage, we need advice on the best and easiest route."

"Weee do not traveel to Eleekron nor reecomeend anyone does. May I suggeest an alteernative?"

Closing my eyes, I draw a deep breath. "Albert, which terminal would I need to travel beyond this galaxy?"

"You would neeed Teerminal 56, but you cannot traveel outside of this galaxy without appropriate papeers, so unfortunately Mr Yardly Thomas, as you only have inteernal papeers, I'm unable to seell you a tickeet to a deestination outside of this galaxy. May I seee your papeers Miss?"

"Oh, okay, thanks."

Albert is exhausting. We don't leave or interrupt him until he has finished, as he may have started all over again, or carried on singing, and I'm already attracting a Reus' attention.

"Over there," Yardly says as he points to the TV screen flashing Terminal 56. It says:

BOARDING.

All passengers need to make their way to the terminal and go through security.

– CHAPTER TWENTY –
Terminal 56

"This way." I grab Yardly's arm.

The board next to the escalator shows Terminal 56 is on level five, the top floor. As I'm racing up the escalator, Yardly, with much shorter legs, is trying to keep up. Checking on him, I knock into a man like Lora.

"Oh, sorry."

"Look where you're going. This isn't a playground," he gargles, pointing to a sign that says *Walk Only*.

"Sorry."

Doing my best not to annoy anyone else, I speed-walk up the remaining escalators. Yardly is taking ages. A Reus on Promenade Square glares up at me; he knows something isn't right. His eyes follow me as I pace backwards and forwards on the fifth floor, waiting for Yardly to catch up. My throat dries as a tingling sensation washes over my body. I'm in danger of being caught. I wave at Yardly to hurry.

"Comin' frew, comin' frew." He barges his way past the other passengers on the escalator. "Pardon, 'cuse me, fank you."

This floor branches off into twenty terminals. I pull at Yardly's sleeve as soon as he gets to the top of the escalator. We head along the corridor, following signs to *Terminals 55 – 60*. Time is running out. As soon as Lionel goes through security, we will lose the Luxlumen. We tear along the corridor towards Terminal 56. With my hip throbbing and my hair determined to stick to my face, I soon lose balance and tumble. Yardly is no longer huffing and puffing behind me.

Scurrying to my feet, I turn the corner. The length of the corridor in front of me is humongous; there is no end to it, but according to the sign, Terminal 56 isn't too far. A travelator runs along its entire length. It's like a conveyor belt, which escorts passengers from one end of the corridor to the other. It's packed. It'll be quicker for me to run.

I build up speed, sprinting along the corridor, passing all the standing passengers on the travelator. I'm free. I'm not stuck in an alien traffic jam crammed together sharing germs. I've got my own private lane.

As I check back for Yardly, my hair splats across my face, causing me to swerve off-course and trip over an abandoned briefcase. I instinctively use my hands to save myself from banging my face for at least the third time today. As I roll onto my back, the figure towering over me and raises his eyebrows; he tuts. It's a Menax; his milky beard drapes on the floor and he's wearing a rather battered top hat. I'm sure he's the Menax from Crystals Emporium and maybe it was his reflection in the museum too.

"Oh dear, oh my, it seems like it's tangled you up, Miss."

The briefcase's handle is wrapped around my foot.

"Why did you leave it in the middle of the floor?" My voice is agitated as I try desperately to unravel my foot. I kick at the bag. "Did you leave it there on purpose?"

"Oh my, Miss, you'll break it. I had simply put it on the floor to fasten my laces and had to hop out of the way or you'd have surely knocked me over, too."

The laces of his boots go from his toes to his knees, a mammoth task if they came undone. Some passengers on the travelator snigger as they trundle by.

"I'm sorry; I shouldn't be running and didn't see you." The impact of running into and kicking the bag over has popped it open. Crouching over, I untangle the handle of the case from my foot and fasten the clips. I stand and pass the briefcase to the Menax. "Sorry."

"Oh dear, no harm done, no harm done at all," he says. He unhooks his watch from his waistcoat pocket, flicks it open, tuts as though he is late for something and replaces it. He lifts his hat in a goodbye gesture and walks away.

Yardly is coming around the corner; I wave at him to hurry as I drag my wild hair into a high ponytail.

There is something on the floor. I'm sure it wasn't there a moment ago. Did the Menax drop it? Or has fallen out of his bag? I kick at it. It's a Carcer, the confinement beam gadget Anton had in the museum. What's a Menax doing with one of them? Is it meant for me?

Shoving the Carcer in my pocket, I sprint to the next corner and as I arrive at Terminal 56, Lionel from Swindlers Road, as predicted, is standing in the queue to go through security. He's planning to travel outside of this galaxy.

"Lionel," I wheeze, grabbing my hip and trying to relieve the stitch piercing through my side. "Lovely to see you." My fingers sink into his squidgy skin. It's an odd yet pleasant sensation. "C-come with me." I prise him from the queue. "W-where's the stone?"

"Don't know and don't care!"

"Well, you did when you came through the wormhole with it, so what's happened?"

"Maddison took it off me." He stares at the ground. "You can't trust her."

Taking a deep breath, I try not to get worked-up.

"You mean Cecelia. To be honest, Lionel, we can't trust you either; didn't you say Anton was the decoy?"

"He was. They wanted you to follow him, whilst Maddison took the Luxlumen. But the emergency exit door wasn't open, at the museum, as planned, so she couldn't get in, and had to rethink her strategy. I told you he was a decoy and to follow Maddison."

"Lionel, let's get this straight. Maddison's actual name is Cecelia."

I'm struggling to get my head around all of this. Did they actually involve my dad in the theft of the Luxlumen, after all? Was he meant to leave the emergency exit door open at the museum, as Anton said, so Cecelia could get in? Did he regret leaving it open and the Reus guards noticed and closed it? Or did he regret never opening it in the first place? It now makes sense why Cecelia went back to the ground floor when she arrived at the museum. She was opening the emergency exit to let Appollo and Anton in.

"Whatever! She's Maddison to me," Lionel says.

"Why did you let her have the stone?"

"She pretended to be Anton." Lionel thumps his cane on the ground and shakes his head. "She was at the terminal and was waiting for–"

"And the Viscorpus, Appollo?"

Lionel takes a deep breath. "He came through too."

I'm guessing Cecelia and the Viscorpus have teamed up and have the Luxlumen.

"Okay, so why are you taking the only flight out of the galaxy?"

"Cause, according to Appollo, they can't trust Urbes, so I need to leave."

"What? Appollo knows you told us about Anton being a decoy?"

The family with the little girl queue at the Terminal. The little girl sticks out a snake-like tongue at me as the mother pulls her away. I tug Lionel further into the corner, so our conversation is more private.

"Well, no, he doesn't know that I told you about Anton."

Lionel bows his head, stretching his neck so his nose would stick in his belly button if his coat wasn't in the way.

"Do you know where Cecelia is?"

"No idea, but she'll not be on this flight."

His neck towers above me, like a towering string of spaghetti, before he shortens it, lowering his head back to its nearly normal height.

"Can you stop that? It's distracting." Lionel tries to keep

still, holding his neck as his head flops backwards. "So, tell me why Cecelia won't be on this flight; isn't it the only one out of the galaxy?"

"Yes, but I didn't prepare her papers to allow her to go outside the galaxy. I only prepared internal papers for her. They won't allow her on this intergalactic flight."

"Does she know?"

"She does now. She was furious and so was Appollo. I did it as an insurance policy, so if the Urbes failed to smuggle the Luxlumen stone for the Viscorpus, I wouldn't make it easy for the Simulos, either."

"So, you double crossed the Simulos and Appollo, and they've dumped you."

"I was trying to save my race. I made it to the Terminal as planned, but they dropped me anyway. They were using the Urbes. It seems like the Simulos are more useful to them. They can shapeshift and are better fighters."

I let Lionel's arm go.

"She ran off. She will probably travel to another space station or planet and try to travel out of this galaxy, with Appollo, from there."

"So, we don't know where she will travel to?"

"No," he says. A tear rolls over his cheek. "But if I know anything at all, they'll be on the first available flight or wormhole out of here." He gulps. "We're all doomed. It's my fault; I'm so sorry."

His thoughts match what he is saying. He is genuinely sorry. I'm positive he doesn't have the Luxlumen.

The information board has rebooted itself. There have been no departures, and none are due for the next twenty minutes. I reach into my pocket for a napkin for Lionel, but my hand cups the Insync Harmoniser. I'd forgotten I had it. As I lift it out, Lionel ducks. He flexes his body in a wave type motion.

"You, okay?" As he nods towards the Harmoniser, I'm again reminded of how TrueBias did the same thing to me, when the Reus slashed my face. "Don't be silly."

Yardly trundles towards us, huffing and puffing. He curls over, thumping his chest with his fist.

"Sorry, I took ages, but needed a rest and a snack. I was starvin'. What 'ave I missed?" He's wheezing so heavily he is making a whistling sound through his nostrils. "Oh wow! Where did you get that?" He's looking at the Harmoniser.

"It's okay; I took it off a friend."

"Of course you did. What sort of friend has one of them?" Yardly steps backwards. "You're askin' for 'rouble havin' one of them, 'rouble with a capital T."

"TrueBias wasn't well. I didn't know what to do."

"So, of course, the only option was to steal his weapon?" Yardly says.

Leaving your friend on the curb suffering should be the last option, not the first. No ambulance could save him, but instead of coming through the wormhole, maybe I should have gone straight to Daisy for help. Too late now, though, but at least, whilst I was going through the wormhole, I told her about him. I shove the Harmoniser back into my pocket.

"Yardly, we've got a problem. We're now after a Simulos called Cecelia instead, and we're running out of time."

"Of course we are. They're 'bout as easy to find as a Caecus."

"Your funeral if you find her because Appollo will definitely be with her," Lionel says.

"Lionel, do you know whether she has shifted into another form?" Both Yardly and Lionel are staring and snarling at each other whilst I'm trying to figure out what to do next. "Hey." I grab their shoulders. "Stop it! We haven't got time for this." They both look towards the ground like naughty school children. "We can't let anybody leave Conexus until we've found the Luxlumen.

"No," Lionel says. "You can't trust that double-crossing Simulos self-centred, lying trickster wh–"

"So, you don't like her anymore, Lionel?"

"Sounds like it," Yardly says.

I'm warming to Lionel, and it may be because he has

seen Cecelia for who she is; it's funny he judges Cecelia for the exact same things he was planning to do himself.

"Well, she'll have to go with Appollo now, because he can't cloak the Luxlumen himself," Lionel says.

"Okay, but why? It was buried underground and carried in a bag. Why can't he cloak it?"

I must be sure Lionel hasn't swapped sides again.

"It's Elekron's life source, like our suns." Lionel twists his neck as though my question irritates him. "A cloaking device bends light using particle radiation to alter the molecular structure of an object. It can't alter the molecular structure of the Luxlumen."

"Of course, that makes absolute sense," Yardly nods his head like he knows what Lionel is on about.

"Well, now we know Appollo needs Cecelia or someone to get the Luxlumen off Conexus. How do we stop everyone from leaving?" I look at Lionel. "Lionel, how do we do it?"

"Other than setting the fire alarms off, nothing will shut this place down," he says.

"Brilliant idea!" To me, that's a plan.

Yardly is hopping from one foot to the other.

"That's madness. You can't go startin' a fire. No, no, no you... you might kill someone. Some of these creatures need a fine balance of gases to survive. Fire could–"

"It's okay, Yardly; I'm not planning on starting an actual fire, just setting the alarms off."

"Impossible," Lionel says. "You'd have to convince a lot of complex high-tech equipment and computers, sensors and artificial intelligence of a genuine fire before they would even consider triggering their shutdown protocol."

"Of course, it's difficult to fool tech," Yardly says.

I roll the Insync Harmoniser between my thumb and forefingers and pull it out of my pocket.

"Can we use this?"

"Problem is, if you get caught with that, they'll vaporise you," Yardly says. "It's a weapon. Of course, they'll vaporise us all for bein' your accomplices. They don't even allow security to carry those types of weapons."

"Oh, yeah, I guess you're right."

Although it's a cool gadget, using it when I haven't got a clue how might be disastrous. I understand why Yardly is much more nervous than he was before; it's probably because he may now be vaporised for helping me.

"Do you know how to use it?" I offer it to Lionel rather than Yardly. Lionel has all the technology in his bookshop; he can surely figure out how to use the Harmoniser.

"Let me see," Lionel says. With a glint is his eye, he holds out his hand.

"No, nooo, I'm not sure you're finkin' straight," Yardly says. "Isn't this fine gentleman the same one who smuggled the Luxlumen through the wormhole in the first place?"

"You're right, Yardly."

I'm sure Lionel isn't being dishonest, but can I risk handing over the Harmoniser all the same? If Appollo gets hold of it, he'll transport himself out of here with the Luxlumen, if he knows how to use it, with no need for a wormhole, a space shuttle or Cecelia.

"Fine, see how useful this parasite-hosting fool is to you," Lionel spits. He shuffles towards the back of the queue to go through security clearance for the next intergalactic flight.

"At least parasites got purpose; you're just a flexible freak," Yardly says.

"Speak to the Reus," Lionel says, "before I do it for you. If I wasn't getting out of this dump..."

Lionel and Yardly's argument attract the attention of the check-in assistant. She glances at us as the little girl with the snake-like tongue, who owns a clump of my hair, stamps on her foot.

Whilst the check-in assistant squeals, Yardly has snuck into a room, which says *PRIVATE* on the door.

"In here," he beckons me. "Quick, before we get caught."

— CHAPTER TWENTY-ONE —

An Unintentional Terrorist

Yardly has lured me into a food storage area; I pull myself up onto the counter by the door.

"What are we doing in here?" Bags of snacks, from peanuts, crisps, popcorn to bottled water, pop, tea bags, cakes and biscuits, plus loads of other edible food and drink, are crammed into every available space; the mesh racking bulges under its weight. "Lionel saw us come in. You know he'll report us."

"This must be the café's stash," Yardly says, as he rips open a packet of Cricket Crunch and munches through the contents. "Of course, the problem with these," he splutters, "is they get stuck in your teeth." As he smiles, the dried insects clog the gaps between the few teeth he has left.

"Why here?"

"Oh, sorry, fought we could try workin' out your gadget. Of course, I'm hopin' there's no cameras in 'ere."

"Oh, okay, but I really don't know what I'm doing."

I roll the Harmoniser in the palm of my hand. I'm not sure this is a brilliant plan, but it's all we have. TrueBias specifically pointed out to me that it's not a toy.

"Of course, if you have any other ideas on how to shut Conexus down, I'm all ears."

Yardly pulls back his hair to reveal a rather round

shaped ear; a tail of a yellow worm is dangling from it.

"Okay, we can try." As I'm nodding at Yardly, I have this sinking feeling that this may not turn out very well. "Let's get behind that." I drag a large metal trolley, used to transport snacks to different bars and cafés, to the centre of the room. "Load it with some of those boxes, just in case."

Once Yardly has stacked some boxes onto its shelves for added protection, we kneel behind it. The Harmoniser has no buttons, only the blue flashing light pulses at the tip. Concentrating, I point the light at a solid stone wall, close my eyes and hold my breath. I squeeze the handle.

"Fire!"

Nothing happens.

"Of course, it was always worth a try, but maybe it's time for you to surrender, but don't go tellin' the Reus anyfink 'bout that," Yardly says, waving his finger at the Harmoniser. He stands, his coat scrunched up around his waist; he pulls it down as he heads towards the door.

"Hey, we can't give up yet! Let me try again."

We've gone to an awful lot of trouble to try only once.

"You gave it your best shot." Yardly shrugs. "Fink we should leave it for now before we get into real rouble and this all gets out of hand."

I can't believe he is giving up so soon, and although I'm frustrated with his lack of commitment. I try not to show it.

"Have you forgotten why we're here? The Luxlumen might be heading its way out of Conexus right now!"

Yardly turns the handle of the door.

"Of course, but it's not our responsibility, is it?" he says. "Look, I've helped as promised, but you got to admit, when I asked whether you were hidin' somefink, I couldn't have imagined this was it, not in me wildest dreams."

"The first planet the Viscorpus could destroy might be, Loquor, the planet I'm guessing your family lives on?"

Yardly taps the door with his forehead. Each blow dislodges the creatures he hosts. A spider decides enough is enough, spins the most delicate thread and abseils from his shiny hair to the ground.

"Stop it or you'll get us both caught!"

Spinning round with a frustrated sigh, he grabs another bag of Cricket Crunch before he squats down with me behind the loaded trolley.

"Okay, you win, but let this be the last time. If it don't fire this time, we must fink of somethin' else."

"Agreed."

Whacking the Harmoniser several times on the edge of the trolley, I'm hoping the vibration will fix it. This is the only plan we have, so naturally it's the best one we've got.

"Dumb thing! Where's the button?" Closing my eyes again, I aim the Harmoniser, but this time I imagine the hole I'm going to make in the wall, and with every ounce of concentration and focus I can muster, I call out: "*FIRE,* you stupid thing!"

"*STOP!*" Yardly screeches.

The solid wall is not solid after all; there's now a massive hole through it, just like I imagined. The beam has burnt through the wall into the café next door, at such an angle, it sliced through the suspended ceiling above. Wires dangle and the lights flash and crackle.

"You hit the lightin' cables by the looks of it."

The short-circuiting of the lights causes chaos. Sparks flash in every direction as the live wires brush against each other and swing away. Aliens, who were previously relaxing in the café, are now screaming and shouting, herding their families and gathering their belongings before trying to escape. Many bounce off each other as they run in every direction. Furniture is being knocked and tripped over, as the cables continue to swing and spark. But no fire alarm goes off. Other than a bit of chaos, nothing much has changed. As we both peer stunned through the whacking great hole in the wall, the tapping of the Reus' claws are bounding along the corridor towards the café.

"Quick this way."

I drag Yardly out of the food store and along the corridor

away from the Reus. Beside us is a row of leather-covered padded seats with glass domes. The sign above them says *Meditation Booths*.

"In here."

We both climb into a double booth. The Reus hovers outside the food store before kicking in the unlocked door. A flashing virtual notice pops in front of our eyes, saying an announcement is being made. As the meditation booth is soundproof, I crack open the door:

"Due to terrorist activity, we've suspended all movement from Conexus until further notice. All staff and travellers are politely requested to make their way to Promenade Square immediately."

"We did it!" Yardly cheers.

"Yeah, but we aren't terrorists. We need to speak to someone."

How irritating, I'm not a criminal. Why does trying to do the right thing and saving the galaxy make me a criminal?

As I'm about to leave the meditation booth, Yardly grabs my arm. His smile transforms into a frown and his mouth turns down.

"Firin' a weapon in a terminal, a weapon which, if you don't mind me sayin' Eliza, you smuggled through a wormhole, and have no papers for, ain't lookin' promisin' for you, is it? All the signs of a terrorist if you fink about it." He stares down at his other hand, which is gripping the arm of the chair; he's trembling. "Of course, I'm not sayin' it's intentional, but I'm just lookin' at it for what it is. Doubt you'd have time to say anythin'; my reckonin' is you'll be vaporised on the spot before you open your mouth."

Yardly has a point. Leaving the doors to the booth ajar, we listen to shutters clunking shut and virtual assistants helping and encouraging travellers to return to Promenade Square. We sit in silence, frozen to our seats; only the drumming of my heart and the panic of Yardly's thoughts distract me. Although we've shut the space station, we haven't thought our plan through. I never seem to think through anything properly.

"We have to go. It looks odd if we stay here, they'll suspect somethin'."

Yardly is right, but his advice comes too late as a Reus appears in front of us. He flings the booth open.

"What are you doing here?" His voice is booming.

I hold my breath.

"S-soo sorry, Sir, is there a problem?" Yardly is playing it cool, well cool, in a stammering way.

"Conexuss iss in lockdown; there are terrorisstss loosse and everyone is to return to Promenade Ssquare."

"What, so nobody can leave?" I need to be sure.

"That'ss what lockdown meanss Misss."

"Please beg our pardon, Sir. As you can see, we were in the meditation booth and, by its nature, it blocks out all external noise. We were not–"

"Make your way to Promenade Ssquare." This Reus has no patience for our excuses.

As we head down the escalator, Lionel is shooting visual daggers at us. He points as though he's going to snitch on us, typical! He's swapped sides again. Yardly was right; he can't be trusted, but the Reus, he is trying to attract the attention of, isn't taking any notice of him, and pulls him off the bottom of the escalator, shuffling him towards the far side of the room. Travellers are being organised into rows and their papers are being checked.

I squeeze Yardly's hand. "What are we going to do?"

"This has got way too risky for me. Of course, if I'm caught helpin' you, they'll vaporise me too. I'm too young to die. Sorry, Eliza, you're on your own."

Yardly nods his head as we arrive at the floor above Promenade Square. He jumps on the next escalator. I could force him to help me, but considering it's me who doesn't have papers, and it's me who smuggled in a weapon, it hardly seems fair. Although he encouraged me to use it, it's still me who fired it. He's probably right. I am an unintentional terrorist. I can't end up on Promenade Square; my lack of papers will be the problem, never mind the weapon in my pocket, plus Lionel will definitely report me.

I sneak under the half-opened shutter of a café. The server behind the counter hasn't noticed and is busily bagging the day's takings from the till. As she leaves, I hide behind the fur coated sofa, which reminds me of a lounging bear; the hairs tickle my nose. She crawls out under the metal shutters and presses a button. The shutters whine closed, clunk and lock. I snuggle into the sofa; my neck is stiff and aching, but I'm safe. An enormous sigh of relief washes over me. Well, I'm safe for now, anyway. An announcement comes over the tannoy:

"We are in the process of locating the terrorists, so we are scanning the space station. Please be aware, there's danger to life. All passengers must remain in Promenade Square. Failure to do so will result in your termination."

"Wow."

Surely the priority of the space station is to protect its passengers, not scare them to death. It must be terrifying to hear such a negative message over the tannoy. The passengers don't know I'm not a real terrorist, and that they're not in any real immediate danger! Although, I guess Appollo is still loose in the space station, and he is a terrorist. They're in danger from him, not me! Being an unintentional terrorist isn't recommended. I'm being hunted by the Reus and if they catch me, then they'll probably kill me, and if I try to get the Luxlumen, Appollo will probably kill me. It's not looking good either way.

The Reus knows I'm still on the space station, because no one has left. They won't abandon their search until they find me. Yardly is right, they probably won't listen, so it's pointless surrendering. Well, they aren't the friendliest of aliens, and TrueBias warned me to keep away from them.

Lionel is bound to snitch on me; he's out to save his own skin, but hiding here is just delaying things. I won't get the Luxlumen back or save my dad by staying here. Using the Harmoniser was a dumb idea. I could've killed someone.

Lying back on the bear's belly, I allow my fluttering heart and trembling knees to settle. I need to plan my next move carefully. Wandering around the café may inspire me, or maybe I'll find an exit because, by not thinking this through properly, I've managed to get myself trapped. Some voices are getting closer.

"We'll do a ssweep of the floorss." A Reus rattles the café shutters. "The prisson sshuttle needss to be disspatched to Phylaca, it'ss protocol."

Did he say they will launch the prison shuttle? My dad is probably on board, and so is the invisible bank-robbing Caecus. If the prison shuttle is the only thing leaving Conexus, then, according to Lionel, Appollo will probably be on board too. I've got to get to the shuttle. I head towards the back room, but my reflection in the mirror behind the counter distracts me. My face isn't absolutely familiar. This is about the third time I've seen the true me, but I like it. An announcement comes over the tannoy:

"Scan level one."

As I'm checking for a bald patch where my hair was ripped out by the screaming little girl, behind me, a solid turquoise grid fills the entire room; it's heading across the floor towards me.

"I'm on level one!"

I duck down behind the counter and hold my breath, trying to avoid being scanned. The light passes straight through my body. A hologram, dressed as a human security guard, appears in front of me.

"Stand and surrender."

I do as I'm told.

"Stand and surrender. Refusal to do so will result in

your termination."

"I am standing."

Backing away from the hologram, I see that the departure boards have transformed into TV screens showing me in the café. A message comes over the tannoy:

"We have located the terrorist and are terminating life. All passengers must remain on Promenade Square as our guards are heavily armed. Please be assured we will do all we can to protect all travellers at Conexus."

Wow, they've changed their tune! The hologram draws what must be a weapon from his holster. From the tannoy message, he's definitely planning to kill me. I need to get out of here. The hologram fires as I dive behind the bear sofa. Shouting and booing comes from the crowds on the floor below as they watch me trying to escape with my life.

My enemy aims and fires again. This shot misses my head by millimetres; he fires again, but this time not at me, but intentionally at the bear sofa, which disintegrates in front of me. I'm now crouched behind a pile of dust. Again, the crowd in Promenade Square below respond, but this time they roar. I scurry, scrambling underneath different tables, whilst the hologram transforms the furniture, in the café, into various forms of dust.

The Reus smash their way in, distracting the hologram as they noisily squeeze under the once locked shutters. They struggle to bend them high enough to fit their vast bodies underneath, so the shutters soon become bent and out of shape. Whilst they are busily struggling to get in, I see my only chance to escape; I dive under the warped shutters, back out into the walkway, and head away from the café. With my back against the wall, I try to keep out of sight, but the Reus, now inside the café, shout orders at the ones outside, who have no idea I've escaped.

With no plan, I'm hoping something will come to me. The crowd on Promenade Square gasp and shout, annoyed I've escaped; they applaud as a virtual guard pops up in front of me, insisting I surrender. Instead, I run.

Sprinting through the virtual assistant guard and along the corridor, I scramble onto the travelator; my speed is turbo-boasted on the moving platform. The Reus bound behind me, their claws clanking on the marble floor, whilst the travellers shout and cheer on the floor below, as they watch the pursuit being streamed live on all screens. The TV in front of me shows a Reus closing in. An announcement comes over the tannoy:

"We are in pursuit of the terrorist. Our guards are armed. Please ensure you stay within the boundaries of Promenade Square. We apologise for any inconvenience caused."

A door at the end of this section of the travelator says *Services*. Is this a way out? Leaping off the travelator, I burst through it; there's a waste-disposal chute in front of me. I kick at the flap; it'll surely kill me going through there. Bottles of chemicals are stacked high on shelves and tea towels are folded neatly on a counter. A service lift is to my right, with the doors slightly open. I squeeze my way through the thinnest gap. They slam shut behind me, just as a Reus bursts into the room. Sinking to the floor, I shut my eyes.

"Lookss like sshe'ss gone through the wasste dispossal unit, flap sstill moving. Sshe will be dissssolved or incinerated; no chance of ssurvival."

The Reus is moving around the room. Is he checking to see if I'm hiding? He's pressing buttons as he tries to force the lift doors to open.

"Please don't open! Please don't open!"

"Shush."

I breathe out a sigh of relief as the door shuts to the service room.

"Is that you, Jack?"

— CHAPTER TWENTY-TWO —
The Prison Shuttle

It's only been a few hours since I was last trapped in a lift. Last night I was terrified. Not only did the lift rhyme, but I met TrueBias, a complete stranger in a dim, dank basement of a room. It's hardly surprising that I freaked out; anyone would, wouldn't they? Most people would think that this was traumatic enough for a thirteen-year-old, but here I am again, but this time I'm being hunted by aliens who genuinely see me as a threat and want to kill me. This unfamiliar world is real and dangerous, and let's be honest, it's a world which, for me, didn't exist until a few hours ago.

There's another announcement:

"Thank you for your patience. We have terminated the terrorist. We will reschedule departures once our communication links are up and running."

Leaning against the wall, I draw in a deep breath, lifting my arms above my head. My back twinges as I stretch out my shoulders. My entire body aches.

"Do not worry, do not fear.
Your favourite empath, Jack, is here.
The Luxlumen is on the basement floor.

By the prison shuttle and waste store.
Caution is needed; you must be smart.
Retrieve the stone before the shuttle departs."

"Jack! I knew it was you. It's great to hear your voice!"

The lift rumbles, and Jack lowers me, presumably to the basement.

"Is TrueBias okay?"

Jack opens the doors into the bowels of the space station. I pinch my nose.

"It stinks down here."

The plushness of upstairs has disappeared. With plain walls and rubberised flooring, this corridor isn't much different from the walkways at Lowry Heights.

The arrow outside the lift points to the *Waste Facility* and a sign below it says:

Full Personal Protective Equipment must be worn at all times
NO EXCEPTIONS, NO EXCUSES

"Caution is needed*,"* Jack says, and he is right. Around the corner, Cecelia and Appollo are chatting.

Cecelia is transforming from a Reus to a human whilst she drags a Reus by the tail. It's an incredible sight watching her mutate. I may seem impressed, but she's really nothing but a selfish coward, so what's there to be impressed about?

"We have no choice," Appollo says, lifting the Reus under his arms and helping her move the body.

She must have tricked the Reus. As they lay him on the ground, Cecelia snaps the card from the cord around his neck.

"What if I bring the Luxlumen through later?" she says.

"As soon as the communication links are up, they will find us. No Simulos will be able to travel to or from this station again. They'll vaporise you; Lionel will make sure of that. You'll have to leave; you've no choice."

Appollo picks up the canvas bag, probably with the

Luxlumen stone inside.

"Well, if it wasn't for that cretinous girl, dead now though, good riddance to her." Cecelia swivels on one foot. I bolt back out of sight. "And you fried her android pal!" She laughs like she used to laugh when she was teasing me. She has an evil, gruesome laugh.

No, I don't believe it, TrueBias can't be dead, but Jack never answered me when I asked him. A darting pain shoots from my chest to my head. Maybe I could have saved him, if only I had stayed to help.

"The prison shuttle is our only hope," Appollo says.

He takes the card from Cecelia and scans the keypad on the door. I step towards them. It's gloomy down here with only the gentle glow of a singular low-level strip light.

"What's the passcode?" he asks.

Cecelia types in a code and the doors open, not to a space shuttle but to another corridor. The doors swish behind them. I dive forwards; it's possible I'll be able to jam the doors open or squeeze through before they shut, but not even my fingernail can crack the seal.

The Reus beside me is groaning. Great, they've got the Luxlumen and my dad, and left me with this Reus, who will surely vent his frustration out on me as soon as he wakes. I've no choice but to use the Insync Harmoniser. How did TrueBias do this?

Pointing the Harmoniser at the door, I face away, concentrating, my brain screams in agony as my eyes bulge. I'm visualising the doors changing, so I can step through them, like TrueBias did in the HoloSuite.

To my amazement, the surface of the door transforms into a shimmering water-like substance. I poke my hand through. The gooeyness of the jelly-like substances circles around it, and there is a sucking sound as I drag it back out. Phew! It's still attached to my arm. I put my face through, but only to check if Appollo and Cecelia are still on the other side; they're not. Stepping through the door, there is a dragging sensation like the door is holding me back. I emerge out into the next corridor.

This corridor is different; it's like a huge metal tube. An acidic taste lurches in my throat; I hope I'm not trapped in here. Another key-coded door is at the far end, and the light above it is red. I aim the Insync Harmoniser at it, but this time, I've no idea what's behind it. Is the red light telling me that there is nothing but outer space? If they've already launched the shuttle, that's how it would be. Oh, no! What am I supposed to do now?

I clasp my hands to the back of my neck; I'm way out of my depth. If I go through the doors and the shuttle has gone, it's likely I'll be dragged out into space and suffocate, or freeze to death or both. If my finger goes through, it will probably freeze off! This is madness; I'd be an idiot to risk a finger or a hand, but what's a finger against saving my dad's life? What should I do? Daisy's voice echoes in my head.

Be brave and believe in yourself.

There's a difference between being brave and being dumb, Daisy.

Should I go back and find something or someone to help? But, if I do that, the Reus outside may have regained consciousness, and I doubt he'll have any patience to listen to anything I say. As I pace around in circles, a slight click clicking echoes up from the floor. The laces on my trainers are undone; I crouch down to do them up. My shoe!

Taking off a trainer, I grab the laces, and with the other hand, I use the Harmoniser to create the opening. I shove my shoe through the door, and with a tug, it reappears intact; I do it again and again and each time my trainer comes back undamaged. I slip it back on. Closing my eyes, I push the tips of my fingers through the jelly-like substance, circles around my hand. My mouth is dry; I lick my lips and open my eyes as I pull them out.

Phew! My heart thumps a cheer. They're all okay. I push my hand through the door and again pull it back. It's still attached to my wrist. Risking everything I leap through.

As I emerge on the other side, a chill creeps down my

spine. The air is icy and as I blow onto the tips of my fingers, my escaping breath swirls up to the ceiling. The plushness of the space station has definitely gone; even the connecting corridor was more impressive than this. This corridor is built of riveted steel. I must be inside the shuttle. Shadows loom everywhere with low-level strip lights running through the centre of the floor, and although there's a door to my left, the rubber treads on the floor lead me to a brightly lit room at the end of the corridor, where there's a great deal of commotion.

"...lucky day. We have high-jacked this shuttle and will *NOT* be taking it to Phylaca," Appollo says.

There's a tremendous amount of clapping, cheering and whistling.

The room is well lit; it's obvious it's a holding room for prisoners. I stay out of sight. Two rows of aliens are trapped in orange-tinged transparent metal-framed boxes. Each row is about 10 cells long and three storeys high.

Appollo is raising his arms and standing at the end of the rows; he's smiling, but he doesn't have the attention of all the prisoners, as they busily chat amongst themselves.

Cecelia has shapeshifted into a female version of a Viscorpus. Well, or else there's more than one Viscorpus here. She spins round. Has she sensed me behind her again? I duck further into the shadows, holding my breath, keeping silent. She places her hand on Appollo's shoulder before she motions with her other hand for the prisoners to settle.

"Silence! Show some respect for our esteemed leader, Appollo," she says.

It's Cecelia's voice. She hasn't disguised it this time, but her request has the opposite effect of silencing the prisoners. Some cheer, others argue; none are keen on Appollo being their leader. I don't recognise many of the species trapped in the cells. Opposite me is an enormous round one who squeaks as he tries to turn the walls of his cell force him into one position. He's next to a stick insect type, who has, by contrast, loads of room.

There's a wiry-haired polar bear, a Menax, some with

wings and many others, but from where I'm hiding, I can't see any humans. I slump against the wall behind me, closing my eyes and letting out a puff of air. My dad is probably not in any of them. Neither is Mrs Shufflebottom. Maybe they're both still on the space station.

"Comrades! It will delight you to know we have liberated the Luxlumen." Appollo's voice is quaking yet booming over the bickering prisoners. "And we will all be travelling to Elekron."

There is a deafening mixture of both cheers and boos. Most of the prisoners are banging their boxes, trying to escape. I bet they regret committing their crimes now. I'm positive life on Elekron will be worse than the prison planet Phylaca.

Appollo ignores the negative responses, but instead stands on tiptoes. He pulls the stone from the bag and raises the Luxlumen to the highest point he can reach. The stone's vibrant lustre fades to the dullest cream as he parades it through the centre of the room.

"Oi Mister, let us out," shouts the prisoner standing in the box in front of him.

"Yeah, come on," says another.

The prisoners chant, "Out! Out! Out!"

Appollo raises his hand. "All in good time; be patient!"

He places his hand on Cecelia's back and they stride out of the room through some automatic doors. They must be heading for the bridge of the shuttle.

What a brilliant idea. The last thing Appollo needs is a hoard of unpredictable prisoners running around the shuttle. He won't be able to launch then, will he? But how am I going to free them all? I creep further into the room. If my father isn't here, do I need to do anything at all? A little sole-squeak from my trainers reminds me of everything I've gone through to get here. I crouch against the wall in the shadows behind an empty holding cell. Just because he's not in this room doesn't mean he's not here. I need to get the Luxlumen as planned. Wherever he is, I'll be able to get him back if I have that.

"Oh, you again!" a voice says, "you weren't sorry, they never are."

"Ah." The closeness of the voice sends shock waves through my body. The holding cell I'm hiding behind has a slight outline of someone in it. "Jeez, you gave me a fright?"

I can barely hear my own voice over the bellowing prisoners. They seem to disagree about everything.

"I'm sorry I sat on you, and made you rob the Currency Exchange. It really was an accident."

"So, *you* did this?" the Caecus says.

"Yes, but not intentionally." I draw in a deep breath. My chest is heavy; it's my fault this guy's here. "I've come to put things right, unless, of course, you want to go to Elekron?"

"No..." His voice is closer. "My name is Zeno. What's your plan?"

"Well, I was thinking of releasing the prisoners and whilst Appollo is distracted, get the Luxlumen and you out of here?"

"Yeah! Like they're going to forget that I tried to rob the Currency Exchange!"

"Stop being so miserable; I'm here to help you." I can feel my patience running out, but it's the deafening noise of arguing prisoners, rather than Zeno that's sending my head in a spin. "What if we said it was part of the plan?"

"Doubt they'll believe you. Anyway, the only way to release all the prisoners is to turn off the confinement beams, and that can only be done from the bridge. You have no chance."

The more they argue, the more agitated the prisoners become. One is unwinding his neck, clicking it from side to side whilst focusing on the prisoner next to him; he's shouting and spraying spit inside his cell. The other is punching on the wall in what can only be described as a threatening manner.

"Confinement beams?"

"Yeah look."

"At what?"

If you're invisible, you must know that people can't see what you're pointing at.

"The ceiling!" From the ceiling, beams of orange light shoot from a central disc to each cell. "You'd have to disable that."

The confinement beam, attached to the ceiling, is the same as the one that trapped TrueBias at the museum, but much bigger.

"Umm, I've got it. I found a confinement beam gadget thingy. We might be able to use that."

I pull the Carcer out of my pocket, the one I found when I tripped over the Menax's briefcase. My head is pounding. It's impossible to concentrate over the wailing noise of the prisoners.

"What are you doing with one of them?" Zeno's voice is shrieking. "It might work if you aim at the disc in the middle to disrupt the downward beams."

The prisoners hammer on their individual boxes, some with their fists, a few with their heads. It's ridiculous that so many are spitting at each other. Their saliva only splats onto the inside pane of their own cells, and sometimes even bounces back onto them.

"If they're free, they might attack us."

Standing, I shudder at the thought.

"It's our only choice," Zeno says.

Nodding, I fiddle with the Carcer and creep from behind Zeno's cell.

"Wait! You're right! We need to have a better plan," he says. "It's pointless getting hurt."

"Okay, I'm rubbish at plans, but how about I'll release the cells using the Carcer, and as soon as Appollo comes out to see what's going on, I'll get the Luxlumen?"

Yes, I know, a rubbish plan, but at least it's something. The more the prisoners argue, the more my heart races. My brain is screaming at me to get away from this madness. Shaking my head, I place the Carcer on the floor and clap my hands over my ears. It's not so much what they are saying, but what's going through their heads that's upsetting me. To be honest, some of these aliens should be locked away. They're dangerous. But nothing is drowning out this noise.

"...Hey, hello! Are you listening?" Zeno says as I pick up the Carcer. "As I was saying, let's release the prisoners and as soon as someone comes out, I'll get the Luxlumen; it's more difficult to see me, and you can hide in the shadows out of the way."

"Okay, right; let's do that."

I'll follow any plan which reduces the chances of me being killed. Rolling my shoulders back and swallowing a gulp of air, I edge out in-between the two rows of prisoners. I need to figure out how to line the Carcer up. A hushed silence smothers the room; the arguing settles as the prisoners focus on me, curious why a red-skinned human is standing in the middle of a prison shuttle. Father is not here, but he might be on the bridge with Appollo.

The prisoners watch me as I turn the Carcer on. A beam of light shoots out. All I need to do now is figure out how I will align it with the confinement beams in the ceiling.

"Go on girl, just open mine," one prisoner shouts.

"Release him and he'll kill us all, the murdering fool!" says another.

"You can talk, mate! Elekron is the only planet who'll have you."

The name Elekron generates enormous amounts of emotion. Some prisoners can't wait to leave for Elekron, whilst others cannot believe that the Viscorpus, Appollo, has hijacked the shuttle.

The arguments again escalate, and I try to focus, switching off, in my head, their horrible thoughts. I direct the Carcer towards the disc in the ceiling; it's important to get the right angle, but as I swing it into position, the beam intermittently interrupts individual downward beams; cells are being unlocked and locked as I work out the best position. This causes a great deal of frustration as the prisoners are released and trapped again as the beam passes though. I need to attach the Carcer to a cell wall. Making sure it's clear of the cell door, I put it in position. The Carcer suckers come out and it sticks itself to the wall of the cell. The prisoners cheer and bang on the cell doors as they try to escape.

I certainly didn't, and I don't think Zeno appreciated how desperate these prisoners are to be freed. The Carcer, within seconds, disrupts the confinement beam mechanism in the ceiling, blocking the orange beams feeding out from it. Every cell is instantly unlocked at exactly the same time. Each prisoner scrambles, recklessly forcing their doors open to escape. The polar bear alien lands on the stick insect and splats him. There is absolute chaos as they either land on each other, or are landed on, causing the arguments amongst them to escalate to deafening levels.

– CHAPTER TWENTY-THREE –

The Bridge

I dash back to Zeno's cell and sink to the floor.

"Hope we've done the right thing."

Zeno's cell door is open, but I get the sneaky feeling I'm talking to myself.

Aliens scramble everywhere. Some race past me into the corridor, desperate to leave the shuttle. Most squabble amongst themselves, whilst others head in the same direction as Appollo and Cecelia.

I can't see the doors to the bridge, as the brawling prisoners are blocking my view. The fighting is definitely getting worse. I hide back in the darkness; my chest heaves, my hands are clammy, and the noise, from the shouting and screaming prisoners, thunders through my head. My tiny flat at Lowry Heights seems like a perfect sanctuary right at this very moment, but I can't go anywhere, not without Dad.

Has Zeno left me on my own, or is he following our agreed plan? Is he making his way to the bridge or trying to escape the shuttle to save himself? What if Zeno can't be trusted? What a prize idiot I am, relying on someone who robbed the Currency Exchange, and who I barely know. I need to find out for sure.

"Well done, Eliza! Another lousy plan!"

Telling myself off attracts the attention of a passing

prisoner. How can he hear me over such a racket? He unintentionally answers my question as the tentacles around his face swish upwards, revealing some exceptionally huge dish-like ears. He makes a beeline for me. As he gets within a metre, a flying alien picks him up and carries him across the room, dropping him from quite a height. I thrust my back further into the shadows; my legs are frozen and welded to the spot. These prisoners should be nice to me; after all, I'm the one who released them.

Maybe my father is on the bridge. Plus, I need to find out where Zeno is. My heart gallops through my body like I'm waiting to start a race. I inhale a deep breath before darting off into the brawl. The prisoners swing and dive towards me, but I dodge them all. The doors Appollo and Cecelia went through are only a few metres away. *WHACK!* Something knocks me and flings me a metre into the air. My hip screams as it slams onto the rubberised floor, and my back twitches as my spine spasms. I scurry like a crab to squat against the side of a cell wall, whilst my attackers, two brawling goblin-type aliens, continue to roll like spinning acrobats, fists flying, knocking anyone and everything out of their way. They bounce off the cells like a ball in a pin-ball machine. Whizzing and twirling, it's impossible to judge, with the yelps and squeals, whether they're fighting or just messing about and having fun.

One of those revolting creatures with the snake-tongued daughter races towards me and yanks me by my hair. What is the fascination with it? This creature dangles me at arm's length, my toes barely brushing the floor. He screams as he jerks me about.

"Oi, stop it!" I'm desperate to avoid any more hair being plucked out of my head. My squeal attracts the attention of a Menax who comes to my rescue. He stamps on the ugly creature's large, balloon-like toes. The creature alters his scream to a howl, dropping me in favour of chasing the Menax, who skilfully dodges his grasp each time the creature lunges for him.

My heart pounds as I brush my fingers through my hair,

feeling for bald patches. A creature, like a stick insect, approaches me and holds out his hand to help me up. Smiling, he grabs my wrist, but instead of being kind and helpful, he flings me into the air. He's amazingly powerful despite how spindly he is. Tossing me about exhausts him, so instead he swings me around and around making my stomach spin and the acids, which were digesting my burger, travel back up into my throat.

"Hey, enough!"

A darling Garrae hobbles towards me; swirling around with my head pirouetting, it's impossible to focus on what he's doing, but I'm released, and shoot through the air, landing heavily on my side. My hip and back again wail in agony. The stick insect zooms past me, hopping and shrieking, swiping imaginary insects off his body, whilst swinging his arms to swat non-existent flies.

"Odd creatures, they hate anyfink with six legs," the Garrae says as he dashes over and offers me his hand, but this time I stand by myself.

Disorientated, I get my bearings; I'm at the far end of the holding room, the wrong end. My Carcer is still in place, undisturbed, containing the central beams. It's being guarded unintentionally by a particularly tall alien, who has trapped the edge of his shoulder in the upward beam, and although he tries, he can't reach the Carcer to divert it away.

The hair-obsessed creature is still after the Menax, who is giggling uncontrollably while being chased. The stick insect is still batting off imaginary insects and the bowling ball goblins clear a perfect pathway, as they rumble through the centre of the two rows of cells. I chase after them. I'm within a metre of the doors to the bridge as they clunk and swish open. Cecelia is standing there, and as I creep towards her, she raises her hands in the air, pivots and strides back through the doors. I sneak in after her.

This isn't the door to the bridge, but to a further corridor. It's like the first one: fairly gloomy with low-level strip lighting. Cecelia is rushing towards the door at the far end.

The prisoners, who earlier headed in this direction are groaning and moaning, lying wounded, sprawled out on the floor.

Cecelia spins round. I dive into an alcove in the shadows, next to another doorway leading off from the corridor. She senses me behind her, again.

"Who's there?" she says, as she switches from a Viscorpus back to human.

She pauses for a moment and as she is about to go through the door at the end of the corridor, Appollo strides out from the bridge.

"Huh! I preferred the Viscorpus look," he says.

"Yeah well, I'm more comfortable like this."

"Don't get used to it. Elekron will expect you to live in the image of a Viscorpus," he smiles and taps Cecelia's cheek. "What's going on out there?"

"It looks like the confinement beam has failed. You sure you haven't messed with anything?"

A pulsing golden ball of light zaps past me and hovers in front of Cecelia. The ball shoots a wide beam of light to scan Cecelia from her head to her toes.

"Oh, no!" she says and transforms back into a Viscorpus; the ball scans her again from her toes to her head and shoots off.

"No, the only thing I did was to program Dot," he says with an enormous smile as he watches the ball of light zoom past him. "She's doing an excellent job, by the looks of it." He points to the pile of groaning prisoners scattered across the corridor.

The doors from the holding room swish open and the stick insect prisoner bursts through. I thump back against the door in the alcove as he dashes past; he foolishly ignores the other battered prisoners who are groaning and moaning around him. He's distracted, unaware of the danger he's in. He's screaming, slapping imaginary flies off his painfully skinny legs whilst attracting the attention of Dot. She zaps through the corridor and hovers in front of him.

As with Cecelia, she scans the stick insect alien with a fan of white light. The stick insect, realising he's probably in trouble, tries to out-dodge Dot, but as he leaps and jumps, dives and darts in every direction, Dot tracks his movements perfectly, like a synchronised swimmer. As soon as she gets bored with this game of tag, she fires a constant white beam of light and the stick insect creature collapses to the floor. I shove my hand over my mouth, crushing a squeal, but the slightest noise slips through my lips, attracting Dot's attention. She hovers, pulsing, and waits for another sound, hoping for confirmation that she isn't hearing things. I hold my breath and keep absolutely still.

"I should let Dot loose on them all," Appollo chuckles as he places his hand in the centre of Cecelia's back. "Come on!" he says. "Let's see if we can figure out how to fly this thing!"

"I should be able to," Cecelia replies. "I've flown similar."

They go through the doors at the far end; Dot, distracted by them, has forgotten about me and is zipping through the entire length of the corridor, waiting for her next victim.

I can't risk being caught by Dot. I'm nowhere near as agile as the stick insect and what has Appollo programmed her to recognise as *friendly*? Cecelia had to shift back into a Viscorpus, so maybe Dot only recognises Viscorpus'.

I press the illuminated button to the door I've been leaning against; it swishes open and I creep in. It then swishes shut behind me, just as Dot returns and hovers outside.

The room must be the shuttle's lounge. Spotlights in the ceiling highlight every corner. There are huge plush padded sofas organised around a central glass table, and a machine which, according to the signs, dispenses, *Snacks and Refreshments*; there's also a TV screen moulded into the far wall.

"Eliza?"

A head peeps up from behind the sofa; it's a flushed version of my dad's. How did Cecelia get in here from the bridge so quickly?

"Eliza, is that you?"

"Good try, Cecelia, but the skin colour is all wrong." My chest thumps. "I won't fall for it a second time."

The man in front of me, pretending to be my dad, stands and smiles. His mouth is so wide it makes the corner of his eyes crinkle.

"Sweetheart, it's me!" He holds out his arms as though he's planning to hug the entire world. "Aren't you pleased to see me?"

This man truly believes he's my father; I can sense it, but maybe Cecelia is getting smarter.

"Oh, just give it up! I'm getting bored with your stupid games. What have you done with my real dad?"

"Eliza, it's really me!"

"Okay, if it is you, tell me what you were bringing home last night?"

"Pizza and cake," he roars. "Pizza and chocolate eclairs." He tosses his arms in the air. "It's yours and Daisy's favourite."

"Dad?" An enormous lump of air blocks my throat as I try to swallow, while stumbling towards him. My head tingles. "Is it really you?" Sinking my face into his chest, the familiar aroma of disinfectant and fading aftershave is something even Cecelia couldn't replicate. "We're going home, Dad."

He kisses my forehead.

"But what have they done to you? Why are you so flushed?"

"Sweetheart, it's a long story." He's crushing me. His heartbeat thumps and skips. "Have I ever told you how incredible you are and how much I love you?" he says.

"I love you too, Dad." A tremendous sense of peace washes over me. "I was so worried about you."

"Come on! We need to get out of here before the shuttle leaves," he says, unhooking my arms from around his waist.

"They said you'd left the emergency exit door open at the museum so they could steal the Luxlumen."

"No, I didn't, sweetheart, I promise, but they tried to

make me; they even threatened me saying that they would hurt you. That's why Cecelia was pestering you so much, so I agreed to help, but a building like the museum has alarms on all its doors. If I had left it open, an alarm would have gone off." He slumps onto the sofa and buries his head in his hands. "I knew what they were planning, but I..."

"But what, Dad? Why didn't you tell me?"

It all makes sense now. Cecelia has been hounding me because she and Appollo were blackmailing my dad, trying to force him to break the law.

"I thought it was impossible to get into the museum. I didn't believe they could *ever* get their hands on the stone. If I knew they could, I would have reported it." Dad holds my hands and plays with my fingers; he peers into my eyes. "I'm sorry Eliza; it's my job to protect the stone and you, and because I didn't, I've got us all in this mess and have let you down." He stares at the floor. "I was so fed up with being trapped in our tiny flat with Daisy, and life is so difficult for us both. For a moment, I thought it was our only way out–but I promise I didn't leave the door open."

"It felt like you'd left me." Tears swell in my eyes, as both fear and relief wash over me at exactly the same time.

"Sweetheart, the last thing I remember is being in the lift with Rose Shufflebottom and then I was in a holding cell. Appollo came in a while ago and released me. I didn't know what his plans were, nor that you were here." He clenches my hands, blocking the natural flow of blood to my fingers. "I would never leave you. You know that, right?" He stares straight into my eyes and winks. The corner of his mouth curls.

"We need to find mum, my real mum, Poppy."

"I know, sweetheart, but the Flos Region are fussy about which species they let in, and at the moment she can't leave."

"What, I'm her daughter and a Dolce; surely being a human as well isn't a threat to them?"

Dad sighs and nods his head.

"Let's sort this mess out first, shall we?" he says.

"Yeah, we need to get the Luxlumen back. Do you know if it's on the bridge?"

"I guess so, but I'm not sure. As soon as they released me, I came in here to sort myself out. Those prisoners are pretty frightening. Then I heard a lot of shouting in the corridor; I panicked and hid."

"Yeah, I released all the prisoners, but an electronic security guard called Dot monitors the corridor outside and is zapping anyone who tries to make it to the bridge."

Dad's mouth drops open, his eyes wide. "What, *you* released the prisoners?"

"Why didn't you tell me I'm a hybrid?"

He pulls me towards him. "You're exquisite, a perfect hybrid, with the courage and determination of your mother." He kisses my cheek. "Come on!"

"We really need to find her."

"Who, your mother? We will," he says. "But for now, we need to sort this mess out. I'll get the stone from the bridge. You wait here; it's safer." He places a finger on my lips as I open my mouth to protest. "We'll then make a run for it."

"What about Dot?"

"Oh." He flaps his hand. "She likes me." He smiles as he stands and makes his way to the door. "Wait here!"

"No, Dad! Dot will kill you."

"Eliza, it's fine."

He presses the button to open the door, and as he does so, Dot is still hovering outside.

"Daaaad noooo..."

She double scans my dad and shoots off.

He marches along the corridor, stepping over the groaning bodies and goes through the main doors to the bridge. A tremendous rush of fear gushes over me. What if he doesn't come back? What if he needs my help?

Dot is zooming around the bottom half of the corridor. With my back in the shadows, I creep tentatively towards the bridge. The slight squeak of my trainers causes Dot to stop. She hovers as though she's again waiting for confirmation that she's not alone. With so much moaning, I'm surprised she can even hear it. As soon as she gets bored, she manically shoots around the corridor. I continue, and hide in the shadows wherever I can.

Within a metre of the bridge, the door swishes open. Diving back into the alcove, Dot is on maximum alert as Appollo strides out. Cecelia calls after him as my dad stands on the threshold of the door, keeping it open.

"It's the outside door; they've jammed it open," she says.

"I'll sort it," Appollo says, striding along the corridor towards the holding room. He points at my dad. "Help her."

As my dad goes back onto the bridge, I sneak through the closing doors with him.

Cecelia is in human form and is at the controls of what is definitely a cockpit of an aeroplane, but massively bigger. The windows look out onto another corridor, like a short runway with lights on either side. I hide behind a workstation towards the back of the room.

"What do you need me to do?" Dad says.

"You didn't leave the emergency exit open, did you?" she says. "We would have been out of here already, if it weren't for you."

"I did. Security must have closed it," Dad says.

"You're a rubbish liar and useless, like your daughter." Cecelia presses some buttons on the console. I'm trying to focus on her mind. "You're only here because Appollo likes you, but that won't last." She sniggers in a way which sends chills down my spine.

Dad's fists clench.

"Where's the Luxlumen," he says.

"Safe," she says. She swings around in her chair and her eyes transform into the most piercing metallic colour. As she stands, she shapeshifts into a terrifyingly huge alien creature with fangs and huge claws. Dad gasps and stumbles backwards. She's towering above him. "I'm not sure we need Eliza's daddy anymore," she says, in a voice which is pure evil.

My dad dashes towards the doors, but before he can get there, Cecelia grabs his shirt collar and swings him in the air. She flings him against the workstation that I'm hiding behind. He slides to the floor. I jam my fist into my mouth, suppressing a scream from escaping.

"You're just an inconvenience to my plan," she says, "just like your whiny daughter was."

My dad's head is flopping backwards and forwards. He is barely conscious; he moans. Although he is aware of Cecelia, he's not quick enough to dodge her. She grabs him by his arm and drags him off the ground, pinning him against the wall. I sense she's preparing to kill him.

"Hey! Leave him alone!"

Standing by the workstation, I focus on Cecelia's mind. My head is pounding. The creature she has transformed into sends a chill through my spine. More terrifyingly, since she can only replicate creatures that she has seen, this alien must exist somewhere. Her head darts in my direction and she releases a high-pitched squeal. She drops my dad and shoots towards me. She prowls around me like a hungry lion before she fingers the zip of my jacket with her enormous claws. All I can sense is fear; she's terrified of me, but why? I hope she can't sense how terrified I am of her too.

"Don't touch me!" I step forward, forcing her backwards. "Leave us alone and tell me where the Luxlumen is."

I'm concentrating so intently, I'm literally crawling into Cecelia's bleak mind, a baron place of hatred, false friends and isolation, but despite this, her feeble brain is grappling with mine.

Her eyes flick towards a cupboard near where she was sitting under the main console, but she's still trying to hold my gaze. She's physically much tougher than me. My dad is still barely conscious, rolling and moaning on the floor. She's eager to kill us both, and I need to hold on to her mind until Dad comes round. I must remain focused.

The door to the bridge swishes open. We're expecting Appollo, but it's only Dot hovering outside. Dad rolls sideways, forcing his leg into the threshold of the door, blocking them from closing. Dot continues to hover; she first scans Dad and then scans Cecelia, who instantly transforms back into a Viscorpus. As she's about to scan me, Dad moves his leg and the doors close.

"There you are," Zeno says. "I can't find it anywhere."

Cecelia's eyes shoot around the room.

"Who's there?" she says.

My dad grabs her from behind and holds her arms behind her back. She transforms back into the terrifying creature as I leap towards the cupboard under the console and grab the canvas bag with the Luxlumen stone inside.

"Come on, let's go! I've got it."

Dad is struggling to hold on to Cecelia, and as he releases her, we dart towards the door. She lunges after us, but trips over an invisible object toppling headfirst onto the ground. She's dazed, and as Dad goes through the doors, I follow, using him to screen myself against Dot.

"Are you with us, Zeno?" I ask.

A hand grabs mine. "Yeah, do you like my trip manoeuvre?" he says.

The main doors to the holding room swish open. Appollo continues to wrestle off prisoners as he tries to come back through. We dive into an alcove, and as he strides towards the bridge, we bolt through the doors to the holding room, just as Cecelia screams from the bridge.

"They've got the stone."

– CHAPTER TWENTY-FOUR –
Dad!

It seems the more determined we are to head towards the main exit of the shuttle, the further into the room the prisoners' brawl drags us. Dad's hand slips from my fingers as he defends me from the fighting aliens. The doors to the bridge corridor swish open. Appollo is standing on the threshold searching for us.

"*Dooot*!" he screams. Dot is obediently by his side, hovering like a faithful dog. "Clear this madness," he says as he shoves her out into the holding room.

Once over the threshold, she ventures into the chaos. It doesn't take her long to select her victims; she's having an incredible time scanning and zapping brawling prisoners, and is systematically making her way through quite a few. Some prisoners, realising Dot is the new enemy, sacrifice others by using them as alien shields to protect themselves from her.

"Where are you?" Appollo's voice bellows, his eyes bulging. Veins pulse through his neck and up into his skull.

Hidden in the shadows, terrified to draw attention, we squat at the far end of the room, the wrong end. Zeno's hand is squeezing mine so tightly, my fingers are going numb. Peering through the cell walls, I can no longer see or hear my dad. Appollo stands at the doors of the bridge corridor, admiring Dot's attempts to flush us out by eliminating everyone else.

"We need to go," Zeno says.

His warm breath brushes past my ears as he tugs at my hand.

"What about Dad?"

"He'll be waiting outside."

Zeno has a point; our plan was to escape, but would my dad leave me here on my own? We creep out into the room, intending to head for the main doors, but Dot appears, hovering in front of us. Air blocks my throat as she scans my body, and despite Zeno yanking my arm, desperately trying to get me to run, my feet are stuck to the floor.

As Dot completes her first scan, the alien, trapped in the confinement beam next to me, is thrashing about so wildly that he distracts her. With his flailing arms he strikes her–*THWACK!* Shooting her off, like a cannonball, directly into the upward confinement beam.

Appollo's piercing eyes penetrate through me; he bulldozes past other aliens, shoving them out of his path as he makes a direct beeline for us.

"He's coming." My words get trapped as I squeeze Zeno's hand.

Zeno is excellent at ambushing prisoners; he trips and shoves aliens out of our path as we try to make our way to the exit, but Appollo is too quick and blocks our escape. We head back into the room as Appollo powers through the brawl after us. He's not much more than an arm's length away, and as I put the Luxlumen in my pocket, I launch the canvas bag in the opposite direction.

As planned, this distracts Appollo. After all, he's only after the stone. He scurries towards the bag just as a rather monstrous ball-shaped creature charges at him, bowling him over, propelling him several metres across the floor. Appollo is lying flat on his back. Is he unconscious? The round creature charges him again, but this time he dives on top, forcing them both to slide across the room, bowling prisoners out of their path and flattening a stick insect creature as they do so, stopping only when Appollo is squashed against the wall at the far end of the room.

A blue human-like alien, with huge muscles and a wrinkly head, yanks the ball-shaped creature off Appollo. The round creature tumbles backwards, landing on two other aliens, who are taking it in turns to face slap each other.

Appollo stands with the help of the blue alien and rubs the back of his neck. His hands are clenched as he picks up the canvas bag and looks inside. He then scurries around knocking prisoners out of his way as he inspects the floor; I guess checking to see if the stone has rolled out.

"Where is it?" he says, his voice bellowing. His eyes dart around the room. We're hiding. I still can't see Dad and there is no clear path to the exit either. Appollo shoves an alien, who has fallen back onto him, out of his way and draws the Terminator from its holster, aiming it at the prisoners.

"Stop now," he says, wiping spit from his mouth.

He's doesn't notice us creeping along the edge of the cells; he's entirely preoccupied with his search on the floor for the stone, and is distracted by the furious mob of prisoners who are now focusing their attention entirely on him. They charge at him, and dive away from his beams of fire, as they do so.

We head towards the exit just as the Reus stampede into the shuttle. They knock me back into the centre of the room as they ambush the other prisoners and cause an incredible amount of chaos. They climb across the ceiling and on top of cells, dropping on anything which moves. The Reus, the new enemy, creates a fresh wave of confusion. More Reus stream through from the corridor, and as they enter the room, the intensity and anger of everyone escalates. The Reus leap in every direction, whilst flying aliens rise beyond the Reus' reach, and grab other aliens, dropping them from the highest point onto the Reus. The Reus tries to grab the flying aliens, but instead miss and dive-bomb into groups of brawling prisoners.

Appollo disappears. Has he cloaked himself or has he

returned to the bridge?

I scramble backwards, desperate to avoid any more attention, but as I do so I'm thrusted further into the middle of the brawl, as the pin-ball goblins once again bowl me over. Zeno's hand grabs mine and pulls, dragging me back to the cell walls. This is so intense and dangerous; despite the Reus being here, the situation is getting worse.

We dash along the cell walls towards the exit, but something grabs me by my hair and instantly stops me. Is it the ugly creature again, the one with the snake-tongued daughter? But I'm not being dragged or lifted. Twisting around, the confinement beam has trapped the tip of my ponytail. The Carcer is behind me; at first, I yank at my hair and then at the Carcer, trying to force the suckers to release. The alien who is confined in it, and who unintentionally saved me from Dot, is thrashing his arms backwards, trying to grab hold of me. The suckers don't budge. If I switch off the Carcer, I can free my hair, but that would release all the downward beams from the ceiling and Dot. My only other option is to pull out a huge clump of hair. At this point, I really have no choice, do I? I need to get out of here. I move the top of the Carcer to the off position, and as I do so, I charge to the end of the row of cells.

My Carcer releases all the downward beams at exactly the same time. So, if any alien is standing on top, or inside a cell, or in mid-air, or in fact, if they're caught in any beam lines at all, they're confined. It traps a Reus in mid-flight as he was about to land on a prisoner. The flying aliens dangle in mid-air. One has a wing caught, the other his leg, all trapped by the beams. Dot has escaped one beam but shoots off directly into another. The prisoners and the Reus, who are still free from the beams, continue to fight amongst themselves, trying to ram each other into a confinement beam. Partially trapped prisoners still battle using any freely moving parts of their bodies.

"Come on!" Zeno grabs my hand and pulls me towards the shuttle entrance. The shuttle engines rumble.

A computerised voice says:

"Instigating launch procedures."

The Luxlumen is still in my pocket and we dash toward the shuttle doors. Other aliens are forcing their way out, unwilling to be on the prison shuttle when it leaves.

The doors have just reopened. A Reus is pinning the blue human-like alien, by his neck, against the shuttle doorframe. He's the alien who protected Appollo from the ball-shaped creature. He must have been clearing the doors so they could launch. It's an equally matched fight; neither the Reus nor the blue alien is winning.

As we escape the shuttle and into the corridor that links Conexus to it, the Reus, fighting with the blue alien at the shuttle door, lands at our feet; he must have smacked his head as he's unconscious. The aliens at the door drag his body clear of the shuttle. The shuttle door starts to close, as a familiar voice calls:

"Eliza."

My dad is still on the prison shuttle; he's battling back aliens trying to get to the closing doors. He hadn't abandoned me; he was probably trying to find me.

"Daaaaad."

Aliens knock him in every direction as he and other desperate creatures struggle to get to the doors, trying to escape. Zeno clings to my hand and then grabs my shoulders, stopping me from rushing back in.

"It may not be your dad, Eliza; it may be a Simulos."

Zeno is right. It could be Cecelia trying to trick me and get her hands on the Luxlumen, but if it is Dad, I can't simply leave him. I try desperately to concentrate on his thoughts. Having been in Cecelia's hollow mind, I'd know the difference, but the surrounding chaos isn't helping. All I can sense is an overwhelming feeling of fear pulsing through Zeno's body.

"We need to leave," Zeno says.

Dad is grappling with the stick insect alien and as soon

as he frees himself from it, he sprints towards the door as another alien pulls his legs from underneath him, forcing him to the floor. He's crawling towards me, desperate to get off the ship before they again clear the closing doors of the shuttle.

"Go Eliza," Dad says, "save yourself!"

I pull myself free from Zeno and scoot back to help him, but the once unconscious Reus grabs at my ankle and pulls me over, and as my dad is being dragged backwards by several aliens, the shuttle doors finally close and my heart sinks.

I scramble to my feet, my chest pounds and my voice bursts into a scream, "*Daaad!*"

The dazed Reus releases his grip as I pull out the Insync Harmoniser. Zeno jerks my arm.

"If we don't go now, and the shuttle leaves, then we'll be sucked into outer space."

"I need to help Dad."

"He doesn't want you to die! Come on!"

"No, I–I can save him."

"He said to go. Eliza, this is madness–"

"I know–"

"We don't even know if that is your dad, and even if it is him, by going back they will seize the stone, and everything will be for nothing." Zeno is pulling me towards the doors to Conexus. "With the Luxlumen, Elekron will destroy this galaxy, and trillions of dads may die."

The Reus lunges for my leg. "Help me!" he cries.

The Reus' claws are trapped in the runners of the corridor door, preventing it from closing. He's trying to free himself, desperately thrashing his body in all directions, but he's twisted so much that he has wedged his claw into the mechanism. I can't budge it. The light above the door switches from green to red. The door thinks it is shut.

"Eliza! The airlock door is busted. We're going to die!"

We have no choice but to leave the Reus and escape through the door at the other end of the corridor into

Conexus. There is no digital pad on this side, but the doors into the space station refuse to open.

"The system detects the airlock corridor is faulty; it's trapped us on the wrong side of the door. If the prison shuttle leaves now, we're dead," Zeno says, banging on the door to the space station. "*HELP!*"

I point the Harmoniser at the door and shut my eyes. I'm trying to concentrate, but Zeno keeps tugging at my arm; he's like an excitable puppy, scratching at me. His hands pull on my jacket sleeve, like a dog pulls at its toy. I open my eyes, but the door hasn't changed.

"Help me, pleasse," the Reus says, swishing around, trying to free himself. I point the Harmoniser again, trying to block out Zeno's panicking thoughts and the sounds of the Reus, who is now screaming. *"I'm going to die! Help me pleasse help!"*

I open my eyes. "Hold tight." I drag Zeno with me and we squelch out through the other side of the door into the corridor with the service lift and the waste store.

"Oh, thank you so much." Zeno slumps to the floor, sobbing deeply.

The ground groans and shivers beneath us like a mini earthquake.

"The prison s-shuttle has launched. The c-corridor has..." Zeno says.

I have a vague hope that Cecelia is trying to trick me, and that my real dad has escaped the shuttle and is waiting here for me, but it's only me and Zeno. It's obvious it was my dad trying to get out; Cecelia would never say, "Save yourself." She is too heartless to consider anyone else. The Luxlumen is still in my pocket. I saved the stone and Zeno over my father. I don't know what Appollo will do to him, if he's even still on the shuttle. Dad was never a traitor. If security wasn't so atrocious at the museum, they wouldn't have been able to get in, but I guess they didn't expect a Simulos' level of manipulation.

My heart slumps in my chest as my legs collapse. I sink

to the floor against the door next to Zeno. My mind is in a muddle.

"What just happened?" Bringing my knees to my chest, I hug them. My stomach flips. "The Reus." I guess he's dead; outer space would have claimed him by now. My heart thumps as I wipe my nose on the sleeve of my jacket. "Sorry, Mr Reus."

"You did all you could."

"Yeah, maybe, you called me Eliza before, but I didn't tell you my name?"

"No," he says, "but your dad did." He squeezes my hand. "Thank you, Eliza, for saving my life."

— CHAPTER TWENTY-FIVE —

Appollo

The waste store doors swish open.

"Hand it over!" Appollo materialises in front of us, holding out his hand and blocking our way out.

My breath hitches in my throat. I shut my eyes and focus on Appollo's mind. *You don't want the stone.*

He's standing a few metres away; he lifts an eyelid and twists his head to one side. His shockingly bright eyes narrow as he peers down at me.

"Yes, I do!" He steps towards me. "Your mind games won't work with me."

This mind reading thing is a bit unreliable. Well, I definitely don't have the abilities of a Dolce like Daisy, and I know with certainty I can't read the Reus' minds, and Cecelia's, well, that was purely a battle of wills, humans are simple to read, but TrueBias said that, as a hybrid, I may only be able to read some aliens' minds, if any at all, and that it might even be intermittent. It's not something I can completely rely on, but he said nothing about aliens reading my mind. Appollo seems different. When he grabbed me in the museum, he didn't let me go until he was ready to, and now he's answering my thoughts out loud. Is he a Dolce too? Have I lost my abilities already? Did I have any real abilities in the first place? Anyway, I won't be giving up the Luxlumen. No way, not without a fight.

"You can't have it; I'm taking it to the Federation of Nobles and they will decide its fate. Come with me! I'm sure we can sort this out."

"You sound so pathetic, just like your android pal. Federation of Nobles! There's nothing *noble* about them!"

"Considering I have the stone, and you don't, I'm not sure I'm the pathetic one."

"Have you no idea who you are?" Appollo leans against the wall and smiles. "You are an incredible feisty creation, Eliza. We're not enemies."

"Course I know who I am." Is Appollo trying to trick me?

"You understand why your dad has been helping us?"

"So, you say, but has he?"

"Your dad is half Viscorpus, which makes you part Viscorpus."

"No–no way! I'm half Dolce. My mum, Poppy, is a Dolce from the Flos Region."

What is he saying? I lick my lips and swallow the lump of air which has accumulated in my throat. This guy will do and say anything to get his hands on the Luxlumen.

"Yes, and your father is half Viscorpus from Elekron. His father is a pure Viscorpus and his mother a human. Your grandfather is a Viscorpus and your father adores him, just as you love your father." Appollo stands upright. I try to scramble backwards, but I'm cornered. "Your father helped us because he's terrified that his father, your grandfather, will die if I do not return with the stone. You can understand that, can't you, Eliza?"

"I've a–a grandfather?" I bite the inside of my mouth a little too hard. The metallic taste of blood trickles down my throat. "Are... huh."

My mind is spinning, but is he trying to trick me all over again? I've no idea what to do. The thought of having a living relative on another planet would have been insane a few hours ago, but now it's so exciting. I have a grandfather! It makes sense now why Dot didn't zap my father; he's half

Viscorpus, a hybrid too.

"Yes, your grandfather lives on Elekron in the dark, as we all do; he is suffering as we all are."

"How do I know you're not lying?"

"Eliza, look at the colour of your skin; you're one of us. Elekron would celebrate having you, a Dolce-Viscorpus-human hybrid, as part of our community."

"So, you're saying my mum is a Dolce, my dad is half Viscorpus and half human?"

Wow... Before I could see aliens, I wasn't any different from any other human. Well, let's be honest, I was completely different, but not noticeably, not really. But he's right. I don't have the skin colour of a human or a Dolce, and neither does Dad. When I asked him on the shuttle about his skin, he said it was *a long story*. Why isn't he just honest with me? Life would be easier if we talked properly, and I didn't have to work everything out for myself. My head is spinning, I'm not sure how much more of this I can take, it's a small mercy, I guess, but at least I'm shaped like a human. I'd hate to look like a Dolce.

"Your dad's job at the museum was to guard the stone; he was our spy, in case they planned on moving it." Appollo steps towards us. "Come with me; be with your father and your grandfather?" He holds out his hand to help me from the floor.

Dad always said he was a *secret agent,* and the museum was his base. Was he trying to tell the truth all along? When Dad said he was planning for us to leave Cresco, was he planning for us to move to Elekron? Is that why I only saw darkness and suffering when we talked about it?

"No, because once you get the stone, you'll destroy all planets in Earth's galaxy."

"On Elekron we follow the dictum: *We fight in the name of our fathers; we live by the honour of our grandfathers*." He stands in front of me. "You have spent hours searching and fighting for your father. Now you know of the existence of your grandfather. You, as your father, need to protect him.

You're a true Viscorpus to your core, whether you like it or not."

"You tricked me at the museum. You used my love for my father to manipulate and lie." I stand and lean against the doors behind me. Zeno's fingers grip my arm. He hasn't made a sound. "If I hadn't got the stone back, you'd have taken my father to Elekron with you and left me here. You would have destroyed me and Daisy and everyone else on this planet."

"I gave you the opportunity to come with us at the museum." Appollo's voice vibrates. His patience with me is evaporating.

"Yeah, well, I've heard the Viscorpus are liars, and you're probably being so creepy because you need me to carry the stone for you. I know you can't cloak it, and now the shuttle's gone, you're stuck on Conexus."

"Huh!" Appollo raises his eyebrows as the veins in his neck throb up through his jawline. Maybe he doesn't like being called creepy. "I can get anyone to transport the stone for me, but I'd like you to do it, Eliza."

"You're not having it."

Appollo pulls out his Terminator from its holster; he points it at me.

"It isn't really a choice, sorry! Pass the stone to me or I shall get it myself."

My hands jam into my pockets; the stone is in one and the Insync Harmoniser is in the other. If I surrender the stone, he will probably kill me. If I try to shoot him with the Harmoniser, then he'll definitely kill me. I flick my lips, which make a popping sound and draw in a huge puff of air. What should I do? To my astonishment and his Terminator shoots out of his hand and skids across the floor; Zeno is helping.

Appollo dives to grab the Terminator behind him, and whilst he's distracted, I hurtle towards him, running straight into and knocking him off balance. He stumbles and shoots forwards, landing face first through the automatic doors into the waste store. I land flat on his back.

Springing up, I shield my mouth and nose from the

incredible acidic stench which wafts around us. I sprint back towards the lift and leave Appollo on the floor with the waste store doors repeatedly trying to close, banging his waist, before they spring back open again.

As Jack opens the doors to the lift, Appollo grabs the collar of my jacket and drags me back towards the faulty airlock. I'm unable to stand, as he pulls me continually off balance; he shoves me against the doors.

"This is your last chance; hand me the stone! Your father is desperate to save his race, to save *your* race."

Gulping, Appollo lifts me by my neck against the door; my feet dangle in mid-air. He shoves his hand in my jacket pocket as a beam of light catches the tip of his ear. He screams, grabs his ear and releases me. Blood oozes through his fingers; my legs, unprepared for the sudden drop, collapse, and my backside wallops the floor. Pain shoots through my hip and up through my spine.

The beam has come from Appollo's Terminator; it's hovering in mid-air. Zeno is by the lift firing, but he keeps missing. Staying as low as I can, I'm not sure whether it's Appollo, or me, who's in more danger. Appollo dives at it, wrestling Zeno to the ground; it's a bizarre sight watching Appollo fight with an imaginary person: a perfect mime. Zeno is moaning and groaning as Appollo snatches the Terminator out of his hand and staggers off balance. Zeno grabs at his foot and pulls him over. Appollo falls flat on his face again, but this time he's blocking the lift. I leap over him and head through the waste store doors to find another way out.

The waste store has a network of metal gangways, which are suspended above huge vats brimming with stinking amber liquid and gases. Appollo follows me. He's firing the Terminator; the beams spark off the metal handrails. All I can do to escape being vaporised is to dodge Appollo's shots. I dash in a zig-zag motion whilst keeping my fingers crossed. The gangways ribbon throughout this vast room like a massive game of snakes and ladders. I scale some stairs and rhythmically bounce, with each step, along a metal grated gangway.

"Stop! This is your last chance, or I *will* kill you and your father."

Appollo has blocked me; he's standing at the other end of the short gangway, aiming the Terminator directly at my head. This time, he'd be a blind idiot if he missed. Is my father safe? I doubt the prison shuttle will still go to Elekron. What would be the point? Neither Appollo nor the Luxlumen are on board. My dad is definitely safer from Appollo than I am.

"Last chance."

"Okay..."

As usual, I've no plan, but what's odd is the Menax with the top hat, whose briefcase I tripped over, is standing by a door on a higher level. He's frantically huffing and puffing whilst spinning several round wheels. Appollo, distracted by the Menax, aims the Terminator at him, and fires. I watch the beam of light hit the Menax in the back of his jacket.

"*Nooooo!*"

I clamp my hand over my mouth, waiting for the Menax to vaporise into dust. But he doesn't. He must have a bullet-proof vest on or something; he's not fazed at all by being shot, but continues to swivel the wheels. The vats rumble, popping steaming liquid below us. Appollo inspects his Terminator as I clasp the Luxlumen in my pocket and shuffle quickly away.

I don't get very far before a hissing, whistling, bubbling sound comes from the vats below us; it's so fierce that it vibrates the gangways, causing me to lose my balance.

Stumbling sideways, I narrowly avoid a sudden jet of steamy stinky chemicals erupting from below me, and another from behind, and then a huge series of them, popping and splattering, sending balloons of steam and colourful scorching liquid in massive columns through the gangway. I dodge most of them, protecting my face with my jacket as a whole series of shooting rods of liquid explodes into the air. One splatters my jacket, instantly burning holes in it. Appollo, by avoiding one, steps back into another.

"Argh," he howls, dropping the Terminator.

He dives to retrieve it but slips and accidentally knocks it through the railings; it plunges into a vat of boiling crimson liquid. With a glow of the purest light, it disappears.

"Oh dear, oh my, this isn't going as I planned," the Menax says, his hat wobbling and tilting oddly as he frantically spins the gigantic wheels backwards and forwards.

Is he trying to kill us?

Appollo's clothes melt, peeling and dripping off his right side.

"Enough of these foolish games," he says.

He's lolloping towards me. The gangway groans and bounces under his weight. I race in the opposite direction; heading to the door nearest the Menax. Appollo's footsteps are booming.

This place is a maze in mid-air, gangways all suspended at different levels above different vats. I travel down a set of steps and along another metal gangway, around the corner and up a ramp. Has Appollo disappeared? Round another corner and *WHACK!* I splat my face right into a metal-caged door. I fiddle with the padlocked bolt; it's hopeless. It's locked and there's no way through. I retrace my steps around the corner and *THUMP!* I charge into Appollo with such force I bounce off his chest, tumbling to the floor.

The skin on his face and hands is blistering and peeling where the chemicals have burnt him. Scurrying backwards, I stand with my back pressed against the caged door. My hands are in my pockets: the Insync Harmoniser is still in one and the Luxlumen in the other. I'm not a killer, so using the Harmoniser is not an option. Instead, I pull out the stone and hold it in front of me. It transforms to the palest pink, with shapes and candyfloss type strands dancing around it. My heart races: the fine hairs all over my body tingle with anticipation, mixed with fear. My lungs scream with every breath I inhale of the boiling acidic air. Appollo steps forward as I wipe the sweat from my forehead with the sleeve of my jacket. If I hand the stone over, everything I've gone through will be for nothing. The entire galaxy will be destroyed, and I may never see my father again.

"Give me the stone!" Appollo's voice is gentle, even pleading. He steps towards me. "Please, or you and your father will suffer."

"We already suffer, living as hybrids."

The stone is bewitching. It's singing to me: we're connected somehow. I'm no longer afraid of Appollo. I dangle it over the edge of the walkway above the vats.

"Come any closer and I'll destroy it."

"No! If you do, you'll destroy your own race." Appollo stumbles; he touches his blistered face and winces. "You know, you're a coward, just like your father. Both of you are pathetic." He is getting more animated as his voice grows louder. "You're a disgrace to your grandfather and your species." He thumps his fist onto the handrail and lunges at me. "The Viscorpus race denounces you."

"I'm not pathetic!"

Dodging his grasp, I grip the stone harder; it's so tempting to hurl it at Appollo. Such rage is building inside of me; it's like my blood is bubbling as my heart pounds in my head. Appollo grabs hold of my other arm, squeezing it whilst stretching over me for the stone.

"Leave me alone!"

The stone levitates above the palm of my hand. The power from it is incredible as the pulsating energy travels through my arm and engulfs my whole body; it's as though I have channelled the cosmic energy of the universe. A blinding light flashes through the room like a sheet of lightning, and as quickly as it comes, it's gone. Reminding myself to breathe, I half open one eye. Appollo has gone and so has the Menax.

I slide to the floor. The stone still sits in the palm of my hand, glowing, pulsing like a heartbeat. Popping it back in my pocket, I draw in a deep breath and scramble along the maze and out of the waste store, back into the corridor with the service lift.

"Zeno, where are you?" A groan comes from where

Appollo abandoned him on the floor in front of the lift. "Are you okay? Can you get up?"

"What happened?" he says, "where am I?"

"You're at Conexus." I shuffle, making sure I don't accidentally kick him; he grabs my ankle and I help him to his feet. We clamber into the lift and he slides to the floor, pulling me down with him.

"Jack, I just want to go home... please?"

"Well done, Eliza, you're a star.
Your abilities have got you far.
In your pocket, the Luxlumen sits.
Used your bravery and your wits.
You've saved the galaxy, that's for sure.
Many trials you surely did endure.
Be proud of achieving such a goal.
The whole galaxy will be so grateful."

How does Jack know I've the Luxlumen? He's an empath; he reads emotions, not minds.

"Thanks, Jack. I won't be vaporised when the doors open, will I?"

"The communication links are working fine.
Daisy has only just supplied a detailed timeline.
It will be safe for you to leave.
You must see the Federation, I believe."

Jack opens the doors into the service room. I open the main door into Conexus. Everything seems so normal.

"Are you with me, Zeno?"

"Yeah, it's been, um, a bit much."

"Well, we'll see the Federation, and I'll explain everything to them."

I've the most valuable stone in my pocket, yet there are no guards escorting me or anyone paying me any attention at all.

– CHAPTER TWENTY-SIX –

The Federation of Nobles

"Eliza, it's fantastic to see you!" TrueBias appears from nowhere, his arms wide and his Cheshire cat grin stretches from ear to ear. "I heard you've had a right old precarious journey."

He seems to have repaired himself, well, sort of. There are bald patches on his head where his skin is damaged, and one eye is a bit, well, bulgy.

"It's great to be back." As I smile at him, he wraps his arms around me and lifts me in the air. "Sorry I left you, but Jack said–" He spins me around and around; it reminds me of Dad. "I'm going to be sick!"

Every part of my body is aching and creaking; my knees give way as he finally puts me down. I stagger dizzily forwards. Zeno places his hand on my shoulder to steady me. He's being silent, but why? Maybe he's shy; maybe that's why Caecus' are invisible.

"It must have been horrific for you. Jack has told me everything, and, wow, you saved the galaxy. Well done!" He grabs my hand and punches it in the air. "We knew you could do it."

Well, that's not entirely true, is it? He didn't know I could do it at all. He thought I would be a useless, stroppy teenager, and was keen, on so many occasions, to get rid of me. It's only Daisy who has true faith in me.

"How's Daisy?"

"She's a very proud, relieved Dolce," he says. "More importantly, how are you?"

"Tired and achy, I'll be glad to get home. It's been a–"

"Triumph! Be very proud of yourself!" TrueBias swings my arm in the air as he skips, dragging me through the corridor. "You still have the stone, don't you?"

"Um, Appollo was desperate for it. He kept turning up. I'm not sure whether he's still on Conexus."

"Not your problem anymore," TrueBias says, winking.

In my pocket, I finger both the Luxlumen and Insync Harmoniser.

"Oh, I have something which belongs to you."

TrueBias stops so abruptly that I walk right into him. Zeno thumps into me, he groans.

"Great, I wondered where it went. I thought I'd lost it." He raises his hand to shield his mouth and tilts towards me as though he is telling me a secret. "I thought Appollo got hold of it. We would have been in infinite trouble then." Flicking the Harmoniser in the air like a baton, he inspects it as it lands. "You haven't dropped it, have you? This is a sensitive piece of equipment."

"No, I definitely didn't drop it." I shan't mention the fact that I banged it vigorously on the metal trolley. "You were shooting at everything. I took it off you so you didn't hurt yourself or anyone else."

"The key to the Insync Harmoniser is to make it an extension of you. Think and believe in your desires, and if it can, it will harmonise with you."

"Yeah, it was a bit... um." We stride arm in arm through the space station. "I couldn't have defeated Appollo without it."

"You didn't say. You still have the stone, right?" TrueBias is staring at me. How many ways can I avoid the Luxlumen question? I breathe out a huge puff of air. "Um, you don't look well, Eliza. Is everything okay?"

"Yeah, of course, I'm knackered that's all. I really just

want to go home."

"Sure, it's been a phenomenal experience for you, but we need to see the Federation of Nobles before you go back." TrueBias drums his fingers on his chest and pulls an odd face. "They've called a special meeting."

The café with the hole in the ceiling has robotic cleaners sucking up the mess, whilst androids disconnect the warped shutters.

"They'll need to know about the Luxlumen. You have still got it, haven't you?"

There's no avoiding this...

"It's incinerated. We were arguing over it and it bounced and dropped into a vat. Sorry, it's destroyed."

TrueBias stops, drops his head to one side and his eyes narrow. By the look of him, if he is going to say anything at all, I imagine it would be a sarcastic, "Really?" or an outright "Liar!"

"Oh, I'm sorry, this is my friend, Zeno. He's helped a lot."

TrueBias spins around. "Okay, um, he isn't here."

"No, he's a Caecus. Zeno, this is TrueBias; can you shake his hand please?"

TrueBias' arm swings up and down in mid-air. "Pleased to meet you and thank you for helping my great friend, Eliza," TrueBias says. "So, you saw the Luxlumen being incinerated, did you?"

How does TrueBias know I'm lying? He obviously doesn't trust me. I've told him it's incinerated. Why doesn't he just accept what I've said and believe me? Why is he asking Zeno, someone who he's never met before? Why does he think Zeno is more trustworthy than me? Maybe I should mention that Zeno is a bank robber!

"I told you it was incinerated, so stop interrogating Zeno."

"No idea," Zeno says, "Appollo gave me a right old bashing and the next thing, there was a brilliant light. Thought I was dead, and then Eliza helped me into the lift."

"Yeah, the light was the Luxlumen in the incinerator, as I

said."

Now I know you know I'm lying, but why is Zeno lying too? He heard Jack say the Luxlumen is in my pocket. Do I need a friend who calls me out on my lies, or one who covers them up?

"Where are we meeting the Federation of Nobles?" Zeno says, destroying the awkward silence.

"A little further," TrueBias replies, straggling the handrail of the escalator.

It's gone 5 am. My belly rumbles; it's not sure whether it's time for breakfast or for my midnight snack. Saving the galaxy is exhausting.

The terminal is deserted. Most of the passengers have left; well, it's an odd time for anyone to be travelling.

"Is my dad helping the Viscorpus race?"

"He was supposed to," TrueBias says, "I can't categorically say whether he did." TrueBias knows the same as me. "Here we are."

The metal circular doors automatically open, taking us into a short corridor. Before us is another set of doors. These doors differ from anything else here. They are huge antique double wooden doors with mouldings and shiny brass-coloured handles. TrueBias knocks and, without waiting for an answer, bursts in.

The room is enormous, with highly decorated ceilings with wooden panelled walls. In front of us is a long rectangle oak table with a row of aliens seated at it. They stand and nod at us before they all sit, except one.

"Welcome, welcome, welcome!" A plum-coloured lady is smiling; her teeth are brilliant white and she sweeps back her mass of shiny caramel tinted hair and tucks it behind her slightly pointed ears. My knees tremble. She has the most incredible emerald coloured cat-like eyes. "My name is Binarti and you must be Eliza? It's lovely to meet you. We've heard so much about you from Daisy and TrueBias, and from Yardly, of course." She looks over to the corner of the room where Yardly is standing. He smiles, shuffles his feet and lifts his hand slightly. "You're all welcome here."

"She's an Adoron," TrueBias says, squeezing my hand. "Everyone loves her."

"Hi!" I raise my hand in a mini wave and smile, nodding my head towards Yardly. What's he doing here? He must have tried to help me, after all. Maybe that's why the Reus came into the space shuttle. Maybe Yardly explained everything, but all of this, to be honest, is a little overwhelming. What will they ask me? What do they know? A Dolce, sitting at the table, scans me. I can tell because I'm listening to her thoughts. I nod at her, keeping my mind blank, well mostly; is she Poppy, my real mum?

"Okay?"

No darling, I'm Jasmine. She reads my mind and answers my question telepathically.

"Eliza," TrueBias says, "this is the Federation of Nobles, and they represent all the planets in this galaxy. They form part of The Universal Federation of Planets." The Nobles again nod their heads.

I recognise some species, the Dolce, a Reus and an Urbe because his neck is too long. There's a creature like Lora and a stick insect one. The spare chair keeps moving, so I'm guessing it's a Caecus like Zeno. Another species I recognise is the Menax, but one is sitting at the table and the other is standing by the back wall, in the shadows, wearing a battered top hat and cuddling a black cat. He's the Menax who was in the waste store, and the one who dropped the Carcer. I hope he's not waiting to get it back; it's on the prison shuttle, and I've no idea where that's gone. Jasmine, the Dolce, twists round to face the Menax in the top hat. She seems bewildered. She can't see him.

I explain my entire experience from start to finish; telling them how helpful Zeno was in recovering the stone before it was incinerated, and how, without him, the stone would be in Elekron by now. I told them about being an unintentional terrorist, which they knew about, as Yardly had already told them, and how the Reus were difficult to communicate with. The Reus Noble got a little fidgety at this point.

"Did you try young Misss?"

I explained that I tried to tell Lora, but she didn't listen and went on to tell them how I found the Carcer on the floor as I was heading for Terminal 56. I didn't say the Menax dropped it; he'd be in real trouble. The Nobles' eyes turn towards the Reus. I'm guessing we shouldn't find weapons lying around on the space station floor.

I also told them about Lionel and Anton, and that Cecelia had flown with the prison shuttle, and Appollo may still be around somewhere.

"We have Appollo in custody," Binarti says. "He claims that you still have the Luxlumen."

She tilts her head to one side as though she's waiting for a confession.

"Oh." I'm not sure whether I'm surprised because they caught Apollo, or that he's snitched on me. Jasmine, the Dolce, is staring at me, so I settle my thoughts. "He'd say anything; I've heard that they are all liars."

"So, you are saying that the stone has definitely been incinerated?" Binarti asks.

"Well, it went into the vat." I swallow a huge lump of spit.

Jasmine glances towards Binarti and nods. Clearly, they are trying to read my mind.

"We are in the process of adding additional security measures so that the Luxlumen cannot leave or pass through this space station, just in case," Binarti says as she curls her lip and glares at the Reus. "It's taking longer to set up than I would like."

"Is my dad definitely on the prison shuttle?" There is some shuffling and typing on the computer screens.

"He is," Jasmine, the Dolce, says.

"Did he help Appollo steal the Luxlumen?"

"We don't know; we've spoken to Mrs Shufflebottom, and she's not aware of your father being involved, but there are discrepancies, and we're not entirely clear."

"Well, I spoke to him on the shuttle and he said he didn't help them. Cecelia tried to kill us both. He was trying to escape with me."

The Federation of Nobles nod at my explanation, but I'm pretty sure, well let's say I get the impression that they didn't believe me, nor, more importantly, didn't seem to care about my father.

Apparently, they transported Mrs Shufflebottom back to the Flos Region and warrants were issued for the arrest of the aliens involved in the theft of the Luxlumen. I'm thanked for my help and granted free passage through any federation space station, so I don't need to, as they say, manipulate anyone in the future. When they say 'manipulate', they mean lie.

As they dismiss us from the meeting, the Menax with the top hat and cat disappear, but before I can say anything, we're ushered out by the Reus.

"Thanks, Eliza, for your help, but I'm off. My mum worries, so I need to go home." Zeno grabs my hand. "I'll never again complain that I'm invisible."

"H-how old are you?" It didn't enter my head that he was anything but an adult.

"Fifteen in Earth years, I was exploring this galaxy, but I've had enough excitement for the moment. It's time to go."

"Well, it was lovely to get to know you. Thanks for your help, Zeno. I couldn't have done it without you, remember work with what you have." As I shake his hand, I wish he wasn't invisible. It would be brilliant to see him in the flesh and give him an enormous hug. "See you again on my next adventure?"

"Unlikely, you'll ever see me."

Chuckling, his voice fades as he moves further away. He then materialises in form, a skinny boy with curly blond hair. He winks a sparkly eye before he disappears.

"Of course, it's great to see you," Yardly says, as he waddles towards us. "I couldn't go leavin', not while you were in danger. I had to try."

"Thank you."

I wrap my arms around him, ignoring the maggot, the worm and the spider all competing for space in his hairline.

"Need to go. Of course, I missed me shuttle for Loquor, so they're lettin' me on the same one as Zeno, and travel back from there." He holds me at arm's length. "It's been fun." Yardly smiles as a dried insect dislodges from between his teeth. He whips it from his mouth, inspects it and pops it back in. "An adventure," he giggles. "See you again sometime."

As I wave Yardly off, TrueBias and I head towards the wormhole back to Earth. "Were you going to vaporise me when we arrived outside the flats? You know, when you said sorry and took out the Harmoniser?"

"Oh, you mean when George dropped us off?"

"Yeah, then."

"No, of course not. Jack was messaging me through the Harmoniser about all the crazy stuff going on outside the flats. I asked him to tell me. He did, as we arrived; a coincidence, that's all."

"Oh okay, good to know."

"Eliza, we're friends, aren't we?"

"Yeah, True, I guess we are!"

As I smile at TrueBias, we arrive at the wormhole for Earth. I hope they haven't added additional security for the Luxlumen yet, or I'm in real trouble. Lora is waiting for me.

"This way," she gargles as she directs me into a side room. "Place your hand out on the table, please." She scans my wrist with a laser. "All done; your papers are embedded."

A wave of elation washes over me. I'm involved in this crazy unfamiliar existence I know nothing about, but equally I'm terrified of how crazy and unpredictable this life is.

TrueBias is waiting for me outside. He holds out his arms and hugs me.

"Thank you, Eliza; without you this would have ended badly."

We stand by the open wormhole.

"What about Dad?"

"I'll call. We will sort it out." He waves as I step into the wormhole. "Trust me!"

Trust him? I hope this wormhole is definitely the one to Earth!

— CHAPTER TWENTY-SEVEN —

The Menax

As I emerge out the other end, the Luxlumen is still nestled in my pocket. Jack opens his doors to level six, and I amble along the passageway and in through my front door. Clunking is coming from the kitchen; Daisy is doing the dishes. She's the Dolce version of Daisy, dull grey, bony and scaly. I don't think I've seen her in the kitchen before.

"Hello darling, I'm so proud of you."

It's great to be home with Daisy; it's the first time she's ever said she's proud.

"I was going to make you breakfast." She smiles and wipes her hands on the tea towel.

"Is Dad back?"

"No, I'm afraid not; he's off somewhere. TrueBias is going to track the shuttle; it can't go far, so he'll find out where it's docked."

"Is Dad a Viscorpus?"

Daisy flicks her lips and makes a popping sound as she folds the tea towel neatly on the side.

"Who told you that?"

"Appollo, the Viscorpus."

"Um, yes, he's part Viscorpus." She leans against the stool and grabs my hands. "There was never a right time to tell you," she sighs. "He finds it frustrating trapped here with me, but because he loves you so much, he stays for you."

As my knees give way, I lean against the table. So, Appollo was telling the truth and I have a grandfather in Elekron. Dad said he was an orphan. Why did he lie to me? Daisy picks up the papers Dad threw at her last night.

"What are they?"

"This is the contract your dad signed many years ago so that he could stay on Earth." Daisy smiles and pops the papers under a cracked ceramic pot on top of the fridge. "When he gets back, he'll explain everything."

"Did he help steal the Luxlumen?"

"Honestly, Eliza, I don't know." She holds onto my shoulders and looks directly at me. Is she scanning my brain for information? "Your dad lies, and he seems to have a knack for tricking me." She turns away. "I don't have an answer, darling."

"Would you tell me if you knew?"

A lady dashes past the kitchen window.

"Oh, we have a new neighbour, darling, a Dolce called Heather." She passes me a mug of stewed tea. "She's lovely."

"I'm knackered." I plonk the mug on the counter.

"Have a nap; I'll wake you later."

I go into my room and kick off my shoes. I close my eyes and...

xxxxxxxxxxxxxxxxx

Nearly a week has passed and things have got back to normal. My dad has not come home; Heather next door is much nicer than Mrs Shufflebottom, and the parking-bay lads only hated me and my dad because we are part Viscorpus. They seem to be okay with me now, now that I've saved the galaxy. Jack and I create the most ridiculous rhymes. Daisy and Heather work tirelessly, telepathically brainwashing every human who uses the lift, into believing that they have seen nothing, just like Mrs Shufflebottom told my dad, before she knocked him through the wormhole.

I've hidden the Luxlumen in a box under my bed. My head has been buzzing. I'm not sure who I can trust, nor who I am. I'm not sure of much really, but what I do know is that without the Luxlumen, my dad's species, my grandfather and part of me will die. The other part of me also knows that if Elekron and the Viscorpus race have the Luxlumen, then Daisy, humans and thousands of other species like George, the Garrae CabCar driver will die, including millions if not trillions of other fathers. It's so confusing.

I'm not ready to hand over the stone, well not until I decide on what's the best thing to do, and before you say it, I know, I shouldn't lie or steal, but honestly, under the circumstance what choice do I have? It was clear from my conversation with the Federation that they care little about my dad, and they probably don't care much about the Viscorpus race either. It's also clear from Appollo that saving this galaxy from being destroyed isn't an option. So, tell me, do I choose between Daisy, the human race, all my new friends or my dad and grandfather? In this situation, what would you do?

There's a knock on the front door.

"Eliza, can you get that?" Daisy shouts from the lounge.

The Menax with the top hat is standing at the threshold; his cat meanders between his legs, and he taps the brim of his hat as the cat purrs.

"Oh dear, oh my Miss, we need to talk."

"Who is it?" Daisy says.

"Oh my, Miss have I caught you at an inconvenient time?" The Menax's milky beard dances on the floor as he talks; he hooks his fingers together in front of his chest and smiles.

"Um, yeah, you have really." I'm not a genius, but even I can guess why this guy is here. "Can you come back tomorrow?"

"Oh dear, but unfortunately it's not possible to delay my visit any longer." He removes his top hat and steps forward into the flat. "May I?"

Without his hat, he is even shorter than me. He doesn't appear to be at all threatening; quite the opposite really. He must know or, at least suspect that I have the Luxlumen. Were there cameras in the waste store, or is there a tracking device on the stone? Again, I've several questions popping into my head, but no answers. I've not really thought this through. I can imagine the headlines on the front page of the local *Intergalactic Journal*:

LUXLUMEN STONE STOLEN

Traitor, Eliza Berry, a mutated human, is thought to have stolen the stone and is considered extremely dangerous...

Why else would this guy be loitering around, or am I just being paranoid? I've lied to TrueBias and Daisy. They will be furious with me once they find out, but Dad and my grandad...

"Okay, but out here." Squeezing past the Menax, I pull the door behind me, encouraging him to shuffle backwards; it's too risky letting him in the flat. He may be planning to raid it, and steal the Luxlumen for himself. After all, I have no idea who he is.

"As you like, Miss, as you like."

I amble over to the railings. Dad's bike is still padlocked in the same place where he left it nearly a week ago. The cat skips onto the handrail and balances like an insane acrobat.

"May I introduce you to Slugmug?" The Menax points to the cat that's clearly suicidal. "And my name is Jidrit, the Universal Watchman." He holds out his hand.

His hand is soft and warm. "I'm Eliza–"

"Oh, yes, I know who you are, Miss."

"So is a Universal Watchman like TrueBias?"

He replaces his hat and adjusts it using his reflection in my kitchen window.

"I'm appointed by the universe to protect all living species, Miss. I help to correct the wrongs, make them right, if you follow my drift."

My heart pounds through my head, making wrongs right? He's here for the stone. "You know, don't you?"

"That you have the Luxlumen? Yes, of course, hence the urgency of my visit."

The moisture in my throat seems to evaporate in an instant. I gulp to generate spit; my voice is reluctant to raise any questions. It's obvious I'm in serious trouble, if not danger.

"W-what are you going to do?"

My heart sinks through my body like a lead weight. If Jidrit knows I have the stone, who else does?

"Oh, dear Miss, do not concern yourself. I'm not here to take it from you."

This all sounds a little confusing. Is he telling me it's alright to steal and lie? Well, that doesn't sound right. His mind is blank and my attempts to appear cool fade as a bead of sweat rolls across my forehead.

"Oh dear oh my, you seem a little flustered. Let me try to explain myself."

Jidrit pulls out a phone-like device from inside his suit jacket pocket.

I flinch. "No!"

"Only my travel journal, Miss, nothing to be alarmed about."

He raises a hand, waving the object in the air as though he is surrendering before tapping it on the handrail.

"Meeeooow."

"Yes, yes, I know," he says to Slugmug, "I'm going as fast as I can."

Jidrit swipes his finger exaggeratedly across the device, muttering to himself. "Ah, here we are, see?" He flashes the screen at me, but it's blank. "Three weeks ago, I was routinely visiting Elekron," he says. "Whilst I was there, there were a lot of rumours surrounding the Luxlumen and how they were planning to steal it from planet Earth." He stares at me, I guess waiting for a response. "I time travelled forward, within their time period to a few points into their future, right until yesterday, when I discovered they had, in fact, got hold of the Luxlumen, and were planning on destroying this galaxy."

"Well, that's impossible"

"Which bit, Miss?"

"I had the Luxlumen yesterday, and I still have it." I only checked in the shoebox this morning, so it's definitely still under my bed. "So, they couldn't have had it yesterday."

"It's a little more complicated than that, Miss. Please bear with me."

I shrug my shoulders, which reminds me of how I reacted when TrueBias told me about aliens, Jack and Dolces, so maybe I should listen, just in case.

"I had no choice but to travel back through Earth's time, and observe the series of events as they unfolded, which led to the Viscorpus securing the stone." He nods his head. "I identified the potential problem."

Having an open mind and taking in what Jidrit says is difficult; my brain already aches. Can time travel really exist? My eyes fuzz over as I stare at this troll-like creature dressed in a business suit. It's all a bit farfetched claiming to be a time traveller. I'm sure TrueBias said that the Menax species were useless, and he definitely wouldn't have said that if he knew they were Universal Watchmen, and could time travel.

"But how can both of us have the same stone at the same time?"

"You can't, well, not within the same time continuum, that is." Jidrit's bushy eyebrows meet in the middle of his forehead as his eyes narrow.

You'd think I'd just asked him the dumbest thing ever.

"If I hadn't travelled back through time to assist you, then Elekron would still have the Luxlumen, but by helping you secure the stone, we've altered the trajectory."

"So, let me get this straight."

Jidrit's amber eyes seem to stare right through me.

"You're saying the Viscorpus originally stole the Luxlumen from Earth, but because you travelled back in time and changed the past, which changed the future, Elekron now don't have it?" My head aches.

The edges of Jidrit's mouth curl and his beard shimmers.

"Oh my, it's not as simple as that, Miss, but in essence, yes. Although as a time traveller, the laws of physics, well the universe, will not allow me to disrupt the natural order of things."

"Well, which one is it? Can you, or can you not change the past and the future?" If Jidrit can alter the past, maybe he can prevent my dad from going through the wormhole in the first place. I pull at strands of my hair. "Can you go back and stop my father from being knocked through the wormhole by Mrs Shufflebottom?"

"Oh, dear Miss, you seem a little upset." Jidrit leans over the railings; his beard swishes gently in the warm breeze. "There's always a natural order to things, but often mistakes are made. Some are more important than others. Your father being forced through the wormhole was of utmost importance. If I travelled back and prevented him from getting into the lift, and thereby saving him from going through the wormhole, then you would never have pursued him, nor have the Luxlumen stone now. Time is a delicate balance, Miss; the slightest alteration to the past can completely transform the future for good, and for bad."

"So, if you can't mess with the natural order, why doesn't Elekron still have the Luxlumen?"

Jidrit lifts Slugmug off the railings, placing him back on the floor.

"You made the tiniest mistake, Miss, which would have ultimately destroyed this whole galaxy, and although I can never tell you what to do, in such circumstances, I'm permitted to offer you *a second chance* to guide you on the right path, before you get it wrong again... if you follow. You've heard about second chances, haven't you, Miss?"

"What mistake?" If the mistake wasn't keeping the stone, then it could have been anything.

"The mistake was–"

Heather, from next door, interrupts Jidrit. She doesn't

acknowledge him at all.

"Hi Eliza," she says, "is he yours?" She points to Slugmug.

"No, he's umm, belongs to a friend."

"Oh, does he have a name?" She kneels right next to Jidrit. "Hello sweetie," she says, tickling Slugmug under the chin.

"Slugmug."

"What an awful name for such a darling," she says, as her scaly hand slides over his back. Slugmug seems to enjoy the attention. "Well must get on; shopping to do." She smiles and hurries towards the lift.

"The mistake, Miss, was simply that you left the Carcer at the museum, yet continued your journey to save your father. When you originally got to the prison shuttle on the first timeline, when the Viscorpus successfully took the stone, it was because you could not release the prisoners, as you had no Carcer; this allowed the Viscorpus to seize the prison shuttle and therefore take the Luxlumen off Conexus."

"So, you did trip me up when I was trying to find Lionel?"

Jidrit smiles.

"I thought so."

He winks.

"What about your stunt in the waste store?"

"Miss, I left the Carcer after you tripped over my bag, but it was already available to you. You could have removed it from the museum. I didn't advise you on what to do with it, nor to even pick it up. I simply gave you another opportunity, *a second chance* to have it; simply providing you with the tools you should have had all along." He draws in a huge breath of air. "I was unsuccessfully attempting to reduce the temperature of the vats in the waste store; nevertheless, my interference was of little consequence."

"I'm not sure Appollo would agree with you. It was only a fluke that I didn't get hurt."

Jidrit drops his head, clasps his hands together and glances at the floor.

"Why didn't you just stop Mrs Shufflebottom from letting in the Viscorpus?"

"Miss, I'm not permitted to interfere with the natural order of things." As Jidrit grabs hold of the handrail, the diamonds, which sparkle in his golden ring, are arranged in an identical pattern as the stones on my star-studded purse. "I always search for the best options for success, and believed, because of the unquestionable love you have for your father, amongst all possibilities, you would achieve the most favourable outcome."

"Well, I've got the Luxlumen, so everything is fine; the natural order should be fine."

Slugmug scowls at me and swishes his tail; it seems an odd name for a cat. Maybe it's short for something like slug-un-mug-it. Jidrit is obviously encouraged by my grin, yet unaware I'm sniggering at my own private joke.

"You're right, Miss. Having travelled to Elekron and visited the same point in time as I did yesterday, they do not have the Luxlumen. You have successfully altered the course of the future, but..." He bows his head. "They know you have the stone and they are coming for it."

"W-what? What am I supposed to do?" My mind whizzes as a tingly, prickly sensation washes over me. "Are they coming here? Have you gone into the future and seen what they are planning?"

"Oh, dear Miss, you misunderstand; my purpose here is done. I can't interfere with the natural order of things, but I thought I should warn you all the same."

It seems that Jidrit is happy to interfere with the 'natural order of things' when it suits him.

"Isn't that messing with the natural order?"

As I tilt back my head, my neck cracks. The Reus in the parking bay are staring up at me, pacing around like caged animals. Can they see Jidrit? Is he invisible to everyone but me? Or is he just in my imagination? Daisy's face appears around the front door.

"Who are you talking to?" she says.

I point towards Jidrit. "It's–"

"Well, your phone has been ringing constantly; it's TrueBias calling, it must be urgent. Call him!" She shuts the front door.

Jidrit unhooks his watch from his waistcoat pocket, flicks it open, tuts as though he is late for something and replaces it.

"Find the Kalsky stone, Miss, but make haste; they're on their way."

He disappears. Slugmug meanders between my legs before trotting off towards the stairs.

TO BE CONTINUED...

Dear Reader,

Thank you for reading my debut novel, *Eliza Berry – A Second Chance.* I hope you enjoyed it, and although I appreciate the story didn't neatly end, I trust you haven't found it too frustrating that Eliza still has the Luxlumen stone. If I'm honest with you, I couldn't decide, whilst writing, what was the right thing for Eliza to do. I was stuck in the same dilemma as Eliza. Hopefully, in my next book in the series, I can sort it out for us all! Please bear with me.

If you enjoyed *Eliza Berry – A Second Chance*, the most helpful thing that you can do is to leave an honest review. So, please consider submitting a review on Amazon. It doesn't cost anything, other than a moment of your time, and can be tremendously beneficial to me. Your quick review helps to get my book into the hands of other readers who may enjoy it.

Thank you once again,

Daniella